M000073393

I am an Island

By Nate Blair

Copyright 2007

Table of Contents

Chapter 1: Cruise Control

The Serengeti Plain is one of God's art projects - a study on the theme of brown. From the light tan shades of dried grasses to the dark muddy browns of the cracked, dried riverbeds. The two-tone brown pelt of the Thompson gazelle shimmers as it feeds on the dried grasses and shrubs. The drying blood of the same gazelle is rusty brown after losing the battle of life. The mane of the lion that killed the gazelle is a golden brown tone. The lion lies beside the carcass of the slain gazelle after satiating his appetite. He rests with his out looking deceptively like an overgrown housecat. And, as the sun beats down on this scene, the wind blows gently, ruffling the lion's fur coat from the mane, across the distended abdomen and down to the tail. The wind dries the remains of the gazelle around his mouth. The king of Africa smells nothing dangerous on the wind. And why should he? For is he not the strongest? He is the master of this brown world, fearing nothing because nothing is unusual and everything is comfortably the same.

And the wind blows on, past the lion and across the plains.
Past the hyenas patiently waiting for the lion to leave.
Past the giraffes.
Past the family of elephants trying to shower each other with dirt and on to the horizon where the shades of brown fuse with the blue of the sky.massive head lolling off to one side and his paws stretched

She sat in the corner of the hospital employee lounge listening closely as Nurse Helen Johnson prattled on and on, obviously happy to have an audience. Like any good single man in his late 20's, Dean Peterson noticed her the minute he walked into the employee lounge. Like most third year medical students, he spent a fair amount of his waking hours either drinking coffee or trying to find coffee which is what brought him to the employee lounge deep in the bowels of University Hospital in Madison, Wisconsin.

As Dean filled his large mug and hunted for some creamer to soften the blow, Nurse Johnson's diatribe was interrupted when she was paged. She scurried past Dean leaving the attractive non-scrubs-wearing woman alone. The woman turned and said to Dean, "Say, do you have a minute?"

Dean smiled into his coffee, "Well, I am supposed to be taking patient histories and with as old as some of these patients are, that could take a lot of time. But that can wait. Sure, I have a minute. My name is Dean Petersen."

She stood to shake his hand, "Nice to meet you Dean. My name is Ellen and I am interviewing people here at the hospital for a sociology research project on the professional interactions between doctors and nurses."

Dean replied, "Oh, are you a graduate student? I am a third year med student."

Ellen replied, ""Yes, I am. PhD in sociology if I can get enough data. I can still use you for the survey if you have time. It should just take 20 minutes or so."

Dean looked at his watch more to give the impression that he was important than anything else. "Sure, I have twenty minutes for you."

Of course, after filling out the survey for Ellen, Dean agreed wholeheartedly that doctor-nurse relations were vitally important and offered to help in any way possible.

He said, "Are you going to be collecting more data?"

Ellen looked around, " Yeah, I try to make appointments with the doctors and nurses and then meet them here or the cafeteria. I just started and it is slow going but hopefully I will get enough data."

Over the next few days, Dean spent all his free time cruising the employee lounge and cafeteria looking for opportunities to stop and talk to Ellen. Finally after a week of this and to celebrate the end of mid-term exams, Dean asked Ellen if she would like to have dinner with him. She said she would love to.

With his dark Greek fishermen looks, he might have been expected to take Ellen to a Greek restaurant. Instead, they had gone to the Russian House, a new ethnic restaurant just off State Street. As Dean always did, he tried to take his date to a restaurant that he had not been to but had heard was good. That way, he got to try something new and could always blame the erroneous critic if it turned out to be bad. The food at the Russian House was interesting and unique, and most importantly for a med student, inexpensive. Dean had a great time with Ellen and the evening had disappeared in a blur of vodka and heavy potato-based foods. Ellen spoke in an intrinsically captivating way. Dean guessed that she could make taking out the trash sound like an exciting adventure. Dean assumed this character trait was a great asset as a grad student in Sociology.

During dinner, Dean and Ellen had argued good naturedly over the value of old movies. Ellen claimed that so-called "classic" movies were really wonderful. Dean said that those old movies really were awful compared to the movies of today.

Over a bowl of gnocchi, Ellen said, "Well, what about Casablanca or some of the Hitchcock films? Cary Grant? I will bet you $20 that I can find a classic film you will like."

Dean said, "Well, for $20 of course I won't like it but you can try."

After dinner, Dean and Ellen went to Blockbuster and she picked out the Hitchcock classic, North by Northwest, which Dean had never seen. "Sounds like a Michael Moore documentary about the airline industry," Dean said trying desperately to prove he was a funny guy. They headed over to Dean's apartment. As they got out of

6

his rusty old Honda Civic (teaching did not pay that well either), Dean informed Ellen, "My roommate will probably be home tonight. His name is Jim. I'm sure he won't mind if we watch this movie though. God knows he watches enough TV."

As she tried unsuccessfully to lock the passenger door, Ellen responded, "Well, most nights I would rather be watching TV too. It beats listening to Nurse Helen Johnson tell me for the umpteenth time how Dr. Wilson is watching her butt ALL THE TIME. I stayed up late one night just so I could watch them interact. You know what? Dr. Wilson is so busy he doesn't have time to rest on his own butt let alone watch anyone else's. I think Helen secretly wants Dr. Wilson to watch her butt. Classic. Just classic."

Dean and Jim live in a spacious two-story two bedroom apartment in a well-kept brick apartment building on the near west side of Madison. The bedrooms are on the upper floor while the kitchen and living room are one large open space partly with a vaulted ceiling on the main floor. The whole place has wood floors and there is even a fireplace in the living room. At $700/month, the rent is low for this apartment and location because Jim's uncle owns the building and had cut them a great deal. Otherwise, this area of town was quite expensive, as students and staff would pay a hefty premium for proximity to both the UW campus and the UW hospital. The ugly winters of Wisconsin make any outdoor travel distance seem much further.

Dean opened the apartment door and brought Ellen into Jim's typical Friday night. Imagine the living room of a typical guy's apartment - couches and chairs that are comfortable but have seen better days share space with an oversized television and stereo. As with all single-guy apartments, the style is "eclectic" at best or "recycled" could even be a better word. Dean was slowly slipping into medical school debt and Jim saw no reason to spend his money on new furniture. In fact, at least one of the couches WAS recycled. In Madison, almost all leases run from

7

August 15th to August 14th of the next year. As a result, everyone is moving simultaneously. Furniture that is no longer desired by graduate students is left on the curb. Other students, in a worse situation or new to town, drive around madly looking for the perfect perch from which to watch TV or drink beer. Jim had found the green couch he was currently lying on during one of these great furniture swap fall rituals.

"Hey, Jim!", said Dean as he walked through the door behind Ellen, "I'd like you to meet Ellen Johansson. She is the sociology grad student I was telling you about. Ellen, this is Jim Wells". Jim had been almost asleep in front of a Milwaukee Bucks game, a half eaten Gumby's pizza (he always got pepperoni and green olive which no one else ever wanted) and a couple of empty cans of Leinenkugels sitting on the coffee table in front of him.

"Hello, Jim. It is very nice to meet you." said Ellen.

"Hey," said Jim as he slowly came out of the pseudo-coma he had been in. "I mean - It is very nice to meet you too, Ellen. How was dinner?"

"Dinner was great," said Ellen, glancing at Dean. "I always like to try new restaurants. Russian food is a little on the starchy side but I can just run it off in the morning."

"Oh great," thought Jim, "she is as high energy as Dean said she was. Dean will like that though. He is a little uptight himself." Out loud he said, "Well, I should probably do the same with this pizza but I think I'll try sleeping it off first."

Dean said, "Well, we rented an old Hitchcock movie in order to settle a bet. North by Northwest. Have you seen it?"

"OH YES!" said Ellen. "It's really great and Dean is about to pay me $20 if he likes it, which, of course, he will."

"Of course," said Dean, smiling and glancing sideways at Ellen.

"You know, I've enjoyed the Hitchcock films I've seen. I'd love to join you." said Jim as he sat back down onto the sofa.

8

As his butt hit the couch, he saw the room from the eyes of a visitor and he suddenly realized that he, and his mess, had taken over the living room even after Dean had reminded him that he was hopefully bringing his date back here tonight. So, just as he was sitting, he jumped up again. He grabbed the pizza box and as many empty beer bottles off of the coffee table as he could. (Why is it that single men never have a messy dining room table? Because they are always eating on the coffee table and the dining room table is reserved for bills and magazines.) Simultaneously, he kicked his Adidas under the couch expecting to retrieve them later. He was not going anywhere this evening. Jim seldom had anyone over at the house and so he was not used to thinking about keeping it clean.

Jim carried the pizza box out to the kitchen where Dean was trying to open a bottle of wine he had. "She's cute and she seems nice." said Jim in a slightly hushed tone.

"Yeah" said Dean. "She's really great. Our conversation has been really interesting so far. I hope she doesn't think that I'm too quiet but I've really enjoyed listening to her stories about all the old fart doctors at the hospital. She sees them completely differently than I do."

"I'll bet", thought Jim. "Her grades don't depend on their approval." "Well, that's great." Jim said aloud. "I hope it works out. You could use a girlfriend to get you out of the library once and awhile. So, do you want me to get out of your way?"

"No. It is just our first date. Are you thinking I am going to make some juvenile yawn-and-put-my-arm-around-her move during the movie? I think we are all getting a little old for that." Dean said.

And so the American tradition of dinner and a rented movie begins. Ellen knows that Dean will sit next to her on the couch. He may or may not try and kiss her. Jim knows to keep his eyes on the screen. Jim also knows he probably should go to bed as soon as the movie ends, if not before.

In the end, the pizza and beer made Jim sleepy and drove him to bed before Dean even got the movie into the DVD player. He said he was getting too tired and could watch the rest in the morning. He asked Dean to check his lottery numbers after the evening news, if they remembered, and dug the slip of paper with the lottery numbers out of his wallet and placed it on the coffee table. "It was very nice to meet you", he said to Ellen. He went up to his room which consisted of a simple bed with no headboard and a corner desk with a computer which sat abandoned and aging quickly under a pile of papers. Jim's company had paid for it in some big "work at home" program, which was shortly discontinued when it became obvious no one got any work done at home. Jim peeled off his clothes leaving them in the usual heap. He ambled down to the bathroom and realized that Dean and Ellen were talking but did not realize they were talking about him. It was just as well as the conversation would not have improved his insomnia, with which he was about to try tangling.

"So, what made you decide to go back to med school?" asked Ellen. As a sociologist studying medical personnel, she had more than a casual interest in the reasons why doctors do what they do. However, Dean had been scoring a lot of points with her this evening and she realized that she was starting to really care about the answers he gave to her questions.

"Well, I think I mentioned that I taught school for several years, right?" Dean said as he stared into Ellen's eyes. He had to keep looking at her eyes because if his gaze were to wander, it would have wandered to the rest of Ellen's body. She had a generally athletic figure. She was a little less distracting because she was wearing something relatively conservative - a lightweight fleece sweater and jeans. She was very thoughtful and had asked Dean if she needed to dress up for the date. Dean had assured her that he would not be taking her to anyplace too fancy on a med student budget. Continuing, he said, "Well, I really enjoyed parts of teaching and working with kids but I did not enjoy teaching the same stuff every year. I had a good friend in town who was a pediatrician and I started volunteering at his practice and really fell in love with the work. Anyway, I want to keep working with kids but I want a bigger challenge intellectually, I guess."

" I think that's a great reason," said Ellen. " I meet a lot of doctors who have never been anything but a doctor or a pre-med student and I think they do not have as good of a perspective on their careers. You did something else first and really found that this is what you wanted to do, which is great."

Dean stood up to start screwing with the DVD player to get the movie going. "Jim seems like a nice guy," said Ellen, to change the subject.

"Yeah, he is. We were friends in college but he has changed a little since then. He is home almost every night and most of the weekends. He has really become a little anti-social. Back when I knew him before, he was REALLY active. He was President of the UW branch of the Sierra Club for two years. He worked for Greenpeace in the summers. I really respected his activism. Now, well, he works for an engineering company here in town and doesn't really do much of anything. His ex-girlfriend really did a number on him, it seems. She was with him in all these activities and then she just took off with some other guy. I guess he was pretty devastated."

"How long has it been?" asked Ellen.

"Well, let's see," said Dean as he took another drink of wine and allowed his hand to rest on Ellen's leg. She did not mind and, in fact, put her hand on top of his. Dean continued, "Umm, it has been five years since we graduated and she took off shortly before graduation. I don't think he has had anything serious since then."

"Too bad", said Ellen as she gazed at the stairs that led up to the bedrooms."He seems like a nice enough guy."

North by Northwest was actually a really captivating movie and so there was almost no chit-chat between the two of them during the movie. After the movie ended, Dean said,

11

"OK, OK, I really liked it. I really did! I owe you twenty bucks."

Ellen smiled and looked over at him and said, "Excellent! I knew you would. Why don't you put that twenty towards taking me out for dinner again?"

Dean smiled back at her and said, "Sure, I would love to." He then happened to glance down and see the lottery tickets on the coffee table and said, "Do you mind if we watch the end of the news? I told Jim I would watch for the lottery numbers. It seems to be the only "sport" that he is playing these days; that, and softball for the company team in the summer. He used to be a varsity baseball player for the University too but..."

"Before his woman done left him," finished Ellen, with a bit of B.B. King inflection in her voice. She watched Dean while he worked the remote to get the TV on the correct channel. She realized that he really cared for the well-being of his roommate – enough to be upset by his lack of "life". She smiled because it was a good sign for a relationship with Dean and he didn't even know it.

Upstairs, Jim was going through the nightly passage down memory lane. He lay there in his boxers and t-shirt under his comforter. His head was on the pillow and his eyes staring through the window at the streetlamp outside. His eyes looked through the streetlamp and beyond to the past. Cecilia had come from Sweden to attend the University. She was as stereotypically Swedish as Jim was stereotypically Midwestern. He liked jeans and flannel shirts. She had blond hair, blue eyes, and the hearty, earthy body that Jim struggled to keep his mind and hands from resting upon. They had met at a rally for the UW-Greens that was in protest of certain copper mining that was polluting the lakes in Northern Wisconsin. Cecilia had been active in the Green party in Sweden and saw immediately that the UW group was not very savvy when it came to organizing protests.

Europeans are generally more environmentally inclined than Americans. They have been living with the signs of environmental damage in Europe much longer and more prominently than Americans; buildings blackened by coal smog, the German Black Forest that is slowly dying of acid rain, the much higher population density. Cecilia had experienced all these things and was committed to improving the environment. She also really enjoyed the company of the people that she met in this process, including Jim. Jim's activism came from an altruism that seemed to guide his every thought and word. They had spent seven hours handcuffed together during the protest that day and by the time the handcuffs were removed, everyone in Madison and Wisconsin knew about the dangers of open-pit mining in Wisconsin. Jim and Cecilia knew they were going to be friends but it took a few more meetings and "chance" encounters before Jim would have the nerve to ask this Swedish beauty out on a date.

For their first date, Jim took her to the University Arboretum to walk through the largest and most interesting piece of nature directly in the heart of the city and then to his favorite restaurant, "Himal Chuli", a small, Himalayan restaurant that survived on State Street only because of the exotic fare (exotic for Wisconsin).

Jim and Cecilia soon were inseparable and inseparable from their clique of other environmental students. With them as a team, there was nothing that could not be done. His engineering training, her good looks, and their combined enthusiasm soon led them to be the driving force behind the local Sierra club student chapter. Under their leadership, membership tripled in a semester. People felt a lot of momentum in the club. It was a momentum that Jim and Cecilia stoked even as they fed their own relationship. Cecilia was very concerned with reducing acid rain and general air pollution issues. Jim was mostly concerned with issues of energy and reducing foreign oil imports.

Their life was the envy of every other couple that knew them. After they had dated for most of the academic year, Jim visited Sweden with Cecilia and fell in love with her family. They were incredibly hospitable. The days were long and filled with coffee and eating. Occasionally, there was some work done but Scandinavians are notoriously lackluster workers during the summers. They make up for it in the winters when the days are only a few hours long and going outside is a much less attractive option. Cecilia's father was an independent business owner of a company that did "something related to banks." Neither Cecilia nor Jim really knew what it was that he did but it provided well for the family. Cecilia's mother ran the house and was now in a more relaxed phase of life after raising Cecilia and her five brothers and sisters. They had a very nice home in southern Sweden outside of Stockholm.

During their visit, Cecilia took Jim to all parts of Sweden on the train. He met all her friends, although he missed much of the conversations, as he did not speak Swedish. Cecilia would always be turning to Jim, causing her blond hair to fly free of her face, and try to explain what was happening. Jim did not really care. He was happy to be with Cecilia and her family. Everyone got very tan from living outside all summer. Jim had grown up in a small family in a small town in Wisconsin and everything about Sweden and Europe and her family was new and fresh and exotic. He almost forgot his melancholy about the problems in the world; he was so busy enjoying it. Unfortunately, summer is followed by fall which meant a return to Wisconsin and school.

When they returned, Jim and Cecilia moved in together with the vision of living the kind of environmentally friendly lifestyle they had always envisioned. They got an apartment with a patch of yard, which they immediately converted into a garden. Cecilia loved herbs and grew basil, thyme and oregano in the garden in addition to tomatoes, cucumbers, onions, and carrots. The apartment was three short blocks from the Williamson Street Coop where they bought their organic and bulk food. Jim built a composting pit in one end of the garden and installed compact fluorescent light bulbs throughout the apartment. He designed a solar water heating system for the whole apartment building but was quite irate when the owner refused to pay the price to install it.

Everything had been wonderful. Unfortunately, as Jim lay on his bed every night staring at the streetlamp, he recalled none of this. None of these images of work and companionship eased his suffering as he lay there. In his minds eye, he saw only the last day. The day she left. It was their senior year. Graduation was only a week away. He and Cecilia had been planning to take the summer off before looking for work with Greenpeace or whatever environmental group would take them. He had just gotten an application to work at Yellowstone for the summer and had biked back to the apartment.

He came bursting through the screen door in the back only to interrupt Cecilia packing her clothes into a huge suitcase. Through the big front windows of the tiny apartment, in front of the building, Jim could also see Ted sitting in his BMW. He knew Ted from the Sierra Club. Ted's father was a rich surgeon in Chicago and Ted claimed to have rejected that when he came to the Sierra club meetings. However, he drove his father's used BMW and dressed like a yuppie so Jim had never been convinced of Ted's environmental conviction. Ted spent most of the meetings talking to or trying to talk to Cecilia. Jim had seen this but not given it much thought because Cecilia was an oddball among environmental women. None of them took any notice of their appearance. Cecilia did not either but would have looked radiant dressed in a burlap sack so most of the men were drawn to her. They had been together for quite a while though and Jim completely trusted Cecilia.

"Where are you going?" Jim remembered asking very innocently. His love for Cecilia was so strong and his innocence so complete that he did not have any paranoia that some men have - who have lost love to the passing storm front or the random BMW. Those men now watch for the signs of the inkling of unhappiness. Jim wasn't one of these men when the day started. So, he asked innocently, "Is Ted taking you somewhere?" She had answered neither question but continued to place her jeans and nicer clothes in the suitcase. She finally paused with her face above the open suitcase and her arms grasping its open sides as if to keep from plunging head first into the huge suitcase.

She said nothing but slowly turned her head to the side to look at Jim. Jim stood in the door of the bedroom where they had shared many nights of passion: both physical and intellectual as they plotted and schemed to save the world. Jim loved to have her merely brush her long straight blond hair over his body during their lovemaking. Now, as her long blond hair fell away from her upturned face, Jim saw the look in her eyes through the tears that ran down her face. "Jim," she stammered with a quivering voice. Jim suddenly became aware of feeling very afraid.

He had felt like this before once. In high school, he had been pulled over by a cop for the very first time. He had only been speeding but the feeling almost gave him a heart attack. A tightness in the crotch, every artery about to burst, the instant desire to run away fast and the hair standing up on the back of your neck.

"Jim" she repeated, "I have something to say that you are not going to like. First, I'm sorry. Second, I love you still even though you will not believe it. Ted is leaving for his new job with Doilette and Touche in International Finance. His first rotation is in Barcelona because he speaks Spanish and he will be there for at least a year and … and I am going with him."

Jim was almost in physical shock just from the look on her face and realized he had not really listened to what she was actually saying. He stammered "What?"

"I am leaving with Ted for Barcelona. Well," she said, now more matter-of-factly, having gotten the worst part over with, "I want to be closer to my family and Ted is going to be very successful. I have to think of my future now and not just everyone else."

Starting to feel like a broken record, Jim repeated "What?"

Cecilia had now closed the suitcase. "I hope that you can save the world, Jim. I really hope you can. It is just not for me anymore." And with that, she was gone, mumbling

something about sending for the rest of the stuff. Jim
followed her out the front door stammering more questions:
"How long?", "How long have you been seeing him?"

She didn't answer any questions nor even look him
in the eye. Ted didn't look at him or say anything either but
silently lifted her suitcase into the trunk as she climbed into
the passenger's seat and looked away from Jim. Ted climbed
in and the car accelerated quickly down the street before it
made a left turn, probably headed over to Ted's place. He
stared after the BMW long after it had turned out of sight
onto Johnson Street. Looking down, he saw the Yellowstone
brochure was still in his hand. He dropped it like a hot
potato then.

And with the brochure, he dropped his entire life.
Cecilia had been such an integral part of his life and his
passion for the environment that it was too painful for him
to continue with any of it. A week later came graduation
which was a very bittersweet event for Jim's family and
friends. So, based on his degree in mechanical engineering,
he applied for and got the job he now had. It was a good,
decent job with benefits and a 401k. Throughout the
summer, he tried to call her and track her down but to no
avail. Even though he found out where she was in
Barcelona, she did not answer or return any of his calls.

However, as Jim stared at the streetlamp trying to
sleep, it was nothing before or anything after that he
considered. It was always the same, simple object he
regarded. Her face as she turned to go. Where once had been
love for him and the apartment and the garden and the
world was now only coldness and a strength that comes
from pulling in all your vulnerable edges. After she left and
after graduation, he had done the same thing and pulled up
the welcome mat of his soul. Like the other song by Simon
and Garfunkel, he was "a rock, an island." Cecilia came to his
thoughts every night but he felt only curiosity. Jim had felt
very little since she had left and that did not seem to bother
him.

17

Finally, Jim drifted off to sleep where Cecilia returned in a dream. Here though, they were happy and she and Jim were enjoying a quiet evening of reading while intertwined in bed. He was reading a new book by Edward Abbey about the western deserts while she held him and played her hair over his body. He always had wondered how he maintained any kind of reading pace with this interference but now, in his dream, he read without thinking and focused on her presence. Her smell, her look, the curves of her body, the small of her back, the movement of her hands as she played them over his skin like a skilled pianist all came back to him. He had known from the moment that they first were handcuffed together that he would love her. He had loved her completely and she had become the main pillar of his life.

As he slept, Jim gratefully only knew that Cecilia's hair had an unimaginable softness and delicacy as it played over his skin.

Chapter 2: The Big Winner

In the Serengeti, the wildebeest is a big slow grass-eater that is not very interesting to look at. Not flashy like the zebra or speedy like the gazelle. However, without the wildebeest, the lion would go hungry and would eat more of the zebra. So, in the end, the flashy depend on the lowly.

Dean and Ellen had sat through a completely boring weather report. "Partly sunny with a chance of snow or rain" they heard.

"Well, that narrows it right down," scoffed Ellen which brought a chuckle from Dean.

"Yeah, I'm sorry to make you sit through this but if we don't watch, then we'll have to get the newspaper tomorrow to find out which almost doubles the cost of the lottery ticket" said Dean holding up the ticket as if showing off a rare treasure. "Frankly, I think this is a pretty stupid activity but Jim seems to enjoy it. He is an engineer so he should know about the odds. I think it his little way of holding out hope for a new life."

"Well, it does add a bit of excitement to the news if you actually have a ticket. It's kind of fun, don't you think?" asked Ellen.

"Yeah, it is. But, well... he does it every Friday though, Ellen, and he always plays the same numbers" Dean said, seemingly a little exasperated. Ellen suspected that Dean had not expected Jim to have changed so much since college.

"I bet it's his birthday."

"Nope, it's May 13th of 1997 as far as I can tell but he won't tell me the significance of the day."

At this point, Dean was trying to figure out what to do in about five minutes after the lottery numbers. Should he try to kiss her or just take her home or what? He turned his attention to the TV which was set to local Channel 3 which broadcast the Powerball jackpot selection. It worked like this: There were six different chambers in which the audience could see a mass of floating ping-pong balls. One by one, the camera would focus on each of the chambers and a woman would allow one of the ping-pong balls to rise to the top of the chamber. She would then turn the ball so that it properly faced the camera. The number would then appear at the bottom of the screen and be added to the complete list of numbers. There were six numbers all together. Jim had picked 0 - 5 - 1 - 3 - 9 - 7.

As the numbers started to come up, Dean started to feel even more excited than he had already been feeling with Ellen. During the news, somehow the war in Iraq had urged Ellen to place her hand on the back of Dean's neck. The story about the local boy who had cancer caused her to lean against him. Dean was secretly hoping for an announcement that nuclear war had broken out just to see Ellen's reaction to that. So, Dean was really not sure what was going to happen next but was thanking Jim for his stupid lottery obsession which kept Ellen in the house a little longer.

But, then the numbers started to come up. The woman slowly turned up a 0. All she ever did was smile and rotate ping-pong balls. She never had a line. Did not even repeat the numbers aloud. Perhaps, she had another job during the day. Although, with the amount of money they were giving away tonight, they could probably afford to have a full-time attractive-ping-pong-ball turning woman. Dean watched as her fingers turned the first ball to reveal a 0.

"Wow, he matched the first one. Usually, it is over at this point already and we can go to bed."

20

"See, it is getting more exciting" said Ellen as she leaned in closer seemingly to read the numbers better.

An electronic 0 appeared at the bottom of the TV. It was a huge TV (ostensibly so Jim could watch the Brewers in the summer but it was on for a lot more than the occasional baseball game) and so the "0" was huge on the bottom.

The camera followed the woman as she walked to the next chamber filled with flying ping-pong balls. She was wearing something red with sequins, Dean noticed, probably to remind people of Vanna White. As she turned the next number, Dean involuntarily sucked his breath in for it was a 5.

"Geez, what are the odds of getting two of them," asked Ellen?

"I don't know", said Dean.

"Does that win you anything – just two of them?"

"No, I don't think so," replied Dean while still looking at the ticket.

When the third ball was a 1, Dean started to simply stare at the screen without turning to look at Ellen when he talked. "He matched the third one as well," he said very matter-of-factly.

"I know" said Ellen who had now removed her head from his shoulder to focus on the screen.

When the fourth ball was a 3, Ellen let out a little yelp and Dean was reminded of his earlier desire to have a nuclear winter. "If Jim wins the lottery, that might be just as effective" went a thought through his mind. He shook it back out of his head- this is just a first date. Aloud, he mentioned offhand "Well, Jim has at least won a hundred bucks for that".

The thought was gone just as quickly and he resumed his focused attention on the screen in front of him. He could almost smell the ping-pong woman now. He noticed that she had diamond earrings as she moved to the fifth chamber. Time slowed as Dean watched the ball pop to the top of the chamber. He could make out the fact that the mute woman had no wedding ring on as she moved with seeming excruciating slowness to turn the ball and reveal the

9 to the entire world to see. "Holy Crap! Jim just won ten thousand bucks," Dean whispered in a hushed voice.

Later, he would wonder why he did not start screaming for Jim to come down. He thought that perhaps he did not want to break the spell of the moment. Like seeing a wild animal while on a hike, you do not want to spook it. Dean and Ellen did not want to spook the lottery. Perhaps if they got too loud, the woman would run away and not reveal the final answer to the question of what the sixth number would be.

What would it be? A random ping-pong ball now held the future of Jim and partly Dean and Ellen inside itself. A two cent spherical piece of plastic controlled their fate. Dean was starting to fidget now but neither he nor Ellen noticed. Ellen had forgotten her date, her growing attraction for Dean, her confusion over if she should stay over if he asked and the fact that she did not want to leave. For the moment, this was far bigger than their date.

The one man to whom this mattered most slumbered restlessly upstairs, lost in his past and avoiding his present.

The final ping-pong ball rose to the top of the chamber like a fly-ball hit high over centerfield. It was grabbed easily by the practiced hand of the lady in red. The cameraman did this almost every week and he knew that now was the moment someone was waiting for and he zoomed in on the ball as she slowly turned it to face the camera. SEVEN! 7 is the number. 7 equals the number. The number is 7!

"Oh my God!, " swore Dean. "Jim's done it. He matched all the numbers! Every single goddam one. Oh my God!" For a moment, Dean felt nauseous and his face flushed. Then, he finally looked at Ellen for the first time in what seemed like forever (and was actually about 2 minutes) and saw that she was slightly pale. She looked like she had just seen an accident. Dean threw her arms around her and gave Ellen a big slobbery first kiss. Ellen returned it with the passion of someone who has just been through a terrifying experience, like parachuting out of a plane.

And just as quickly as it had began, the lottery drawing ended and the channel cut immediately to an advertisement about Ford pick-up trucks, changing the mood in the room. Ellen stopped the kiss and said, rather anti-climactically, "Well, I guess we better tell him, right?"

Dean stopped and looked her in the eye. "Wow, that was incredible. And the kiss was great too." he said with a small smirk. Ellen smiled back at him and flipped her hair out of her face.

She gave him another little peck on the mouth and repeated her question "Shouldn't we go up and tell him?"

So they jumped off the couch and instinctively grabbed hands as they raced up the carpeted staircase side by side. Dean had the ticket clamped tightly between the fingers of his right hand and his left hand clamped squarely on Ellen's right hand. The steps squeaked under their feet as they bounded up the stairs. Ellen was thinking that this was definitely the most exciting first date she had ever had. Dean was doing well. Of course, she knew that the downside was that no restaurant/movie/long walk combination could keep the second date from paling by comparison.

They reached the landing and stopped outside of Jim's bedroom door. The sound of his snoring could be heard echoing around in the bedroom. Jim had finally entered the blissful deep sleep that takes away the dreams. Takes Cecilia away from his mind. Suddenly, a hand reached down and grabbed him by the back of his shirt and started to shake him. "Jim! Wake up. Wake up. It is important." said the voice.

Jim woke with a start. Simultaneously, he shook his head and pulled away from Dean who had grabbed his shoulder. "What the hell?" said Jim. "What the hell is the big emergency?"

Dean was sitting on the edge of Jim's bed. Ellen stood discreetly in the doorway. She suddenly realized that

Jim was sitting in his t-shirt and boxer shorts and she was not sure if it was appropriate for her to enter the room. What would his reaction be, she wondered? She had read the stories about shocking news in her studies. Stories about people who had heart attacks when they won large awards. For some people, winning large sums had rectified a terrible, dead-end life. For others, it had ruined a very satisfactory and normal life. Stories of people who ended up on drugs or simply broke because they horribly mismanaged the winnings. In fact, Ellen had recently read about a bill in Congress to make it a law that for awards of more than one million dollars and for people who were not in poverty previously, no money would be paid out for six months. Some said that even one year would be better. The bill had little chance of passing because it represented big government at its most intrusive but enough people had screwed up their lives this way that the effort was at least being made. So, Ellen stared down at Jim with bated breath wondering what he would do. Would he jump up on the bed? Would he pass out? Would he throw up?

Dean was not sure quite how to tell Jim this. He was also wondering how Jim would take it. He knew that the old Jim of college days would have probably proclaimed that he would give it all to Greenpeace. Dean was much less sure about the new Jim. Dean started to talk as soon as it seemed that Jim was actually awake (although it was difficult to tell in the dim light from the street lamp outside). Dean had not turned on the light yet because he did not want to startle Jim awake. Of course, Jim had woken with a start anyway. Dean looked Jim in the eye and said, with as straight a face as possible, "Jim, I woke you up because you won the lottery." Jim stared right back at him uncomprehendingly. Dean started to talk a little louder and let a little of his excitement creep in. "You WON the lottery! Not just the crap ass four in a row AND not just the "Match 5 for 10000". You won the WHOLE DAMN THING!"

By this time, Dean was shouting in Jim's face. Jim shook his head again. His dreams were often quite vivid and he thought for a second that Cecilia would appear at any time. She did not, however. He stared at Dean for another second as if Dean had suddenly started talking in a loud dialect of Arabic.

"What?" finally came out as the most coherent response that Jim's brain could muster.

"Jim, let me try and make it simple while you try to wake up," said Dean as he realized Jim was still half asleep trying to take in something that wide-awake people would have trouble absorbing. Jim's brown hair was cut pretty short and his stubble had started to grow here at the end of the day. The smell of pizza and beer was still on his breath but his eyes were now clear and the small muscles on the side of his eyes started to squint a little. Jim normally wore contacts and reached for his small John Lennon-style spectacles from the bedside stand. The glasses were a hold over from the old days. He slowly placed them on his face and then looked at Dean to signal him to continue.

"OK, so Ellen and I watched the end of the news and then we watched the Powerball drawing to see if you matched any numbers, just as you asked. The numbers started coming up and they kept matching and matching and...well... you won the whole thing," Dean said. His dark Greek skin and penetrating eyes looked even more serious in the low light.

"How much did I win" whispered Jim? He was fully awake now. He was having another one of those moments that reminded him of being pulled over by the cops. He felt somewhat vulnerable sitting up in his bed mostly naked getting this news.

"206 million dollars," whispered Dean looking right into Jim's eye. And Dean stopped talking, leaving that number just hanging in the air.

Jim started to shake a little. His hands gripped the bedsheet as if trying to hang on. His gaze snapped from Dean to Ellen and snapped back to Dean. He gathered from their faces that they were not kidding – that it was true. Inside, his organs had switched into overdrive. His heart was pounding. He started to breathe heavily and even to hyperventilate. Suddenly, he threw off the big white comforter and dashed into the bathroom. He did not even bother to excuse his boxers as he dashed past Ellen. He threw up just after reaching the toilet. He hung his head there supporting his weight by placing his hands on the top of the toilet lid. "Oh my God," he finally said. "Winning the lottery is a little hard on the stomach, I guess."

Dean and Ellen were standing in Jim's room after he cleaned up and returned. They had turned on the light but Ellen was pretending to study the streetlight outside. Dean was no longer sitting on the bed but had moved to the chair next to the dust-covered computer.

Jim came back in and said "Can I have the ticket?"

"Sure", said Dean who had not relaxed his grip on the ticket since the fifth number had come up and matched. He handed the ticket to Jim who just stared at it. He kept looking at it as if it was about to spontaneously start dancing a jig. "Oh my God," Jim said again and again.

Jim was not really thinking. In fact, he was not really sure that he was even alive and awake. No normal human could even comprehend that kind of fortune. What Jim could comprehend was that he was standing there in his boxer shorts. He grabbed his pants off the floor and put them on. As he did so, he noticed the small rip in the knee of his jeans. "Well, I guess I can afford a pair of jeans that don't have a rip in them now" said Jim as he pulled them on. He grabbed a sweatshirt off another chair and put that on as well.

"Yes, I think a new pair of jeans would be in your budget" said Dean as he sat smiling at Jim.

"Wow. I cannot really believe this. I cannot believe this is happening. It is not really how I imagined it – if I even really did imagine winning." said Jim.

Ellen spoke for the first time, "Well, they say that it takes anywhere from a month to a year before people realize what has happened".

An hour later, Jim and Dean were sitting in the Blue Moon, a bar just a block down from their apartment that was where they went when they didn't want to sit in the apartment. Dean had taken Ellen home. She had to get up and work in the morning unfortunately. She was leading a discussion group among the weekend staff at the hospital. She probably would not be able to sleep anyway but Jim wanted to go out and Ellen at least had to make the attempt at getting some sleep. The ticket was in the lock box that Jim had in his closet. Both he and Dean and Ellen had seen him hide it in there. They thought that was safer than bringing it out of the apartment with them. As they had sat there staring at the lockbox, Ellen had said "Imagine, just an hour ago it could have been a worthless piece of paper and not the most valuable slip of paper in the country tonight."

"Yeah, I am in shock and it isn't even my ticket", said Dean, who had stared at the lockbox as if it would spring up and jump out the window.

In the bar, they chose a booth that was tucked away in a corner behind the pool table – which no one was using. Jim stared into his beer. The wheels started to turn in his head – beer can do that for men. Finally, he said "Well, I can quit my job now, I guess. Think of all the trouble I went to last spring to set up the 401k program. I guess I have a new 401k program now!" He was already done with his first pint. He reached out and poured himself some more of the pitcher of Guinness. Instead of the normal, cheap but good pitcher of Leinenkugels that he normally ordered, Jim had ordered a pitcher of Guinness. He really did prefer Guinness but always ordered Leinie's to save a few bucks.

Dean was inherently a little cautious and glanced around the bar a little nervously. Most of the patrons were milling around the front by the bar. A mix of college students and lonely locals. This caution would serve him well as a doctor and had kept him from getting snowed while he was a teacher. "Are you going to tell everyone?" he asked. "Right now, only I and Ellen know. When I dropped her off, I told her not to tell anyone." He continued with a wry smile on his face, "Actually, it worked pretty well because now we have a little secret that we share. Thanks for making our first date so damn exciting. She already wants to see me again."

27

"Hey, that's great! I'm glad for you. I can't promise to make all your dates exciting though. You are going to have to pull that weight on your own from now on. But, making your date exciting will not be the last present I give you though. You know that, right?" Jim was starting to feel the Guinness and the buzz was making him a little giddy. "What do you want? Huh? Just name it, buddy. A car? A house? Two houses?"

Dean's caution kicked in again and so he proposed to Jim, "Hey, Ellen told me that she had read about lottery winners in one of her sociology classes. She told me that she remembered in the class that experts recommended to the winners that it was best to not spend any of the money for awhile. Of course, pay off your debts and whatever is critical but do not make any big purchases for awhile to give the change a little time to sink in. Seems like kind of a good idea, don't you think?"

Jim looked at Dean for a second, then down at his beer. "Yeah, you are probably right. Did you hear about the guy in West Virginia that won over $300 million a few Christmases ago? HE got robbed at a strip club, spent tons at the track and his granddaughter disappeared right out of his house? His wife said that she wished they had never won the money in the first place. I will probably not tell anyone else until everything is a done deal and then just a few people that I can trust." A little of the responsibility of all this money sank in to Jim.

Dean looked across the booth as Jim started to slump a little lower. "So, are you going to quit your job?" asked Dean trying to regain the euphoria.

A big, broad smile came over Jim's face and he refilled his beer glass. "You better believe it! Those guys are going to split a gut when I do not show up on Monday. Or...Maybe I should go in and screw up until they fire me. No, they're decent guys. I don't want to do something like that. I'll just go in and give my notice on Monday. I'll tell them I got a better job. OK, let's not tell anyone for awhile. I want to make sure that everything is set and the money's for sure going to come in." Jim shrugged his shoulders and stared at his beer. "Who knows? Maybe someone else had the same numbers. The jackpot's 206 million, which is one of the higher amounts given out to date. Probably lots of tickets sold for that amount of prize."

"Well, hard to say if your numbers are very common. Unless someone has that date as a birthday, you might have the whole thing to yourself. Have you ever thought about winning before and what you'd do?" asked Dean. "I mean, you have been playing for years. And, you always play the same numbers. What did you want out of winning?"

Jim sat there for a minute as he took a long pull on his beer. "Well, I started playing the lottery after Cecilia left. I guess I thought that if I won, she would come back. I suppose it was a little silly but it was a very bad time. Eventually, that feeling kind of wore off but I kept playing more or less out of habit. I guess I have a lot of habits. Other than obsessing about my ex, I had the common thoughts. Quitting my job. Buying a boat. Buying a house and getting out of that apartment-no offense." He paused to sip his beer again and then continued, "I guess that I thought the money could free me to do what I want. Options." Taking another long slug, he said "Of course, knowing what I want to do now is not exactly crystal clear though – especially after this pitcher of Guinness! Why aren't you drinking more?"

"OK, OK," said Dean as he finished half a beer in one long sip," Anyway, I'll be here if you need me. And you will. We've been friends for a long time so you do not have to worry about why I'm your friend." Dean winced as he said that. His mind had flown ahead to the point Jim would not reach for some time, unfortunately. Dean winced because he assumed, wrongly, that Cecilia had left only for Ted's money, as Jim used to think. In fact, she had left for several reasons.

"Yep, you're a true friend Dean. I will need you around. Would you mind if I paid for some stuff for both of us?" asked Jim.

"OK," said Dean smiling," but I'm not going to be your kept man!"

29

"Ha," snorted Jim. "I guess I could be a sugar daddy now. Does Ellen have a roommate?"

And so they sat and drank their beer. After they finished that pitcher, they wondered how much it would cost to buy the Milwaukee Brewers. They decided that it was too much hassle and to just get season box seats instead. With drunkenness came a burst of generosity and Jim walked up to the bar to talk to Bill, the very busy college-age bartender, and asked "Can I buy a round for the whole bar? We have something to celebrate."

The Blue Moon was not a high-brow bar, although they did have Guinness on tap which was pretty unusual, and so it never happened that someone wanted to buy a round for the whole bar. Plus, it was quite late on a Friday night so the neighborhood bar was far more full than normal. Bill looked really surprised but said, "Sure, you can. Is that what you want to do?"

Jim replied, "Yeap, a free Guinness to everyone who wants one."

Bill announced it to the patrons who all applauded. In the end, it was about $1500 but Jim deftly put it on his credit card, saying "Well, if you cannot share with 300 of your best friends, who can you share with?" No one else really cared except they liked the free beer. Dean just sat back in his chair and watched Jim give away a little cheer. "No harm in that," he thought.

An hour later, Dean and Jim finally stepped out into the chilly evening with everyone cheering Jim. They headed back to the apartment. It was now pretty late or pretty early. The next day would be Saturday. Jim needed to go down to the Total Gas Station about three blocks away to report that he had the ticket. By the middle of the day, the news stations would have picked up the news that a local person had won the Powerball jackpot. Dean and Jim figured that if they went first thing in the morning, they had a chance of getting in and out without being discovered.

Just as Dean shoved the key into the deadbolt to unlock the apartment door, he stopped and looked up at Jim who had been patiently but drunkenly watching and waiting for the door to be opened. It always seems to be that way. The person who is unlocking a door - either on a car or apartment - is watched by the others somewhat absentmindedly. Dean looked Jim in the eye and said, "So, are you going to try and get Cecilia back now?" Dean had started thinking about what Jim had said about why he played the lottery. For a second, Jim just stared at Dean. Dean saw something in Jim's face that made him want to turn away for a moment but he did not. Finally, the moment passed, Jim rolled his eyes as if to scoff at Dean and said, "Oh, come on, no need to ruin a perfectly good evening bringing her up. Don't worry, it's not like I am going to run in and phone her up if that's what you mean. Now, open the door, it is getting damn cold out here."

*****

The next morning, Jim awoke to the alarm which they had set for 6AM. It was a short night and he was aggravated by the hang-over he had now. Of course, the beer had helped him get any sleep at all. Jim could hear that Dean was in the shower. Dean had promised to go down to the store with him. Dean would drive because Jim seemed pretty distracted. Jim got out of bed and started shaving. As he stared at his face in the mirror, he said, "Well, this is the last time I will look at this face of a man who is not a millionaire." The thought was a little overwhelming so Jim focused on not slashing an artery as he cleaned himself up. Jim realized that he also needed a haircut.

"Well, I can start going to a real barber now, huh Dean?" Jim called out to Dean in the shower.

Dean said, " Uhhh, don't talk to me. I have not had any coffee yet. You and your damn Guinness!" Dean finished in the shower. Soon, they were both dressed, fed and caffeinated. They dressed very casually and hoped not to stand out.

While Jim was in the shower, Dean had called over to the Total Station. "They said that they knew they had the

31

winning ticket. They want us to park in the back of the station and there will be a guy there to let us in. They said, "Bring the ticket and as many forms of ID as you can carry."

"Thanks for calling. That was a good idea. OK, let's go and get this done with".

A small knot had started to form in Jim's belly and he just wanted to get it done with and get on with the rest of the day. Of course, he had not planned anything past this moment. Or rather, he had made some plans but they probably all needed to be re-evaluated. For example, he did not need to spend part of the day changing the oil in his car himself.

So, they went out and got in Dean's rusty Honda and drove down the street to the Total station. The streets were still pretty empty and the station had just opened so there were very few people around. Although it was springtime, it was still pretty cold out this morning and Jim could see his breath.

"Sorry, the Honda heats up really slowly," said Dean.

"No problem, we will just have to get it fixed - maybe by replacing all the parts. I just cannot believe this is happening to me," said Jim smiling a little.

They parked in the back as directed. It did not look like there was anyone in the front. A burly looking man in a dark suit and black winter wool coat stood by the unmarked back door of the Total station. He motioned for them to come over and then opened the door for them. "Good morning" he said with all the inflection of a robot. "Bouncer" was what went through Jim's head. "Seems like we're walking into a club," he muttered.

He and Dean were lead into what looked like the storage room for the gas station. On all the walls were shelves containing boxes of window washer fluid, ice scrapers, beef jerky, and so on. In one corner, there was a mop station which gave off a slight odor of ammonia. In the middle of the tiny room, a small table had been set up with several neat piles of paper and an apparatus that looked like a microscope and another apparatus that didn't look like anything. Another man in a suit but containing a lot more personality started shaking their hands vigorously as if he was pumping his joy into them. He was a short man and reminded Jim of pictures of Gandhi. For a moment, he tried to picture this man in a wrapped white cloth but it was impossible to do with the man shaking his arm so hard it was about to fall off.

The happy man said, "Hi, my name is Art. I am with the Powerball organization for the midwest. I come out every morning that there is a winner here in Wisconsin. My job is to make sure the ticket's valid and that you're who you say you are. The rules are listed on the back of the ticket. You do have the ticket, correct?"

"Right" said Jim pulling the ticket out of his pocket. They had put the ticket in a zip-lock bag the night before and it was still inside. The ticket was not that big. Only about 2 inches by 3 inches. It was a little crinkled because Jim had kept it in his pocket at work the day before. He always got coffee and the lottery ticket on Friday morning at the gas station. He recognized the day manager who was standing in a corner. "Hi," he said, "I recognize you. You're the guy normally here in the morning".

"Right," said the man," I'm Jonas Harrison. I'm the day manager and so I open the store. Very nice to meet you officially, Mr. ..."

"Wells, Jim Wells, at your service."

"No," said Art, "we are at your service, Mr. Wells." Art had been studying the ticket using a microscope and had also looked at it with ultra-violet light. He seemed to be convinced that the ticket was authentic. "Congratulations, Mr. Wells. This is the official ticket and it's a winner!"

Everyone in the room started to relax a little. Art explained that, in the recent past, there had been a number of people who had been trying to create fake Powerball tickets. The lottery had secretly added some new hidden features in order to counteract this problem. However, Jim's ticket was genuine. It had the hidden microprint and it had the secret ultraviolet marks. Most importantly, it had the winning numbers on it.

"Ok" said Art, "We need information from you now to prove that you're who you say you are." Jim produced his Wisconsin driver's license, his Social Security card, the lease for his and Dean's apartment, a recent bank statement, his checkbook and several credit card bills. Being an engineer has advantages, as Jim was well organized and was able to gather all these things in a few minutes before driving over.

"Great! That should be all we need," Art said as he started using the small photocopier to copy everything that Jim had brought in. The picture ID's were especially important, Art explained. Finally, Art had finished that and opened another small case. "OK, Jim, I need to take your fingerprints for the file." Jim cast a quick glance over to Dean who was frowning slightly in the corner. Art noticed this and said quickly, "Look, we need to make sure of who you are at this second so that as the years go by it will be easy to maintain your identity should, God forbid, any questions arise. It has happened before. About five years ago, someone who had been getting their yearly check walked into our offices one day only to find that someone else had claimed the check a few days previously. Someone impersonating them had claimed the check instead. Well, that was a huge fiasco and now we fingerprint people when they pick up their yearly check, before we give them their check. Don't worry, we only use it for this purpose. By law, we are sworn to secrecy about this and about everything else regarding the award winners."

"OK," said Jim and allowed Art to fingerprint him. Dean was surprised that Jim would have allowed that, but he guessed for 206 million dollars, it was a small price.

"Well, that's about it" said Art. "I have written out a receipt here. It is being witnessed by Mr. Harrison as well as your friend Dean Peterson. There are, I am sorry to tell you, several other matching tickets that were printed according to the computer. You are the first to come forward but they have 30 days technically to come forward. However, no one has every made a claim after the first week has passed for any of the major jackpots. Therefore, we should know in a week or so your probable fraction of the prize. The final

34

total was actually 224 million due to last minute sales yesterday. The smallest amount you could receive is 44.5 million if all five winning tickets are claimed. Of course, the most you could receive is the entire 224 million. Today, I am authorized to give you a check for $250,000 which should take care of any immediate financial problems that you have."

At this point, Jim's eyebrows went up. Dean could not decide if it was the check for $250,000 or the fact that he might only get $44 million that caused his eyebrows to go up. Dean hoped it was anticipation for the $250,000 and not the early onset of greed. God knows that $44 million would be plenty. Dean could not even fathom an amount of more than $1 million.

Art continued, "OK, once we determine what the final winnings you will receive are, we will divide that amount into 20 equal payments. Each year you will receive that amount in a single lump sum from us on the first of August. You need to go to the local Powerball representative (there is one in every state that has the lottery) and receive the check from them. What you do with the money is your business. You can pick up the first check at the end of this month which will be two million. Our normal address is in the packet on the table. It is here in town so you don't have to travel to get your check as long as you continue living in Madison. You will also need a lawyer and a financial consultant. I suggest you go with the law firm of Rottier and Davis. They have worked with several previous winners. I am also suggesting that you contact the Northstar Resource Group. Their financial advisors have handled several of our people. It is all written down in the packet."

Jim picked up the packet and started to thumb through it. He recognized the names of the lawyers from the TV and knew where the lottery offices were already. He handed the packet to Dean.

"One final question," said Art. "We would like your help. We want to publicize your name and picture to promote the Powerball lottery and present you with a huge

35

check at a press conference. Can we have your permission to do this?" Jim looked at Art who was smiling placidly at him. Jim turned to Dean who slowly shook his head side-to-side.

Jim turned back to Art. "Look, Art. I would like to help you out but I am not sure if that would be wise."

Like Regis Philbin on the Millionaire gameshow, Art said, "So, is NO your final answer?"

Jim replied, "That's right, NO, do not use my picture or name to publicize the Powerball."

Art's face relaxed into a smile. "Smart decision. I have to ask by the regulations but only idiots agree to tell the world that they are now made of money. Everyone around you will know soon enough but at least kooks in Montana won't know your name."

Mr. Harrison and Art shook hands with Dean and Jim. As they turned to go, Art stopped them by saying "One more piece of advice, Jim. You seem like a nice young guy who is going to have a lot of years with this money. Try not to forget who you are today. It is easy to get lost in all this green stuff." And with that the meeting was over and Jim walked out of the small backroom of a gas station and into his new life.

Dean smiled as he thought that perhaps Jim had already forgotten who he was years ago.

Chapter 3: Beginning to Breathe

The giraffe is a graceful creature in spite of its potential to be exceedingly awkward. The length of the neck, if designed by a person, would be unstable and weak. The long legs would seem to break easily. But when you watch a giraffe run, it is as graceful and smooth as a stallion. When you watch the giraffe reaching for the leaves that it needs to survive - up on the highest branches- you begin to understand the purpose and design of the giraffe within the surroundings in which it evolved. The neck transforms in the mind from a gangly exaggeration to an essential and artistic design. The grace of the adult giraffe stands in stark contrast to the giraffe fawn just hours after birth. The fawn struggles to stand almost immediately. The baby needs to get moving in a world filled with predators. But those first steps are slow and awkward. The brain tries to send signals to the legs. These instinctual signals often misfire as the body tries to coordinate the new muscles in totally new ways. Like an orchestra tuning up for the grand performance, the resulting movements seem crazy, disjointed and painful to the casual observer but are all part of the necessary process if the fawn wants to reach adulthood.

"Lean farther out!" called Jim.

Dean thought, "If I lean any farther, my entire body will be outside the boat." He yelled back to Jim, who was manning the rudder while also leaning in the back of the boat, "What the hell is the point of having a boat if you're not inside it?" Jim just smiled behind his sunglasses as he concentrated on guiding this small sailboat. The sailboat was an Interlake. The Interlake is about 17 feet long and has a very, very tiny cabin in the middle which would keep the extra life-preservers and sack lunch dry. With a medium-sized mainsail and a jib sail, it could almost be sailed by a single person.

Jim and Dean were out sailing across Lake Mendota which sits in the middle of Madison. The University of Wisconsin sits along one edge of Lake Mendota. More precisely, the Student Union and the associated sailing club lie directly on the water's edge. For about a month now, since the boats first went out on the lake in April, Jim had been sailing several times a week. This sailboat, along with a navy of other tiny sailboats belongs to the University of Wisconsin Hoofers Sailing Club. On the surface, the name is somewhat misleading because the club has nothing to do with horses. In fact, there are a series of University clubs for everything from hang-gliding to scuba diving to equestrians (the original club from which the name comes). The great feature of the club for most people is that they didn't need to own or rent a sailboat to go sailing. Jim happened to see the boats when they were being moved back into the water shortly after he quit his job; and he started asking around about sailing. He'd never taken any sailing lessons while he went to the University. Dean thought that Jim was starting to think of himself as being rich and so sailing had a natural - albeit stereotypical - appeal. Jim thought it just seemed like a fun thing to do – his only prerequisite for most activities now. Jim had started coming down frequently during the week and had already moved up from the "floating yellow bathtubs" that the beginners use to the Interlakes. Jim felt confident that, with enough practice, he would continue to improve and get certified by the club to take out bigger and faster sailboats that require a bigger crew to do all the necessary tasks.

"Don't worry," yelled Jim, trying to calm down Dean. Dean had only gone out three times with Jim so far this summer as he had been in and out of town with different med school rotations. Jim continued, "I am sure you can still be a doctor even with a wet ass and rope

39

burns." The wind was blowing straight and clean across the lake leading Jim to feel confident about keeping the Interlake aggressively tacked into the wind. The speed continued to grow as they shot across the lake and blew by several canoes and a smaller "bathtub" boat.

Dean relaxed and started to enjoy himself. "This is awesome!" he screamed. "Really, really awesome."

Two hours and a few miles of open water later, they were back on dry land. After putting the boat away, Jim and Dean walked up from the docks and took refuge in the Rathskeller – a very authentic seeming German bar nestled within the very large Student Union. It was one of the only University-owned bars in the country that sold beer in addition to real German food. After collecting a few "Rathskeller Ale" beers and two bratwursts, they found a booth and started to look through a booklet on sailing and discuss sailing with the Hoofer club. Jim said, "Well, the club has a ton of boats but if you can only come down on the weekend, you have a good chance of getting shut out on getting a boat. Everyone wants to sail on Saturday."

Dean took a long sip of his beer, "Well, luckily, you have all the time in the world! In fact, perhaps you need to take up something else to do during the weekend?" He smiled, leaned back and put his hands behind his head.

Jim only half-realized that Dean was making fun of him and replied, "Maybe. The problem is that the weekend is when other friends, such as you, can go sailing. Actually, I don't want you to think I am complaining but the weekdays are getting a little boring when everyone is at work or wherever." Jim looked down into his beer. "In fact", he said, "I rented that movie "About a Boy" the other day. Did you see it? It has Hugh Grant and he doesn't work either. Anyway, I rented it to see how Hugh spent his time during the week. It didn't help because his life seemed pretty boring to me plus he just had enough money not to work – not enough to really do some stuff." Jim gazed out the window to the lake. "I like the sailing though because all this stuff seems so far away while I am out on the lake and there is so much to learn it is really all-encompassing." He paused and

40

then looked back at Dean, smiling. "Once I get the first annual check next month, I'm seriously considering getting a boat over in Lake Michigan! Wouldn't that be sweet?! Drive over; spend the day on some really big waves – far from shore… Stay on the boat, if it has a cabin…"

Dean interrupted, "Hey! I almost forgot to ask you about the place you bought." Even though Dean and Jim were roommates, Dean had been at the hospital all of the time and Jim had also seldom been home when Dean actually was home. Jim took a short trip to see his parents and had told them the truth. He wrote them a big check which he thought they wanted but, when he got back, he said that the whole thing had felt a little weird. His parents were quite set in their ways and I think that Jim's opportunities kind of scared them. Perhaps it just takes some time for them to adjust to being related to a rich son. Dean had told him that hopefully they would adjust to it by the next time he saw them.

Dean continued, "I read that cryptic note you left on the countertop." He looked up at the ceiling as if the note was reproduced up there:

"   Dear Dean, We need to talk. I found a house in Maple Bluff. Hope that you would like to move in or I will pay out the rest of my part of the apartment lease, if you want. – Jim.

"So, what is the deal on that," he asked? Dean was really curious because Maple Bluff was the most exclusive and expensive part of town. The neighborhood of Maple Bluff actually sat on the same lake as the University and the sailing club. However, the social difference between the University and Maple Bluff could not be greater. The Wisconsin Governor's mansion sat on the lakeshore in Maple Bluff. Most of the people living out there were either senior state government officials or senior University officials as it was still far away in mind but close to town by car.

Jim started playing with his thumbs a little bit and then looked Dean straight in the eye as he began his story, "I

41

met someone at one of those sailing parties at the end of the day Saturday, a few weeks ago. He was very happy and a little drunk because he had just gotten a big promotion at work – I forget if it was Intel or IBM. Anyway, he has to move to New York to be the Chief Corporate Counsel or something and he was going to sell his house here out in Maple Bluff. Anyway, he invited some of us over after happy hour and I checked it out. It has really incredible views over the lake!" Jim rapidly counted off the amenities on his fingers:

Index Finger: Right on the bluff with stairs down to a little dock where you can tie up a sailboat.

Middle Finger: Is all set for entertaining with a big screen TV, a pool table, air hockey and a hot tub big enough for 8 people.

Ring Finger: It has a three car garage – so no more parking on the street for us.

Pinky Finger: Five bedrooms, three of which have their own bathrooms, lake views and it faces west so the sunsets are incredible.

Dean leaned back with his eyes very wide and said, "Wow. That sounds incredible. Just out of curiosity, do you mind if I ask how much it costs?"

Jim kind of casts his eyes about and then says, "Well, don't spread this around but he's asking $1.2 Million for the whole package with a bunch of the stuff (like the TV and pool table) included. However, my realtor says that, because this guy needs to move so fast, they will probably come down closer to an even million. So…. I made an offer on it today. Oddly, I have to get a loan but the lottery people were very helpful in talking to the bank so I got qualified really quickly. Actually, that new financial guy, Brian, told me to get a mortgage anyway and invest the check and I'll come out ahead." Suddenly, Jim stopped short as it all sank in, "My God! I am buying a big-ass house! More house than I would ever need!! Woo hoo!! Let's get some more beers!"

Dean and Jim walked up to the bar and got some more beers and Dean said, "That house sounds really awesome. I would be happy to move in...at least for awhile."

Jim ordered some more beers but cast a look over his shoulder at Dean and asked, "Why just for awhile?"

Dean got a little smile on his face and stared at his feet while he says, "Well, everything with Ellen is going really well – when I get a chance to see her. Anyway, I think that we might move in together pretty soon. Mostly so I can see more of her in spite of my hectic schedule."

Jim stopped for a second with a beer in mid-air and stared at Dean. He looked a little...well...almost scared, Dean thought. Then, Jim's features relaxed and, as he moved out of the beer line and back towards the booth, he said, "You can both move in! There is plenty of room."

Dean chuckled and yelled after him, "I don't think you understand the point of moving in with your girlfriend!" Dean shook his head and watched Jim as he walked away. He really hasn't changed too much yet, he thought. Then, he corrected himself – except for quitting his job, learning to sail and buying a mansion in the ritziest part of town. Well, he hasn't changed much on the inside, he decided.

Dean got back to the booth and he and Jim resumed the serious task of going through the sailing manual for Dean's education.

A month later, during the dead heat of summer, we find Dean standing on the top of a thirty foot cliff that drops directly into Lake Mendota below him and wraps around the backyard of Jim's new house. Dean says that he feels a little like Kato Kaihlen staying in O.J. Simpson's house. He's on the far eastern shore of the lake. He is standing there in shorts facing south into the humid, hot haze. He can see the campus through the haze laid out along the southern shore and can just make out the student union. He's watching for the boat that Jim is supposedly sailing towards him. Jim has just called to see if Dean wanted to go for a short sail before he goes in to the hospital for his shift. Dean's only responsibility is to grab some sodas and sandwiches and meet him down at the small dock below the house. Behind Dean lay the new house. Jim and Dean had been moved in the week before. Their paltry amount of furniture barely filled any of the rooms. Luckily, the previous owners had also sold Dean a bunch of their stuff that they didn't want to bring to New York, including the pool table and built-in entertainment system in the basement. And, of course, the hot tub and little pool were the main attractions for Jim so far.

"Oh, there he is" said Dean to no one in particular, as Jim's boat came into view. Jim was looking pretty skillful on this boat which was a class bigger than the Interlake. Dean had been out sailing many more times as well and was becoming pretty good at helping out around the boat as it skimmed along the water. Dean looked up at the sky and across the waves. It was a good day for sailing because the wind was steady and strong. Often, the wind on these inland lakes was really gusty and swirly …but not today.

Jim landed the boat, slightly bumping the dock, and Dean jumped aboard. "Did you get the sandwiches?", asked Jim.

"Yeap, pastrami and rye for you and your arteries and feta and sprouts for me. Plus, some classic generic black cherry soda just like you asked for."

Jim said, "Great! Let's go while the wind is good then. I suggest we sail over to Bishop's Bay and then back toward the Union for starters."

Dean said, "OK, but I need to be back by four to get in for my shift and I DON'T want to have to explain that I was late because the wind died."

Jim stopped adjusting the sail to stare at him and bark, "Hey, that wasn't my fault! Plus, I called to get you a speedboat ride back to the house."

"Relax, relax," said Dean as he settled himself into the cockpit and stowed the sandwiches. "I am just yanking your chain. However, we did wait a while before we called anyone."

Jim settled down and muttered, "The wind could have come back up. Anytime, really…anytime…"

They pushed off and almost immediately were up and hanging out on the side as they rounded the little point on which the new house sat. To the casual observer, they looked like a professional sailing team. Jim had bought them both new waterproof sailing suits and matching sunglasses. Off they cruised, tacking upwind northeast across the lake to the Bishop's Bay Country Club – a majestic piece of property with several golf fairways on the verge of tumbling into the water. There wasn't much time to talk except for ordering directions at each other. Both of the men were still at the level that they had to consider their movements carefully and their occasional mistakes caused them to backtrack. An occasional "DUCK" was heard too as the boom zipped over their heads far too quickly. Well, at least they looked like professionals in their outfits…

They made it over to Bishop's Bay in what was a new record time for Jim. He had started tracking his speeds habitually now as he was racing several times a week. Sailing had morphed from a recreation to practically a new vocation for him. Dean wondered if this is what happened to all wealthy people. That they needed some kind of "work" to do – even if it doesn't involve money or wages and is completely voluntary and fun… Perhaps this is where Jim is headed, Dean thought. Not so bad really and it could be worse. Considering how he used to just go to work and then vegetate in front of the TV, Dean was kind of expecting Jim to just get a huge TV and spend his days sitting in front of it. But, thought Dean, I guess even Jim cannot stomach those daytime soaps.

They rolled across the lake and past the fairways before making a rather abrupt landing against the dock of Bishop's Bay. Luckily, there were no other sailboats at the dock and the speedboats were all safely up in the boathouse. They pulled up to rest for a little and eat their sandwiches.

Between munches, Jim said, "So, is Ellen going to come over tonight or not? She hasn't been around lately much. Is she busy or working or what?"

Dean fumbled with opening his sandwich wrapper and started to mumble, "Well, I don't know. She's seemingly a little upset. It seems that I'm - Dean gestures quotes with his fingers as best as possible while holding a sandwich and soda - "emotionally unavailable" lately. I try to spend time with her but I've been pretty distracted these days. This surgery rotation is pretty tough and so I think she feels a little neglected. Plus, I think she feels a little weird being in the big house when I am not with her. Which reminds me, I am not going to be home for 36 hours starting two hours from now."

"Do we need to get going?" asked Jim.

"No, with that speed, we're fine." responded Dean, still thinking about Ellen.

"I'm sorry to hear that, buddy," said Jim. "Let me know if there's anything I can do…like take her out on the town or something."

Dean laughed, "No, I think that the last thing my relationship needs is my girlfriend going out with the richest man in town!!! So, are we going to sail or sit around acting like women at a coffee shop?"

With that, they took off again. They made it over to the Union pier and back to the house in record time so Dean could get going to the hospital. Dean jumped out and disappeared inside to prepare for hours of saving lives, filling out paperwork, drinking coffee and being exposed to germs and abuse from doctors.

Jim headed back to the Union pier to put away the boat. It takes awhile in the afternoon on a good wind day because of the line up of boats coming in. So, by the time Jim got it tied up and the sails stowed and the rowboat back to shore, it had started to get dark by the time he was driving home. Recently, because of his odd schedule, Jim had not had to worry about traffic, which he proclaimed as one of the hidden perks of being wealthy – the ability to schedule around the rest of the working world. However, today Jim was caught in the traffic around the lake which reminded him that he should start thinking about what kind of car to buy. He liked the lines of the new Volvo AWD wagon. Jim was about to pick out the color for the Volvo in his head just

46

as he pulled into the driveway when a big dog dashed in front of the bumper! He slammed on the brakes and stopped, just in front of the immobilized dog. He thought, "Thank God for ABS brakes, even in this old car." The dog sat frozen in the driveway, peed all over and shook slightly. It looked like a Golden retriever.

Jim didn't know what to do, and as he was sitting there trying to decide, a woman advanced on his position across the lawn. He recognized her, and subsequently the dog, as being one of those attractive suburban women who walked her dog every morning about the time that Katie Couric goes off the air. Jim turned off the car and rolled down the window just in time to hear "...so sorry. I am sooo sorry." she said addressing Jim. Turning and advancing on the dog, she shouted, "Scout! Get over here! You cannot run off like that! You almost got yourself killed!" Then, once she got her hand on the dog's collar, she digressed into disciplining the dog "Bad DOG! Bad boy! Bad Boy!" She rapped him on the nose with her palm. By this point, it had dawned on the dog that he had screwed up. He crouched and turned as far away from her as possible considering she had him by the collar.

Jim suddenly realized that his car was still hanging out of the driveway into the road and that the woman seemed content to discipline the dog in his driveway. Seeing no other way out of the situation, he got out of the car and introduced himself. "Hi, I'm Jim Wells, I just bought this place a month back." The woman suddenly came out of her disciplining trance and turned to Jim, thereby letting go of the dog, which took off in the direction from which it came. As she looked after the dog, she extended her hand to shake Jim's. Finally, turning to face him, she said "Hello. My name is Sable. My husband and I live next door." Throwing her thumb over her shoulder at the monstrous brown brick castle next to Jim's, she continued, "We've been meaning to come over and say hello but just haven't had a chance yet when you're home and we're home. I am sooo sorry about Scout. He thinks that, because of his name, he has to bolt after every squirrel and rabbit in the neighborhood. We have the invisible fence with the shock collar but he just puts up with the pain until he's through it, I guess."

Jim said, "Well, no worries. I'm just glad I didn't hit him! Serves me right to drive a little slower through the neighborhood anyway."

At this point, Jim finally stopped long enough to take a look at Sable. She was young, even younger than Jim perhaps. Late 20's or just over 30. She had the look of someone with time and money to worry about her appearance. Blond with brown highlights in her hair and wearing what must be her "lying about the house clothes" which consisted of some faded Polo jeans and a sweatshirt from the local organic grocery store. Jim assumed that she volunteered there when she wasn't chasing her Golden through the neighborhood.

"Well, I'm glad you didn't hit him either!" she said, finally focusing on Jim as well. "You know, if you don't have any plans, I'm actually cooking a stir-fry tonight for Cliff and I. Are you free to join us? I realize it's rather spontaneous but…well, Cliff travels a lot so it might not work out any other time."

Jim smiled widely, "Sure, I'd love to. Turns out I was just thinking about what to do tonight when I almost hit Scout."

"Great," she said, seeming genuinely pleased to have him agree to it. "Does seven o'clock work for you?"

"Sure," said Jim, "Can I bring anything? Wine perhaps?"

"That would be great, bring anything red as the stir-fry is a little spicy."

Cliff and Sable's house was actually a little bigger than Jim's but Cliff needed all of the space. He just about shook Jim's arm off when he met him and his presence swallowed up Jim. Jim continued to listen to Cliff talk through the handshake and while he went to grab Jim a beer from the fridge. Cliff felt that beer was an excellent appetizer and Jim couldn't agree more. Jim started to drink his Sam Adams from the bottle while he found out that Cliff was a salesman, a career especially suited to his personality and his appearance. Cliff had obviously been a big, well-built guy all his life and it turned out that after a short-lived ("I blew out my knee so far they almost couldn't find it") hockey career, Cliff had become a hockey equipment salesman for CCM. Now, a short six years later, he was the US sales manager. Success brought sacrifice, though, as Cliff traveled all the time. Jim felt a little odd at first that they would share one of their only evenings alone with him but the three of them seemed to get along famously.

Sable felt that the formal dining room was far too formal to eat in (unless twenty relatives or co-workers were coming by) and so she had set plates out on the island in the kitchen. So, the three of them sat on kitchen stools, hunched over the island ladling rice and stir-fry directly out of the rice cooker and the huge Calphalon wok on the stove. Cliff had given Jim a tour of the rest of the house, which, not too surprisingly, was laid out in a similar style to Jim's house to take advantage of the lake views. The similarities ended there though. Jim noticed that they had actual furniture in their rooms and that someone (he assumed Sable) had spent a considerable effort to get the colors to coordinate and the furniture to look like it all belonged together. Jim realized that he had a lot of work to do on his own house. In spite of the size and the exercise in decorating, Jim realized it seemed a little staged and he couldn't put a handle on it until he walked into the large rec room. He realized that this is where Sable and Cliff must actually live. At one end was a small sitting area in front of a huge TV. Behind the sitting area were a pool table, weight-lifting machine and treadmill. There were books and magazine strewn around, a crumpled towel next to the treadmill and a pile of mail and bills sitting next to the couch. There was also a dog bed next to the couch which was probably Scout's normal position when he wasn't taunting the neighborhood drivers.

Cliff said "Well, as you can see, we were not really expecting company but I guess you are a neighbor so you don't really count as company, right?" And he laughed loudly.

As they sat down to dinner, Cliff threw Jim for a loop by asking him, "So, what is it that you do, Jim?"

Jim realized he had not really had to answer that question in the few months since he had become the big winner. "Well...," Jim started and then stopped.

Cliff jumped in, "Well, don't tell us that you work for the CIA because we have too many spooks in the neighborhood already! No one around here likes to or often can explain what they do, it seems."

Jim laughed, and then continued, "No, it's pretty simple. I'm an engineer by background. I recently quit my old job and am looking for something new. I've some money for the moment so I'm not looking real hard for work at the moment. The house was a real bargain so I bought it. A little strange to buy a house and be unemployed but I'm pretty confident about finding something." Jim thought it sounded ridiculous but he really didn't want to tell them the truth until he felt he could trust them a little more.

But, Cliff and Sable had met enough rich people to know that certain questions shouldn't be pursued and that most conversations about money end up being boring anyway. So, Cliff pursued another direction, "Engineer, huh? Do you know anything about cars and engines? You see, I am a car racing nut and am looking for someone else to help me buy a new engine."

"Unfortunately," said Jim, "I'm no expert on engines. I'm more of a heating and cooling engineer, but I have a lot of free time at the moment so let me know what you need." Cliff looked across the island at Sable, whom Jim sensed was starting to get annoyed. Cliff said, "Well, I'm pretty busy for the moment but I'll let you know. If nothing else, you'll have to come out and watch the race next weekend."

"A real car race? Do you drive yourself? Is it stock cars or..."?

As Sable started to set the stir-fry and rice and Cliff leaned into the table and said, "Well, they are Ferraris actually. Ferrari sponsors the races and organizes everything. We just show up with our cars and pocketbooks and do the driving. The races in the north Chicago area are the closest but I'm lobbying for getting one over in Milwaukee next summer. Some of my old hockey buddies got me involved and I bought an older Ferrari just to try it out. I REALLY like it though. Very thrilling, very thrilling. There are only a handful of races left before the end of the season so I'm trying to make it to as many as I can."

Sable cut in," Jim, you should really come. You'd be someone for me to sit with while he is out there trying to kill himself." She glared at Cliff while he glanced back complacently, shrugged his shoulders and continued to shovel stir-fry into his mouth. Jim looked away noticing that the sun was just setting across the lake. Just when the moment was getting ackward, Sable turned to Jim and abruptly changed topics. "Actually, Jim, was it you I saw out sailing today? We can't quite see your dock from our angle up here on the bluff but I thought it looked like you and someone else sailing up to here and then off again. Sorry, I wasn't stalking you but I was working on the yard at the time."

Jim scooped up some more stir-fry onto his plate and answered feeling somewhat proud, 'Yep, that was me. I started sailing at the beginning of the summer when I quit my job and have been doing pretty well actually. I really like it. I was sailing with my roommate Dean today. He's in med school. This stir-fry is really delicious."

Sable was getting more interested now and leaned across the island under the light grabbing the tabletop with both hands. "Really! Would you take me sailing some day? That would be really fun!" And then she leaned back in the chair and tapped Cliff on the arm. "Cliff's not a big fan of the water; which is odd considering he grew up on hockey skates."

"Yeah," said Cliff as he knocked on the granite countertop. "I only like water that's frozen ...or really hot like the Jacuzzi...not much in between."

"Sure," said Jim looking at Sable, "I'd be happy to take you out some time. I'm going for another rating, on a bigger boat, at the end of next week and then it should be a little easier to grab a boat when I want. Oh, and I'm going to a big group sail on Friday afternoon if you're around. Have you seen that larger boat painted like a black and white cow off the dock of the Union?"

"No" and "Yes" said Cliff and Sable respectively and separately. As she reached to pour more of the red wine that Jim had brought, Sable looked at Cliff, "You know I take that class over there, right? Well, I usually get lunch at the Union afterwards and watch all the sailboats out there." She turns to Jim, "I'm taking an English class twice a week on Chaucer. Keeps the mind sharp, you know."

Jim raised his eyebrows involuntarily because, being an engineer, he always felt self-conscious about his literary skills and so was always impressed with highly literate people. He made a mental note not to judge Sable in the future as a simple trophy wife until he learned a little more about her.

Jim left their house with a flurry of exchanging numbers and future dates and volunteering to watch their dog (which had been completely sedate the rest of the evening with no squirrels to scout) occasionally when they both were gone. Jim drifted off to sleep in his double bed (realizing that he could probably get at least a queen-sized bed now) thinking about boat sailing and car racing and Cliff and Sable's big, well-decorated home.

That next Friday turned out to be overcast and cool, the wind was spitting a little drizzle. There didn't seem to be any lightning though, which meant the group sail could go on. Jim had called Sable in the morning and she was still up for it so they arrived together in Jim's old car. Sable actually remarked that it was refreshing that Jim didn't find it necessary to get a new car to match his new house. Jim tried to steer the conversation away from money and cars because he still didn't want to talk about the lottery with Sable and Cliff yet. So, he said, "Sounds like Cliff is pretty passionate about racing the Ferrari?"

Sable just stopped and shrank deeper into the passenger seat and started to stare out the side window.

"Yep," she said. "I really worry about him actually. His car isn't very good compared to some of the others and the man has no fear." Now, her voice started to get a little bit louder and a little bit more strident and she looked directly at Jim, who conveniently had to watch the road, "Plus, he's home so seldom and then to be so involved in this racing crap is annoying me. As if he thinks of ways to be gone even when he's here." Then, she looked a little surprised by her own words and softened her statement with, "Well, I guess I understand really. He needs to spend time with his friends. Also, I don't think he told you but they're going to hire another guy to share some of his traveling responsibilities so, in a few months, everything should settle down some and he can be home more regularly. Oh, you probably didn't want to hear all of that. It just kind of spilled out. Sorry."

Jim attempted again to steer the conversation and hoped that eventually the car steering would help and he thought that somehow the Union had gotten much further away than normal. "Well, I'm sure you'll figure it out." he started out," How's your Chaucer class going?"

Sable seemed relieved and a small smile crept across her face as she glanced out through the drizzled side window and said "Humm, nice subject change, Mr. Diplomat. Anyway, the Chaucer class is a great intellectual simulant. I was an English major in undergrad and I'd actually signed up for a Chaucer class once but was unable to take it. So, when my friend mentioned that non-students could sit in on some of the UW classes, I checked out the schedule and jumped in."

Jim asked, "So, can it count towards another degree or something?"

Sable shook her head. "No, I am just sitting-in. Sit in the back, don't ask too many questions. But…I'm doing all the homework and so I think I'm getting something out of it. I think the prof likes having me around too because it drives the regular kids to do their homework so they don't get shown up by the "soccer mom"." Sable chuckled as she made the air quotes on "soccer mom". Jim smiled too, having found a subject free of drama. Just as the conversation was turning up, they arrived at the Union and started pulling on their raingear and getting their other gear together.

Jim generally knew the other people going out on the group sail and they generally knew him too. Consequently, there were a few questioning looks for the assembled, raincoated Wisconsinites when Jim walked up accompanied by a very attractive blond. It was obvious to Sable that several of these women were really into Jim based on how they watched her every interaction with Jim. She thought, "I guess the wedding ring doesn't mean anything in this crowd."

Finally, Jim introduced her...carefully, much to her relief. "Everyone, I'd like you to meet my next door neighbor, Sable. Sable's the beginner I mentioned I was bringing today."

Sable said "Hi! Thanks for letting me come along!" With that, the captain started putting people to work. A small motorboat with a young college kid working for the Union took them out to the big boat in a couple groups of four. Sable and Jim were in the second group. The trip leader/captain was an older guy named Sammy. Sammy was the kind of guy who worked nights at the grocery store so that he could sail whenever he wanted to even if the job stunk. Single, lived in a small apartment, and he liked it that way. He had moved to Madison from somewhere on the East coast years ago for a woman and had never made it back to the ocean again. He also instructed part time for the sailing club and Jim had been in one of his classes. Sammy leaned over to Jim and said, "So, the girl next door, Jim? How storybook of you..."

Jim looked at him somewhat confused for a second then smiled, "No, no, she's just a friend. She's married but her husband is afraid of water." Jim didn't mention that Cliff was also out of town most of the time. Jim realized that everyone thought he had brought Sable as a date which struck him as funny for some reason.

54

Once on the boat, everyone took their stations. Jim was going to help Sammy in the rear of the boat – not that Sammy really needed much help back there. Sammy was a real expert and had captained this exact vessel hundreds of times. Most novice sailors moved uneasily around a large sailboat. They stepped on lines, they tripped over the cockpit rail, they were constantly craning their necks to see forward of the mainsail. But Sammy moved as if integrally attached to the boat. As if someone had mounted him on the boat as a functioning part of the boat. He grabbed for lines without looking. It seemed as if he saw the entire horizon constantly yet without ever directly looking. His feet were glued to the deck and he moved without error on and above the surface of the boat. Jim often caught himself staring at Sammy to the point that he forgot his own role on the ship. Ever since Jim had met Sammy, he had always taken every opportunity to sail with him. This was made easier by the fact that Jim was always available. Sammy seemed to like turning Jim into a sailor and was always very patient. So, today, they stood in the back of the sailboat watching the beginners and the "Ride-alongs" and the water and the sky and the wind simultaneously. The master and the protégé helping each other as best they could.

Jim kept a special eye on Sable to make sure she was doing ok and not getting in the way or having a bad time. To her credit, Sable seemed to fit right in on the little world of the sailboat. She introduced herself easily to the other women on the short journey. She really seemed to be having fun and suddenly Jim realized that she must be very, very bored in her well-decorated home in posh Maple Bluff. Jim was glad he was able to bring Sable into this world. Hopefully, she'd want to sail again.

The weather started to improve dramatically as the storm broke up and the sun shone through. It was perfect weather for an end of day sail - with a rainbow and the coming sunset combined. Sammy, with Jim's help, handled everything for a leisurely cruise around the lake. He shouted out instructions in "simple-boating" which means he used words like "that thingy by your left hand" and "hold onto that rope with both hands and don't fall in." Jim made sure that nothing got too far away from the position it should be in and answered questions from the beginners as they came up.

Jim was so busy, he lost track of Sable. As he glanced around, he realized that she was manning the winch on the starboard side of the boat as the ship tacked further up in the wind. Sammy was watching her too and telling her exactly how taut to make the line and what to expect as the boat moved smoothly through the turn. "Excellent", said Sammy to Sable.

Sable smiled back up at him, "I think I am getting the hang of this turning thing!"

"Winch," Sammy called over as he smiled at her, "Good job with the winch." Sammy turned to Jim and said, "Are you really sure her husband is afraid of the water or is he just a moron? Damn Jimmy, she's hot. If I'd known that she lived next door, I would have bought that rich guy's house myself!"

Jim kept adjusting the tiller but he was smiling as he said, " Sammy, Sammy, Sammy. She is very attractive but her husband is a big guy so I'd go easy if I were you. Plus, you spend all your money on sailing – you'd have never bought that house."

Sammy was quiet for a moment and kept watching Sable for awhile until he finally said, "You know, she has absolutely no fear of the water at all. She must love that house by the lake. But, why would someone move next to the lake if he didn't like water."

Jim replied, "Good question. I guess he just always wants to own the very best even if he doesn't appreciate it himself. Besides, she's the one who is home most of the time. He's a salesman on the road most of the time."

Sammy jumped on that news, "What! He's gone all the time? She likes to sail? You have no noticeable means of employment yourself. Sounds like the perfect plan to get on the yuppie-version of Jerry Springer."

Jim dropped the line he was holding and turned to Sammy, somewhat frustrated, "Look. I just met her, she has a husband, she's just a friend – end of story!"

Sammy leaned back a little and put up his hands. "Sorry, sorry, just yanking your chain man. By the way, what do you do anyway?"

Jimmy shook it off - literally, as he had gotten wet when he dropped the line he was holding causing the whole boat to rock slightly and kick up spray on him. " I'm an unemployed engineer looking for work. Not looking very hard this evening though!" And with that, he smiled, and Sammy smiled and they never spoke of Sable and her husband again.

As the boat was being put back into storage, a plan developed to hang out at the Union and have some beers. The lakeside part of the union is a very large multi-tiered patio capable of seating hundreds of people. Summer evenings are filled with live music, fresh beer, the smell of grilling bratwursts and the cool breeze off the lake. "Nothing like a beer at sunset!" said Sammy to Jim as they sat around one of the brightly-colored tables on the patio with the other members of the crew.

"Nope," said Jim as he gazed at the sunset, "nothing like it, no matter how much money you have."

Sammy raised his glass and said to the gathered party, "I would like to toast a successful sail, good fun and an excellent sunset." And with that, the crew all raised their beers.

Chapter 4: Friends

The Australian penguin marches on shore in southern New Zealand to the delight of the tourists hunkered down in blinds watching them. Considerably smaller than the more famous King(?) Penguin, they are also more brown and grey than black and white. However, like their genetic siblings, as they waddle around the scrubby areas close to the beach, their stubby wings and webbed feet seem even more out of place and useless. They seem almost handicapped until they get in the water and transform into efficient torpedoes. They seem destined to be trapped between these two worlds – shore and sea. Perhaps they group together on the beach partly because they feel safer to be surrounded by others in the same predicament..

After the sun set and the music ended and bratwursts chased down the beers, Jim and Sable drove back to their neighborhood. Sable constantly peppered Jim with questions about sailing all the way back. She had really enjoyed it and she said, "Jim, that was such a great adventure! And your friends are really nice. I especially liked Sammy. He was very helpful. He seemed to always know when I was screwing up and was there to help."

Jim smiled recalling his conversation with Sammy and thinking, "Yeap, he was watching you the whole time – new hot girl." Aloud, he said, "Yeap, they are all really great people. I think you could really fit in there if you wanted to or had time."

Jim pulled into his driveway. They both got out of the car into the cool night air and found themselves staring at each other across the top of his car. Sable suddenly turned away throwing a "G'Night!" over her shoulder. Jim threw back a "Thanks for coming." and he headed up the drive.

As he glanced up at his large dark house, Jim remembered Dean had said something about living at the hospital this week. Which made him wonder what he would do tonight…Which, in turn, made him think about reading a book…which made him quickly consider what book to read…which reminded him that he really only had several beginning books on sailing…which led him to stop and yell over to Sable, "Hey! Would you want to borrow some of my beginning sailing books?"

She stopped, turned, looked him in the eye and said, "Sure. I was wondering what to read after the new John Grisham novel. They aren't too technical though, are they?" She strolled back over to his driveway even though they could both hear Scout barking for her now and together they walked up to the house and Jim unlocked the door and stepped across the threshold to turn on the lights. As he went to grab the books from the bedroom upstairs, Sable started to look around as this was the first time she had been inside the house. Of course, the house was still relatively devoid of furniture. Sable yelled up to Jim, "This place is great! Graham, that guy that sold you the house, never really let us in. You're kind of into minimalism, huh!?" Jim walked up behind her from the other direction with three books in his hand.

"No," he laughed, "I just haven't really gotten around to decorating much, if at all, yet." He started to look around with fresh eyes and realized he hadn't even thought about the impression that the house gave to someone who didn't know the whole story. Probably looked like someone who had sunk every last dime into the downpayment and had nothing left for furnishings. Of course, he thought, the wall-sized plasma screen and leather couch, which were the sole occupants of the living room, should muddy that impression some.

He looked at Sable and said, "Yeah, I should get on that. Typically, I don't have much of a mind for home decorating. At least this place has some intrinsic appeal. You should've seen the last place!" Then, he looked down and said, "Here are the books - "Sailing for Dummies" and "Sailing 1-2-3" plus the University sailing guidelines book which explains everything about sailing down at the Union like we did today."

Sable took the books and after glancing at them quickly turned up to Jim and said, "So, aren't you going to give me the tour?"

"Ahhh, sure. Of course. I haven't given a tour before so it might not be very polished but why not?" and he looked off trying to decide which direction to head first.

And so Jim led Sable through the living room (also seemingly the in-home theater), the dining room with only the beat-up table and mismatched chairs that had seemed quite fine, if not oversized, in the old apartment, through the kitchen with three random pots hanging from the pot rack. They went upstairs to tour the empty bedrooms (except for two) and down to the basement with the bar and pool room and another big TV from the old apartment. They ended up in the yard after checking out the deck and hot tub, looking at the stars as Sable tried to visualize the slightly different view of the lake from Jim's yard with the view from her yard. Along the way, they grabbed a bottle of wine from the mostly empty wine cellar and so they drank from two of Jim's four wine glasses and talked about the house and what "potential" it had. Finally, Sable turned to Jim and said "So, I'll make you a deal, Jim. I'll help you decorate your house - I practically do it for a living anyway - and you can teach me how to sail. How is that for a deal?"

Jim said, "Well, I am certainly getting the better end of the deal, but that would be great!"

Sable nodded emphatically and even her hair bobbed affirmatively a little, "Great, that's a deal then!" She stuck out her hand very formally towards Jim. Jim paused for a second looking at the hand. He reached forward and held her hand. Touching is another level of contact between

61

two people even if it is quite formal. The French do it right by starting off immediately with two kisses on the cheek. Much harder to dismiss a person once you have kissed them on the cheek. Suddenly, there was an air of decision and finality and the conversation came to a stop. "Oh, I better get home and check on Scout. I have to lock him inside all day now until we can get a fence built or some other solution", Sable said.

"OK, then," said Jim feeling slightly strange. "Well, thanks again for coming along today and for offering to help with the house." Jim took her wine glass and meandered up the flagstone path to his back door while she headed across the lawn to her house and the barking of Scout. He paused on the large patio next to the firepit long enough to make sure that she made it inside. She waved back as she pushed the French doors open on her own patio.

One of the nicest and potentially most destructive aspects of not having to work is the utter control that one has over the morning. If you want to sleep in and then leisurely drink coffee while reading the paper, you can do that. If you want to get up at precisely 6:00 AM, work the treadmill until 6:45, shower, dress, have one cup of coffee, two eggs and two slices of toast (except for Saturday when you have pancakes), then that is up to you too. Or, if you're Howard Hughes and want to be awake while the world sleeps and if you never want to arise until others are going to bed, that is fine as well.

Conventional wisdom says that the rich can do "whatever they want". It isn't true, of course, as they are subject to the same non-financial constraints as everyone else. They can't change their relatives any more than the poor can. But, on the other hand, they seldom have a strict time to get to work, they seldom have to commute and they are never forced to stop at Starbucks because they didn't have time to make coffee.

Jim tended to fall into the "get up late and slowly speed up from there" category. Since he quit his job, he had purposely never set an alarm. Usually, Dean had made enough noise in the morning running off to "body plumber school" (as Jim had taken to calling it) that Jim had woken up and started his day. However, Jim had ended up staying up late after Sable had gone home, just watching TV. Nothing in particular actually but sometimes it seems that people don't want an excellent day to end by going to bed. So, they are trapped in the space between having the energy to really "do something" and giving up on the day and going to bed.

However, the morning after Sable and Jim had gone sailing, Jim's sleeping-in was interrupted by the continued clanging of the doorbell. At first, Jim thought it was Dean but then his foggy mind started rolling and he realized that Dean had to still be at work. So, Jim rolled over but the clanging continued. Finally, he got up, walked over to the bedroom above the front door and looked outside. No delivery trucks, no FedEx, nothing. Jim turned around when the doorbell rang again. He opened the window and yelled down "Who is it?" Slowly, emerging from the patio that surrounded the entrance, he saw Sable slowly backing up onto the front walk. She looked up at him with a big smile and he watched helplessly as it slowly fell off as she realized she had woken him up. She started talking really fast as if she was embarrassed, "Geez, I'm SO sorry. I just assumed that you'd be up already and I was looking at some catalogs over breakfast and I got all excited about decorating your house and I… and I… and I should have called." By this point, she was no longer looking up at him.

Jim leaned against the window sill and said," No problem. I was up," he lied. "I was just reading the book in bed that I was reading when I fell asleep. Why don't you let yourself in down there and take a look around, I'll take a shower and we can DO SOME DECORATING!" Jim started to chuckle at the thought of being infected with the decorating bug while the smile returned to Sable's face. "Take your time! I will start to measure your rooms and that big window that needs some drapes," she said as she pushed through the door beneath him.

63

Within two hours, Jim and Sable were cruising through her favorite furniture store with some rough sketches of his main rooms, a ruler and no limit to the budget. They were a storeowners dream. Very quickly, they had a whole slew of sales people suggesting all kinds of combinations and groupings and accessories, etc. Sable handled them like a professional – asking the right questions, making Jim try out sitting on all the couches (which Jim learned were called "sofas" by professionals), questioning him about his favorite colors and any themes or ideas he had for the rooms. Jim slowly realized how much Sable knew about this and how he knew so little. Not only didn't he know anything but he didn't know there was anything to know about it – which he found fascinating. A whole new world of fabrics and colors and terminology opened up to him. The difference between a window treatment and a valance and a drapery were shocking to him. As Jim wandered through the stores, Sable laughed at almost everything he said:

"You mean that these pieces go together? The fabric doesn't match. This one is green and this one is red"
"Sooo, a valance is like a really short drape?"
"A window treatment? Sounds like something that you spray on the glass."
" A couch is a sofa? Then, what's a couch? Do couches exist? If not, what have I been sitting on all these years?"
"OK, I can see how this table goes with the couch but it's barely big enough to put a drink on let alone a drink, a lamp, the remote and a stack of magazines. For that price, you would think you could get a table that could actually "table" some stuff."
"For the price of that rug, we should stick it on the wall so no one steps on it."

After a couple hours, they took a break to have a late lunch at a little hole-in-the-wall Mediterranean restaurant called "The Saz" close to downtown on State Street. They both liked it and Sable knew there were some really cool

64

shops downtown with some funky lamps, etc. that she wanted to check out.

As they waited for their food, Jim said "Sable, I really have to thank you for all the help today. The house is going to look great with just the new furniture, let alone getting some "window treatments"."

She looked back at Jim, "You're so welcome! This has been great because your house is such a clean slate so we can do whatever we want. And, on top of that, in spite of what you keep saying, you really do have a good sense of what goes together, for a guy! I think that those leather couches for the game room will be really beautiful - yet very masculine. Kind of a George Clooney-Lake Como sort of thing you have going now. You're sure to get all the ladies after this!" Suddenly, Sable stopped talking. She realized that she had just mentioned something that she had previously decided not to talk about. Specifically, Jim's love life or lack thereof. Considering his perceived station, she couldn't understand why he was alone – let alone living with a "roommate". Luckily, the food came at that very moment keeping the moment from lingering oddly.

They ate in relative silence watching the odd-looking people on the sidewalk that add a lot of character to State Street. Suddenly, Sable seemed to come to a decision in her mind and looked at Jim and smiled. Quietly and slowly she said, "Jim, we spent twelve thousand dollars this morning. You never even blinked an eye once and always just went with whatever looked best to you. It didn't seem to matter if it was cheaper or more expensive. Now, you told Cliff and me that you had quit working and were taking a break from work. Most people that I have met who were "taking a break" don't go around spending twelve grand in a morning of furniture shopping. I don't care how you spend your money but I'm just worried that you bought stuff you couldn't afford because I was so excited about the whole process. I mean, we can cancel some of those orders if we go back after lunch."

Jim chuckled and waved her off quickly, "No, no, I wouldn't want to spend that much every morning but it's alright to do it once and awhile." Again, an awkward silence and they both sat and looked at their food. Jim was tormented. He desperately wanted to tell Sable the truth but at the same time he realized that she might (a) not believe him or (b) be upset that he didn't tell her or her husband the truth before or most importantly (c) it might ruin what was a perfect day. Finally, he said, "Don't worry. I know what I can afford and what I can't. I'll draw the line at some point but I do need furniture in the house if I expect anyone besides you to come over. And, I doubt I could impress you with money anyway." Moving on to a lighter subject, he said, "So, shall we move on to the wonderful world of lighting?"

She smiled at him and said, "Sure, I'm quite sure we can find some lamps that are less than twelve grand."

And off they went, Jim still wondering if he should say something else to her or just leave it alone. Eventually, he would have to tell her and Cliff probably because, as she already noticed, people cannot keep spending and not bring in money unless they have something in the bank...from somewhere. He smiled to himself, "Maybe she thinks I'm in the mob or a bank robber or something worse..."

At the end of the endless day of shopping, again, Jim found himself staring at his empty house and asking Sable if she wanted to have dinner, if she didn't have anything else to do. She said, "Well, that's very nice of you but actually, Cliff's flying in tonight, so I need to go home. But, today was really fun. I think I'm definitely getting the better end of our bargain, I get to go sailing and decorating with other people's money." She flashed her grin, which Jim had become very familiar with during the day.

Jim said, "No, no, I'm actually getting the better part of the bargain! I get to go sailing and have someone help me fill up this house and make it a home instead of an empty box. Let me know when you want to go sailing - although tomorrow at sunup is a little early."

She grinned again.

He continued, "Well, thanks again and have a good night. Say hello to Cliff for me." As with the night before, he followed her with his eyes until she went into her house and he heard the dog barking a greeting to her before turning to enter his own home. He slowly walked around the house envisioning how it would look in three to six weeks when all the furniture arrived. He was pleased and wished it could happen tomorrow. "I guess that only happens if you buy your furniture at Walmart like we used to do", he muttered to himself.

The phone rang. Jim had to run up from the basement, where he had been envisioning the new Clooney-esque play room, to catch the phone. It was Sable.

"Hey, Cliff missed his plane and isn't coming in until the morning now. Is your offer for dinner still open?"

Jim paused for a second and said, "Well, I'd made other plans in the intervening ten minutes but I guess the microwave won't hold a grudge if I cancel."

"Very funny," she said. "Do you want to go out, or stay in?"

"Well, I think we were "out" a lot today so if you would feel comfortable working in my kitchen, we might be able to whip something up. Who knows, Dean might come home and join us too."

"Great," she said. "I was going to make Pad Thai for Cliff tonight so, if you like that, I'll just bring it all over."

"Wow," said Jim, "that sounds great." Dean didn't mind being the beneficiary of Cliff's misfortune. "Hey, can I do something? Run out and get a movie or dessert or something?"

"Sure," she said. "Actually, I think that they just released that new Hugh Grant movie...Love Actually I think it is. Would you want to see that?"

"Sure," said Jim, deciding not to mention that he had just watched another Hugh Grant movie, About a Boy, about another independently wealthy guy.

"Oh, and how about some popcorn for dessert? That way, your microwave won't feel so abandoned?" she joked, warming to the idea of the replacement evening.

A few hours later, Dean came home to find a huge stir fry pan still half full of Pad Thai in the kitchen and Jim and some unknown woman on the couch watching a Hugh Grant movie with a big bowl of popcorn between them. There were so many things wrong with this picture that for a good few minutes, Dean just kept peaking around the corner into the living room. Finally, Jim reached up with the remote and paused the movie. "Dean, I hear you out there. Come on in here." As Dean angled around the corner holding his mail in his hand, he gave a little wave. Jim continued still sitting on the couch, "Welcome home. I would like to introduce the woman you have been living next to for the last few months. This is Sable and she lives next door." Sable jumped off the sofa to say hello and shake Dean's hand.

Dean finally started putting everything together and said, "Oh, Jim mentioned that he had been hanging out with the people next door. You all were going to go sailing yesterday, right?"

"Yeap," said Sable," and today I reciprocated by taking Jim shopping to decorate this place. In a few short weeks, this whole house will be filled with furniture."

Dean said, "Well, as long as it continues to be filled with an awesome smell like this Pad Thai instead of smelling like Jim's feet, that would be great!" Dean started following his nose back into the kitchen, yelling over his shoulder, "Unfortunately, I'm just stopping through to get some clean clothes and then I'm headed over to Ellen's place. I've been at the hospital for three days straight basically so I'm way in the dog house with her." Sable followed him into the kitchen to help him dish up the food and Jim followed them both into the kitchen.

Dean ended up staying for over an hour due to the charm of Sable and her food. Jim and Sable took turns telling Dean about the furniture that they had bought and the sailing they had done the day before. Dean listened and ate contentedly. Sable had a thousand questions about med school and residency and "what was the strangest thing you have done so far?" Jim realized that he had never even asked Dean about any of these things nor did he know most of the stories that Dean was telling. Perhaps Dean didn't normally like to talk about his job, Jim thought, or maybe he'd never even asked him about it. Jim made a mental note to try and ask Dean more about his work from now on.

Dean finally left to go visit Ellen – in the process swearing both of them to lie for him that he had been delayed at the hospital a little bit longer if she ever asked. Jim and Sable collapsed back on the couch surrounding the popcorn and took the DVD off of pause. As the movie was ending and the credits were starting to roll, Sable asked "Did you think those relationships were very realistic? Have you ever been in a relationship like any in that movie?"

"Well, I don't know…" said Jim as he tried to find the special features on the DVD.

Sable jumped back in, "Well, I didn't mean to pry. I just thought that they're all kind of unusual, as relationships go…" Jim looked at her, put down the remote, turned towards her and just started talking. He said, "In college, I dated this woman named Cecilia. We met while we were both involved in some environmental causes and really clicked. I thought it was perfect between us. We were living together and I visited her family in Sweden and I really thought she was going to be the one. Anyway, the reason that I bring it up is that I've always thought it was like some kind of weird movie because of how it ended though. She left me for this guy, with a BMW and a new job in international finance, that she thought could maintain her in the style to which she wanted to become accustomed." Suddenly, Jim's eyes got really wide and he sort of stared over her shoulder. "Holy crap!" he thought "I can probably buy and sell that guy now. Dean asked me if I would try to get her back now but I didn't realize I had become that guy." Aloud, he continued, "Well, anyway, that is the only sort of movie-type experience that I have had."

Sable just let him sit there for a few seconds. Then, she gently reached her hand across the bowl of popcorn and touched him on the arm. "Jim, I'm sorry to hear about your awful experience. It sounds like she was going to be trouble no matter what. So, there hasn't been anyone since then?"

Jim roused himself out of his stupor – realized that Sable was still there and had her hand resting on his arm – suddenly, he snapped back into focus. He simply said, "Well, it was a long time ago now." He smiled and then lied. "There have been a few since then but nothing that lasted very long." Sable just sat and stared at Jim for a little while. "What?" he said finally.

"Well, I'm trying to decide which question, of the thousand which popped into my head, I should ask you?" She just looked at him and he looked at her. After a few seconds she said, "I guess I just want to know if you've tried to contact her now that you're much more successful than in college." Before Jim could stammer out anything, she continued, "And, I'm wondering whom you would win her back from as I doubt she's still with the same guy. Do you know where she is?"

Jim started to relax, "No, I haven't talked to her since then. Sorry for zoning out there. As you can tell, I haven't talked about this in quite a while. I didn't mean to get so heavy on you. I guess it was something I haven't thought or talked about for awhile. "

Sable said, "Well, I'm glad you felt like you could share it with me. God knows, I don't have a lot of deep conversations normally so I can handle one once in awhile."

With that, she stood up. "I'd really like to stay and hear more, but I think that I need to get to bed because I have to get up early to pick up the house and go pick up Cliff at the airport – hopefully."

Jim said, "No problem. Really, thanks so much for such a great day again." Jim walked her to the front of the house and she turned suddenly, gave him a big hug and said, "Thanks for everything, Jim. This has been wonderful to have a friend to hang out with who lives next door." And then, she was gone across the yard to her house.

Chapter 5: Drifting Apart

No one disputes the fact that watching birds in flight is something that must be taken for granted – otherwise, everyone would just continually stare in amazement at the feat. Canada Geese are such a fundamentally awe-inspiring sight. Even more so is the impact of an entire flock of geese flying in sync, following the same invisible highway through the sky. Looping and turning and swooping and climbing. In spite of what the biologists tell us about birds flying to migrate or to look for food, one wonders if the sheer joy of flight alone makes them take off sometimes. No one is really sure why the first one takes flight, but the rest take flight because of the first one. Like one unit, they are a team. They take turns leading and following but are always together and always in formation.

A few weeks after Sable had been over and after Jim had qualified on an even bigger sailboat through the club, Dean came home again to find Jim sitting in the kitchen with a slew of papers spread out across the table and a very tan, slightly older man in a slick summer suit sitting across from him. The man seemed to be in mid-ramble when Dean walked in. Dean said "Hi." Jim introduced him to Tad, whose name was perfect for his occupation, which was being a luxury boat broker. Jim said, "Dean, you are looking at the proud owner of a new 62-foot single-hull sailboat named "The Lucky Ticket". Seems appropriate, doesn't it?"

71

Dean said, "Really? That's great! Are there any pictures? I didn't see it parked outside. Is it in the garage?" He was now smiling as he made fun of Jim.

Jim said, "Well, it is docked over in Milwaukee at the Royal City Pier. Actually, I was thinking of going over to look at it again today. Do you wanna go?" Dean stood and looked at him. For a long second, Jim thought he was going to say no because the look on his face said something between exhaustion and exasperation.

But, then Dean kind of came out of it and said, "You know what, that's exactly what I need today. A little drive in the country over to the lake would be perfect. Can you drive though? I just came off a shift and might fall asleep, if I drive."

"Excellent," said Jim, "Of course I can drive."

So, after Dean took an endless shower and Jim finished up with Tad and traded him several sets of keys in exchange for one large check, they were on their way. The entire way over, Jim rambled on and on about the boat. He had applied his entire energies (except for when he was actually sailing or hanging out with the sailing club or decorating with Sable) into selecting a sailboat once he got the first check. Like the furniture he bought with Sable, he didn't buy the most ostentatious boat nor did he buy the bargain bottom boat but really the one that he wanted. Jim kept talking about it until he finally looked over and realized that Dean had fallen asleep.

The chill in the air in Madison was Old Man Winter tipping his hand a little. However, it turned out to be a bright sunny day by the time they pulled up to the marina just north of Milwaukee. Less than two hours from Madison, it was the closest access to big water available. Dean woke up when the car stopped and the two of them got out of the car and started wandering around the marina looking for "The Lucky Ticket". Jim had not gotten the slip number from Stan and so they walked around looking lost. Finally, Dean flagged down one of the guys working at the marina who pointed them to a slip way out at the edge of the marina.

As they walked up to the boat, it slightly rolled in the water and made a little squeaky noise as the gunnels rubbed against the bumpers on the dock as if it was ready and raring to go zipping across the lake. Jim had picked this boat because it had some nice appointments within the cabin. Jim had Dean take a picture of him as he stepped onto the deck for the first time as the owner.

Jim started examining some of the thousands of details that he'd not noticed when he had checked it out before buying it. He was racing around from bow to stern looking for anything amiss or broken or in any way substandard. Dean simply strolled back and forth taking it all in. And there was a lot to take in. The previous owner had spared no expense in outfitting the boat. Glorious wood was everywhere and where the wood ended the polished brass and chrome took over. There were three bedroom cabins, one much bigger and obviously for the "skipper" and his lucky mate. It had a little bathroom of its own. The galley was large and the table could collapse to hold even more sleeping crewmembers. But best of all was the upper deck. The boat was docked with the sail cover over the open cockpit area. It had a bar which collapsed into the wall, a spanking new flat panel TV, more radio and communication gear than anyone could ever want and seating for at least ten people.

That was where Jim found him – looking out across the lake, drink in hand and collapsed into the cushioned seats against the edge of the cockpit. Jim said, "I found a couple broken handles in the galley and they slightly mis-specified the sonar equipment but all in all, everything looks really awesome. What do you think?"

Dean slowly opened his eyes, turned his head to look Jim in the eye (having to squint a little bit due to the sun) and said, completely straight-faced, " Jim, you are - officially - the luckiest son of a bitch that I've ever met." Jim started to chuckle but Dean continued straight faced, "I had a patient die at the hospital today of AIDS-related pneumonia. Not uncommon. But, now it seems that he got AIDS from the guy he was living with because he was too

73

poor to get his own place. He traded sex for a place to live! You're not just the luckiest damn fool in the world - you wear it like it is some natural step on the road of life. A year ago, you were just an engineer without much of a life who occasionally played softball. Now, you're some kind of sailing God, making friends with all the richest people in town and you spend your days watching MTV and doing whatever you please." Dean stopped and just stared out at the water. The silence was pregnant as each man waited for the other to say something to break the tension.

Finally, Jim poured himself a drink from the little bar and sat down next to Dean and joined him in staring out across the water for a few more seconds before he said, "I know I'm really lucky. Do you want me to give money to charity, is that it? Do you want me to give you money?" That question got him an icy stare from Dean. "OK, OK, I will try to be a little more grateful for everything. But, I have to keep living. I cannot just maintain a feeling of intense gratitude every minute of every day. Can't you give me this one moment? Can't you let me enjoy buying this awesome boat? Even Bill Gates gets to indulge his money once in awhile between trips to Africa to rid the world of debt, AIDS and TB."

Dean suddenly relaxed, "Oh, crap, I'm sorry, buddy. I just had an awful day and that guy died and then to come here and see all of this luxury and imagine all the fun you're going to have here…it's just so disconnected from reality. I'm sorry, Jim. You're doing great with all this stuff, finding things you want to do."

By now the sun had begun to set. "It isn't completely easy," said Jim. "Being rich doesn't mean you get everything you want."

"You're talking about Sable, aren't you?" asked Dean.

Jim just stared for a second, "You always could read me like an open book. Is it that obvious to everyone? Don't answer that. Anyway, yeah, she's great, her husband's never home and I think she genuinely likes hanging out with me. Beats watching MTV," he said with a little smile.

Dean sat back down. "Sorry to get all cranky on you. I guess you're going to run into that a lot until I'm done with plumber school."

Jim said, "Hey, don't worry about it. So, should we take it out for a quick sail?"

Dean responded, "Can you do that? It's almost dark and we haven't ever run her before so it might be better to wait. I wouldn't want to get stuck out there if we can't get the motor running or something."

Jim was examining the controls as they spoke, "Yeah, I don't know if we can sail today anyway. I gotta read the manuals on some of this stuff. The UW doesn't have anything this sophisticated…might cut into my MTV time too" he added, casting another jab at Dean.

Dean started to laugh and said, "Perhaps, if I helped you decipher the controls, you'll stop giving me crap about the MTV comment?"

Jim looked up in the air for a second as if considering it, "Ahhhh, nope, you are screwed for the near term … until I forget. Ah, let's go get some dinner downtown before we head back."

Dean really wanted to go to sleep but was now feeling a little guilty and so he said, "Sure, sounds good. Wanna go to the Speakeasy?" The Speakeasy was a fun, concept restaurant in downtown Milwaukee. The concept was that it was a restaurant from the Prohibition. It had a hidden side entrance which looked like an anonymous warehouse door from the street. Once inside, there were several hidden passages (mostly used by the waitstaff) that lead to many small eating areas with a few tables at each. Dean had been there before but Jim hadn't. They walked in, went through the little ritual of swearing not to tell anyone about the Speakeasy and then were led down some strange pathway to one of the dining rooms. They spent most of the dinner talking about the new boat that Jim had bought. However, the conversation eventually turned to Ellen. Dean had continual battles with Ellen over how much time he spent at the hospital. Like most people dating medical residents, Ellen hadn't anticipated what it would really be like and it both surprised and annoyed both of them. Dean kept telling her that it would all be over soon. It didn't help that Ellen had a really open schedule and not many other friends to keep her occupied. Dean asked Jim about Sable which just resulted in another round of drinks with their meal but little else. Dean told Jim that he would shortly find someone single to date – especially with his new boat and new decorating – and then Sable wouldn't occupy so much of his mind.

The tiff they had on the boat was never mentioned again but neither one forgot it. Dean cut down on the remarks he made about Jim's money and Jim started to realize that he needed to watch what he said, even around Dean. This really started to bother him because Dean was one of only a couple of people that knew he even had the money and he had always felt like he could tell Dean anything.

They drove home in a relative food coma not saying much. Dean had Jim drop him off at Ellen's and they promised to get together the next day while Ellen was working to go over the instructions for the new boat. Hopefully, they could take it out on the maiden voyage within a week or so. Jim drove home and turned on the TV to relax. When he found himself watching the Jessica Simpson show on MTV, he shook his head, made a mental note to buy TiVO or something the next day, flipped off the TV and started pacing around the house. The new furniture still had not arrived making the house seem even more empty. He started to ruminate on what Dean had said. "Maybe I should be giving more money to charity," he thought. "Maybe there is something else that I should be doing?" Finally, Jim just shook his head and thought, "I just need to settle into this for a little longer and then I can start making a plan. It'll sort itself out." With that, he went and sat in the hot tub and started reading a new book.

Chapter 6: Reckless

When dogs are left at home all day, especially when they are puppies, destruction happens. Shoes, jackets, the TV remote control, all end up with strange teeth marks or buried in the yard. The cute, adorable dog turns into the mischievous weapon of household destruction. By the time you get home, the guilt has already set in or the action has been forgotten. The remaining question usually is why. Were they truly angry that you left them at home? Do they have an innate need to destroy things? Or, are they bored and lonely? I think that the fact they typically don't destroy things while the owner is home is proof that lonely and bored is probably the real reason. Being alone - for any animal that belongs with others of its kind - is difficult for them to endure.

The next day, Jim woke up late as usual to Dean standing over him wondering if now was a good time to work the boat operations. Jim was a little annoyed. As if, just because his life was pretty unscheduled, Jim had to work around Dean's maniac schedule. "No, he replied, "When... I ... am asleep... is definitely not a good time to talk about boat communication equipment." Immediately, he felt like a baby for saying that. He shook his head and jumped up out of bed. "I just need to take a quick shower and then we can get started."

"OK," said Dean. "I'll go down and make some breakfast. Eggs, toast and bacon, right?"

"Sounds good, "sighed Jim as he headed towards the shower.

Within a few hours, they felt they had figured out what they could from the manuals and pictures and were just in need of the actual boat to practice everything. Unfortunately, the weather was against them with thunderstorms forecast for the afternoon and Dean had to go to the hospital within a few hours anyway. So, Jim was left alone with his manuals and his thoughts again. Not really sure what else to do, he called Sable to see if she was busy or wanted to do something.

She was also dreading a rainy day. She had planned to work in the garden all afternoon but didn't want to get started if it looked like it was going to rain.

"So, what do unemployed people do on a rainy day?" asked Jim.

"Well, whatever they want it seems," said Sable, "But, I have indeed been meaning to go check out the new Ovation Center downtown. You know it? The new performing arts center downtown? They started letting people tour through it last week. It's supposed to be quite impressive inside. Would you be interested in going?"

"Sure," he said. "I haven't even been by there from the outside yet."

"I'll come over after I get cleaned up??"

"Sounds good" he said. Jim hung up and looked at himself in the reflection of the refrigerator. "Hmm," he thought, "a sweatshirt and jeans might not be a stellar look for an art center." So he ran upstairs and changed into some khakis and a button-down shirt – something he used to wear to work.

Sable showed up looking a little fancier than he thought she should have (to go out in the rain) with a simple white lightweight sweater covered by a North Face waterproof shell and something that looked like riding pants tucked into some boots. Whatever comprised it, it all went together in a "look". Jim noticed that it looked good and realized that it all fit together – like the furniture that she had helped him buy. This left him wondering if there was such a thing as Geranimals for adults or do rich people take a class on how to dress in such a coordinated style? He made a mental note to take Sable with him shopping the next time he bought clothes. Jim realized also that he had not bought any new clothes outside of REI since he had received the first check. He had never been much of a clothes shopper before and now the thought of shopping without a budget, for clothes, seemed quite overwhelming to him.

The new art complex was an incredible architectural feat which almost seemed out of place for downtown Madison. State Street had a flurry of bars, restaurants, dingy used book stores, head shops and other stores that catered to college students. Now, this new Arts Complex took up two entire blocks and there was a Gap and several Starbucks too. The place was changing. They parked in the new ramp next door and took the dry skyway across which dumped them into a large glass atrium. Almost cubic, it was about four floors high. The lights were all on because the rain had darkened the sky. The walls were all glass with several levels of white walkways around the edge of the cube. This huge atrium was attached to the side of the new main concert hall so each level in the concert hall opened onto a hall in the atrium. At the moment that Jim and Sable entered the atrium, it reminded Jim of being in a carwash. The rain was coming down quite heavy and water coated all the windows so that everywhere one looked, one only saw water and the faint illusion of reality beyond that. In fact, there were several skylights in the roof which were also darkened and coated by the storm and rain. Jim and Sable simply stood still for a long moment absorbing this new large space. Slowly, they started to stroll around the walkway along the edge of the atrium.

Sable said, "Wow, this is great! And, you know what?"

"What?" said Jim.

"Well, I was thinking that this will be so nice in the middle of the winter. Have you ever been to over the Olbrich Gardens tropical greenhouse? It's so nice to go there in the winter. Cliff and I used to go there all the time when

79

we were dating. It's great for your skin and sinuses. But, this place will be great too – even if it's not as warm. It's almost like you can walk around outside in the winter. I think there's a view of Mendota between those buildings, if it wasn't raining."

Jim said, "Yeah that would be good in the winter. Of course, we could just go to the Caribbean for the winter too."

Sable said, "Yeah! Now you're talking. Cliff is always having trouble planning far enough ahead so that we always end up just flying to Miami for a couple days or something."

They kept walking and came around to the theater entrance and walked in. Suddenly, they were plunged into almost-complete darkness. As their eyes adjusted, they realized that only a smattering of lights were on which were pointed at the stage. An older man in a typical usher's blazer and black pants walked up to them. He was a little heavy set but also looked like he had been through a great deal in his lifetime. "Hello there, folks," he said, "I take it you are just walking around and checking everything out?"

"Yeap," said Jim. "Rainy day and all..." The usher seemed slightly let down by the implication that they were only visiting because it was raining.

"That's fine," he said, "My name is Oscar and I'd be happy to answer any questions you have."

Sable perked up and said, "Oscar, this is a really incredible place you have here. What's the first show going to be?"

Oscar said, "Well, they're going to do Les Miserables as the first public show. However, Tony Robbins has scheduled some big self-help seminar before that but that'll be by invitation only."

"Les Mis it is then," she said. "Oscar, do you mind if we walk around a little?"

"No problem," he said, "Go right ahead. There will be some workmen installing lighting as soon as they get back from lunch so stay out of their way but otherwise everything has been cleared for the public, by the inspectors."

Jim and Sable walked down into the floor of the hall and looked up. There were three balconies that wrapped around the walls of the hall with what looked like crushed red velvet covering on all the surfaces. The ceiling was an abstract collection of shapes which were obviously designed to improve the acoustics. Suddenly, Sable turned and grabbed Jim by the arm. She had a big idea: "Jim, I'd like to figure out where the best seat is. I mean, obviously the middle of the front row or the middle of the first balcony would be the best but they usually cost a ton more and I want to go see if the side boxes work or if part of the stage is hidden."

"Ok, I could use some exercise going up the stairs anyway."

So, up they tramped to the first level boxes and the second level boxes which both had fine views in Sable's opinion. Finally, they made it up to the third level. Jim sat down in the box and Sable sat down next to him. As she sat down, she put her hand on top of his hand which rested on the seat armrest. Like any normal single man, Jim immediately noticed this – just as he had noticed that she had put her hand on his arm before. Jim didn't move his hand and neither did she. The silence grew longer. The silence grew pregnant. The silence grew too long. Neither of them was moving and neither of them was talking.

Finally, Sable said, "Well, I think you can see just fine from these seats."

Jim turned towards her and realized that she was looking a little flushed and so he thought better of saying anything. Like most people, men especially, Jim didn't know what to say at this point. He finally admitted to himself that he was really overwhelmed by his attraction to Sable. From the look on her face, he realized that she was interested in him too. If she had been single or even separated, Jim would have asked her out a month ago. But, she wasn't single nor separated but just alone – a victim of the modern age of long-distance travel and globalization. Ahh, progress…

Before Jim could say anything, Sable abruptly stood up – breaking the moment into shards. Jim was actually a little startled and jumped up as well. The result was the both of them running into each other in the narrow space in the front row of the box on the third level. Sable lost her balance and leaned over the railing. Instinctively, Jim grabbed her by the arm and pulled her back up and close to him. They stopped with their eyes locked. Finally, Jim just started to smile and silently acknowledge the silent and somewhat awkward nature of their situation.

Sable started to grin in return. "So, I guess we better go see the rest of this place before the rain stops outside," she said. Sable slipped past him while, Jim noticed, running her hand across his body. Jim paused, his shoulders rolled slightly forward and he looked up at the ceiling to collect himself. They toured the rest of the Art Center rather quickly while their conversation grew more superficial and cheery.

It looked like the rain had stopped so they decided not to take the skyway. They stepped onto the street in a blaze of sunshine. The sun had found a hole in the clouds to the west and was shooting its rays back to the east underneath the clouds. These rays were in turn bouncing off all the still-wet surfaces creating the effect of a searchlight shining on them. Squinting, they started walking back to the car when Jim said, "Say, are you hungry? I always get hungry in museums for some reason. My mother took me to the Chicago Art Institute when I was a kid and we stayed there through the lunch hour so that I was starving and now, whenever I am in a museum, I get hungry."

Sable seemed a little reluctant but finally said, "We weren't in a museum though. We were in a not-quite-finished Arts Center."

"Well, it has Art in the title."

"OK," she relented. "Do you have something in mind?"

"How about Deb and Lola's? They have a good lunch menu and we can sit in the window and rip on the people walking by?"

"Ha," Sable chuckled, "I am tooooo nice of a woman to rip on people – but, if you're good at it, I promise to laugh."

Deb and Lola's was one of the more upscale restaurants on State Street in Madison. This isn't hard to achieve in a college town that specializes in bars serving beer so plentiful and cheap to so many drunken college students that your feet started sticking to the floor by the end of a long weekend night. Although not one of the very best restaurants in town, it was convenient to where they were standing in the sunshine, especially if it started to rain again. Jim and Sable stepped into the restaurant and convinced the waitress to give them a prime spot by the window.

As Sable sat down, she turned to the window and said to Jim, " OK, start ripping!" Jim, without missing a beat, looked out the window, saw a young college student walking by with a Michael Jordan basketball jersey barely covering his bulging beer gut. "Boy, I bet Michael Jordan isn't happy about having his name on that guy. Must have a vertical jump of about 3 millimeters instead of 3 feet."

Sable smiled. "Not bad, can you do better?"

Jim looked out the window again and spied a young female college student walking away with a very noticeable, big butt. "Hey, someone should tell J. Lo that that woman has stolen her ass!"

Sable chuckled because she had been ripping on J. Lo the other night while they were watching TV. "Even better," she said.

"OK, I think that now I need a drink before I can think of anything wittier than a J. Lo joke." Magically, the waitress appeared. They each ordered a shot of tequila and a beer chaser. "Don't you think we should get some food too?" asked Sable.

"Sure," said Jim, still staring out the window looking for the perfect material for his next joke.

"Well, Jim dear, you're going to have to stop looking out the window and look at the menu in order to figure out what you want."

Jim stopped, turned back to look her in the eye, grinned and said, "Yes, dear, I'll look at the menu." He flipped open the menu without taking his eyes off her and said, "Well, I would like to start with some bruschetta, I'll have the chicken fettuccini in cream sauce with a glass of the house white and then we can talk about dessert. All that should give me plenty of time to find more victims on the sidewalk." Sable just smiled and shook her head which made her hair wave back and forth in a strangely captivating way. Jim thought, "and the drinks aren't even here yet."

And so the ripping continued.

"What was that guy thinking with black dress shoes and shorts?"

"What color is that – vomit?"

"Looks like her hair is trying to make a break for it and escape from her head."

"That guy needs to admit he has a problem with Krispy Kremes before he can get anywhere in life - …"

Soon, the ripping got boring as it usually does for people who aren't fundamentally insecure. Jim started talking about his new boat. Sable was fairly interested and was asking a lot of questions about it. Soon, after the second round of tequila shots, Jim noticed that Sable was starting to get that happy, dopey look that people get when they are pleasantly drunk at the table. They don't have to try to walk because that would be too difficult. They don't try to guide the conversation or be guarded about what they say, they just talk.

Finally, Sable cut Jim off in mid-description of the sonar equipment to say, "Jim, you look really good on a sailboat."

Jim was feeling a little drunk too but was more sober than Sable and still sober enough to notice the red flag that went off in his head – especially based on what had happened earlier in the day. He simply said, "Well, thanks. You look pretty good too especially now that you know what you're doing." Jim and Sable had now been sailing about ten times together and Sable was indeed getting better at knowing what to do, how to do it, and – most importantly – when. However, his response didn't end the moment.

Sable turned towards the window and her eyes started to get a little moist. "Jim, I'm sorry. I'm just so lonely, so much of the time without Cliff here. And, I have such a great time with you and it just sometimes gets hard. Like earlier today." With that, she just banged both her hands on the table out of frustration. Or, she tried to do that but one hand missed the table completely and banged into her thigh. "Ouch!" she said and started to chuckle. "I'm getting a little drunk. You should know that happens pretty easily with me," she said sheepishly.

Jim looked at her for a second and then said, "Sable, Cliff is a fool for not being around more. I shouldn't say this but I think you are the most incredible woman. You deserve better than this and you know it. Cliff does too probably or he should, at least."

There was a long pause as Sable stared out the window again, the intimate turn of the conversation sobering her up quickly now. "But, I'm married. I love Cliff too, I really do. I like you a lot too and I've had the best time with you and things are so easy with you – I guess that's partly because it's safe to hang out with you, but..."

At this point, Jim realized that she had started just thinking half-drunk thoughts completely out loud. He watched her and let her talk and talk and get it out. Lots of stuff about Cliff and how much he was gone and how he was great when he was around. However, he didn't really call or think about her much seemingly when he was on the road. She was mad at him for volunteering for certain trips when it wasn't his turn. She resented his need to have other interests besides her when he was home and resented herself for that resentment.

Finally, Jim got the feeling that she had just about shot her whole magazine of pent-up emotions. He grabbed her hand and held it with his. This got her attention; she stopped talking and looked at him. He put on a very happy face and said, "Hey, I'm attracted to you too and I would like to be involved with you if I could but, you know what, at the moment, I also just really need a friend. Besides, we'd probably break up if we started anything and then, we live next to each other so that would all be weird and I'd have to move all that great furniture to another house."

Sable squeezed his hand and said, "Exactly! Who'd want to move all the Clooney furniture? You know what, you are so great. You really are. So, should we get some dessert?"

Jim laughed. "No more tequila for you! We already had dessert. You had chocolate cake, remember?" Sable looked down at her plate for confirmation and then looked around at the empty restaurant and the dark street outside. Absentmindly, she said, "Wow. It's dark. We spent the whole day together again and it seems like just a few minutes passed."

Jim stood up and said, "I think it's time to get you home to an aspirin, water and a long sleep. Don't you?"

"Anything you say, skipper," she shot back.

Chapter 7: Just Being a Guy

The squirrel is the fastest rodent, with speeds up to 17 miles/hour. That speed keeps them free of the black mamba, the fastest snake, which goes 12 miles/hour in short bursts. Greyhounds, the fastest dog, has been clocked at 45 miles/hour. The fastest bird is the Peregrine Falcon which can dive at an unbelievable 200 miles/hour.. The sailfish has been known to unreel fishing line at up to 64 miles/hour. Typically, a human can run at most around 15 miles/hour - a 4 minute mile. However, it is the human in the end that can travel over 100 miles/hour in even a typical car if they like. Only a human can fly along at over 600 miles/hour while reading a book, watching a movie or even sleeping.

Cliff came back into town a few days after Jim and Sable had toured the Ovation Center, for which Jim was somewhat relieved. He needed a little physical distance from Sable in turn to get some emotional distance and to try and put some perspective on his feelings for her. He busied himself getting his boat in working order, ready to sail and learning about all the fancy systems on board. He also did a fair amount of shopping to decorate it and get some clothes and other supplies so he didn't have to bring anything over from Madison.

He had just gotten home from Milwaukee the following Saturday afternoon when the doorbell rang. Jim was a little startled because the bell almost never rang. Dean and Ellen just walked in, Sable called first and then walked in, and the delivery guys usually woke him up. Jim figured they would do that so they could just leave whatever it was on the step and do a little less effort.

So, Jim looked out the door and was startled to see Cliff standing out there. Jim immediately felt guilty. Then, in the next second, he felt mad at himself for feeling guilty. He hadn't done anything…really. He was just spending a lot of time with this guy's wife and would probably drag her up to his bed if he had even the thought that they might be getting separated. So, he thought often about doing the wrong thing but it hadn't happened in reality. Jim shook his head vigorously. "I wish Dean was here," he thought. "I need a third party to intervene and tell this guy that I havn't done anything untoward to his wife." Jim shook his head again and the doorbell rang again.

Jim opened the door and put on his best car dealer smile. "Cliff!" he said, "How are you? Long time, no see." He could see immediately that Cliff was happy to see him for some reason too and immediately relaxed. How car dealers keep that fake attitude up all day was beyond him.

"Jim, remember me telling you about the Ferrari racing that we do? Anyway, I'm going to a race today and was interested in seeing if you would like to come along? They have a course all blocked off down by Alpine Valley - good roads, safe route, remote. They pay for the cops to block off access and everything."

'You don't race on a track?" was the only thing that came out of Jim's mouth.

Cliff laughed, "Well, no. That is NASCAR! This is more like a Formula 1 race with a big road course."

Jim said, "Sure, when are we going?" because it was starting to get late into the afternoon.

"Right now," said Cliff and pointed over to his driveway. Jim stepped out of his doorway and looked over to behold one of the most beautiful cars he had ever seen. The soundtrack to Magnum P.I. suddenly raced through his brain. Without realizing he didn't have shoes on, Jim ran over to the Ferrari and practically sniffed it like a puppy. Cliff walked over, smiling broadly - pleased that Jim was impressed with the car. "350 hp with a new turbocharger, racing tires and I stripped out some of the extra weight," said Cliff.

Jim never stopped looking at the car and said, "Wow. This is great! I never thought I'd see one of these in Wisconsin though."

"Yeah," said Cliff, "It's not something that I'd drive down University Avenue in the January salt but summertime is still here and the baby is ready to run! So, how's 'bout it? Wanna come with?"

Jim finally pried his eyes off the car and looked Cliff in the eye trying to discern if Cliff somehow knew how Jim felt about his wife or perhaps how she felt about him. Learning nothing from those steely hockey-player eyes, Jim went back to boring holes through the red paint of the car and said, "Of course, that would be excellent. Can you really race with two people?"

"Actually," said Cliff," they don't allow that unless you are also a registered driver for the team. However, there's a place for friends to sit and watch with lots of food and eye candy. We can drive down together and I can give you an idea of what she'll do along the way!"

Jim ran and got dressed, threw on a fleece jacket and a hat and went out to join Cliff. Cliff was just in the process of hugging Sable goodbye and giving her a kiss.

Sable saw Jim, smiled and yelled over, "I'm glad you can go. I hate to watch. Don't let him do anything too dangerous - OK, Jim?"

Cliff said, "Hey, wait! Isn't this the guy that races sailboats across the lake at 30 MPH or more with his butt hanging off the side?"

"Yeap," said Jim, "but the lake hurts a lot less than asphalt if you fall" With that, Cliff and Jim got in the car. Jim wondered what Sable thought. "They look like they have been best pals for twenty years" was what Sable was actually thinking. Cliff started it up and they listened to it thunder to life. Cliff slowly backed it out of the driveway,

89

looked for any traffic. Seeing none, he stomped on the accelerator, causing the car to skid along the entire length of the street until the tires finally grabbed hold of the pavement. Then, he let off the accelerator and Jim was finally able to peel his body off the seat. At this point, they were going about 60 MPH on their little residential street and Cliff slowed down to pull onto the main Madison beltway for the half hour drive down to the race area. Cliff yelled over the engine and wind noise telling Jim the details of the car and the racing system. Jim caught about two thirds of what he was saying. Mostly, Jim was just sucking in the experience. He had never owned a convertible and had NEVER been riding in a sports car of this caliber. He thought that only sailing could really bring him this kind of a thrill but the open top of the Ferrari, the stares of the people that they flew by, and the anticipation of actually letting the car run without the hindrance of a speed limit really made him want to just scream.

They finally pulled off of the main highway and onto a side road. Cliff was forced to drive a little slower behind a row of cars. Cliff looked over at Jim and said, "You know, I have been meaning to tell you how great it is that you have been hanging out with Sable. You know, I am gone so much and she has such trouble making friends that it has been really great that the two of you can hang out! She says that you are teaching her to sail, right?"

Jim's guilt was suddenly as chilling as the cold breeze swirling around his head and shoulders. "Yeah, she has been going out with me and the crew. She is really picking it up and I think that she has started to meet a few other people in the club as well, which is good."

"Yes, yes, yes," said Cliff. "She really needs friends."

Jim risked another statement, "I hope this doesn't bother you if I say this but she really misses you when you're gone. You know that, right?"

Cliff continued to navigate deftly and said, "Yeah, I know that. Well, I was planning on cutting back my travel time this next quarter but I was recently offered a promotion to the international sales team which would mean a huge raise and an opportunity to shoot for the CEO spot in a few years. I could be the youngest CEO that the company has had in recent history. Plus, I am hoping to get Sable to travel with me more if it is international travel. I told them they had to fly her with me if she wants to go."

"Sable wouldn't view this as good news," Jim thought. She didn't want to travel; she wanted to have a life with some structure and some meaning. She wanted to be a Mom, not in charge of Cliff's luggage. However, all he said was, "That sounds like a great opportunity." Suddenly, Jim realized that he was actually happy about the news because it might mean that Sable just leaves Cliff. He shook his head to clear that idea out of his mind.

Cliff leaned over and said, "You aren't getting car sick, are you?"

"Ha! No. No. I'm not."

Jim expected the car race to be the Indy 500 with endless laps around an oval track with a bunch of people in white t-shirts watching from the stands and drinking Bud Light. None of that was even close to correct. He realized it was much more like a polo match with cars replacing horses. He should have realized that Cliff didn't belong in the Bud Light scene and obviously belonged in this scene. They pulled up and came to a stop on the road in a long line of other Ferraris. They got out and walked over to what looked like a huge lawn party in a park next to the road. "We are on some rich guy's farm supposedly but I don't see any cows here," said Cliff as they walked up to the crowd. Lots of over-dressed men and women who looked like they had stepped out of the Italian countryside or a Ralph Lauren ad. High priced champagne was flowing freely (for everyone but the drivers) and various Italian antipastas were being handed out by well-dressed waiters. Jim was markedly under-dressed which made him feel a little sheepish until he remembered that he could probably buy and sell most of these people. Then, he felt a little better. Of course, he didn't know anyone either and so he stuck close to Cliff. Cliff, of course, knew everyone. "Hi there, Commissioner." ... "Hello,

Your Honor. Of course, I will win!" After a few of these conversations, Jim was happy about his anonymity as opposed to Cliff's local celebrity status.

One of the groups that welcomed Cliff with open arms was his pack of highly successful former hockey players. They had matching jackets that Cliff had bought and welcomed him as the captain. They welcomed Jim because he showed up with Cliff, of course. Not all of them were drivers, though, and some were just along to watch, like Jim. They started by giving Cliff crap for having missed most of the season while he was traveling and now showing up for the final race of the season and the glory. It turns out that the "Team" that Cliff was on was doing quite well in the standings and that several of them had won races. Suddenly, Cliff said, "So, what will it cost me to buy this race from you guys?"

"You ain't got enough money!" one of the other hockey-player-come-business-man said.

"Bet I do. I just got another promotion at work. You guys are now looking at the new Head of International Development for CCM International."

"Great," said the same guy again, "Now there won't be any strippers in the whole world that you don't know on a first name basis!" This drew a huge laugh from the rest of the guys and even Cliff had a chortle about it. Just as when Cliff told him about the promotion, another red flag went off in Jim's head as he considered the implications for Sable and her life. Jim thought, "I guess if Cliff was happy on the road in most ways - then it didn't matter when he came home." Sable was just another part of the world that revolved around Cliff, it seemed. Of course, on the way home, Cliff tried denying going to strip clubs and getting hookers especially after he met Sable, writing it off to locker room antics left over from being a hockey player.

The actual racing was relatively anti-climactic in Jim's opinion. Jim sat in the stands with several of Cliff's buddies who were sipping champagne and checking out the women in the audience as much as watching the racing. The racing was quite fast on the straight sections of the road but even Jim could see that all but one of the drivers over-slowed into the corners. Jim could tell why Cliff liked it. Cliff was two or three times as aggressive as the average driver. He slowed incrementally before the corners and just slammed through them on the accelerator. He drove within inches of the other drivers through the corner, who invariably let off the gas just a hair which allowed him to squeak by in front of them. Most of the drivers were just in it for the sheer fun and to say that they raced their Ferrari on the weekend. Cliff, however, was in it for the same reason that he lived the rest of his life, to win. Not contentment nor inner satisfaction or any of that crap, but pure, unadulterated...competition. That's why he was great at sales, why he had been great at hockey and why he had the biggest house, the prettiest wife and the fastest car. Cliff didn't exist comfortably outside of the winner's circle.

Jim stopped himself and shook his head. He thought "I'm probably not objective about it considering I have "a thing" for the man's wife." Jim decided he'd better hang out with Sable a little less the next time Cliff was out of town. But, for the moment, Jim was enjoying the sound of the racing, the smell of the rubber and ozone, the taste of champagne and the blurry vision of the luxury rockets cruising over the rolling hills of Wisconsin through the late summer evening.

Cliff came in second, which thrilled his teammates who hated when he showed up for every fifth race and still won. Cliff was cranky all the way back to Maple Bluff and kept saying "I just couldn't catch him on that last corner. I'll have to see what the mechanic can do about that. Just have to see the mechanic." Jim found out that normally Cliff just left the car with the mechanic and didn't keep it at home. A good idea, Jim thought, as they peeled rubber at yet another stop light bursting through the speed limit for the umpteenth time on the way home.

By the time they had talked to the boys and hung out for a little award ceremony after the race and drove home, it was pretty late, cold and dark. There were still a few lights on in Cliff and Sable's house. Jim was sure that Sable would not be able to sleep until Cliff got home safely. Hopefully, she was a little worried about Jim as well. Jim thanked Cliff profusely for the opportunity and promised to take him out on his boat on Lake Michigan at the next convenient opportunity. Cliff said that sounded good to him if they could stay at the dock and drink so he didn't get sea-sick. Jim laughed and promised him a completely flat water adventure.

Jim found himself shortly thereafter checking for used Ferraris online while he was reading his emails. He started to chuckle and thought "Well, I'd probably better finish up getting my current toy working and on the water first."

Chapter 8: Crash

Hyenas run across the savannah hunting for a victim. One would assume that they approach it like a civilized man would approach going to the grocery store.. Their prey might be weaker than the rest, sick or injured in an accident. Perhaps it wandered away from the rest of the herd, tripped in a hole, skittered on some loose gravel, or just was not able to find food or water. It doesn't mean that the gazelle they pick is inherently worse than the rest. It just happens that, on that particular day, in that particular piece of ground, the gazelle they have chosen has a lot of bad luck. The hyenas don't really care. They circle the victim, taunting it for some time and making sure it's all out of fight before ending the game. They rip the gazelle apart, scattering blood and entrails across the dirt praire. Unlike the man at the grocery store, the hyenas comes to the table with true hunger and feast indulgently on the prey.

A week later there was a beautiful blue sky warm day in the end of September. Jim realized that it was getting pretty late in the year and he needed to hurry to try out his boat a couple of times before he had to put it in storage for the winter. The problem with Lake Michigan is that the heavy ice pushed onto the shore during the winter, meaning that all the boats (especially the expensive boats) needed to be pulled from the lake at the end of the fall season. When the sailboat is pulled out depends on the boat owner, but the lift operators quit working about a week into November. So, time was getting short and Jim headed over to the marina first thing in the morning. He was installing a new sonar system and a system to improve the ability to sail the boat alone. He had talked with Dean about coming over in the afternoon but wasn't sure that he would make it. Dean had not been around much, as he had basically moved in with Ellen. Jim had hoped that the two of them would spend more time at the house but her little place was much closer to the hospital than driving most of the way around Lake Mendota to Maple Bluff. The University hospital was on the opposite corner of the lake which didn't seem far until you had to drive directly through town to get back and forth. Anyway, Jim had not seen Dean much at all in a few weeks and so had called to see if he wanted to come over. So, it made Jim smile when Dean showed up just after lunchtime in his beat up Honda and extracted himself from the car looking a little hungover. Jim decided that this must be due to the hospital as Dean didn't normally drink before noon. The feeling was confirmed when Jim saw that Dean was still wearing his scrub pants on the bottom.

"Hey," said Dean, "How is it going? Need a doctor?"

"No," fired back Jim. "But, I could use an extra set of hands if you don't mind getting your doctor paws all covered with grease and grime."

"Well", said Dean smiling, "What if I just get some nurses and tell them what to do?"

They both chuckled. Jim put down the spinnaker gear he was working on to shake hands with Dean and fetch both of them a couple of beers from the fridge. "I guess we don't need nurses if we have beer," said Dean. "That seems like the good way to work into this working stuff."

And so it went, and they got lost in the work and the time passed. Because of how late it was in the season, it got completely dark pretty early and soon it was getting too dark to work. They took a break and sat down with another set of beers and some frozen lobster that Jim threw in a pot of boiling water down in the galley.

"Did ya catch that lobster around here?", asked Dean with a grin.

"Very funny," said Jim, "I could get you some Mac and cheese if you'd prefer?"

"No," said Dean, "I haven't had lobster yet today so that would be fine." He continued, "Say, I have some news."

"WAIT! Let me guess," interjected Jim. "My bet is that you and Ellen are engaged!"

"Uhh, well no, we aren't but that is probably in the works too. She has this thing about waiting until I finish all of body plumber school before getting engaged. Remember, she had that friend who had a horrible first marriage?"

"Oh, yeah, I remember, they got married in Vegas after only two weeks which seems romantic until you find out that the guy was in prison three times and didn't tell you that he broke parole."

Dean shook his head, "Yeah, so that isn't the news. And… and I am thinking this might bug you a little so I am just going to say it – I graduate in December because I had to retake those two rotations, remember? Anyway, I just got a residency interview in Denver and it sounds like I could easily get a spot there. I think I'm going to take it, if I get it." Dean paused and looked at Jim before continuing, "Ellen should be defending her thesis sometime in January too so that timing is perfect and she has a few leads of places in Denver. We both love the mountains and everything so it's a really great fit for us, all around."

Jim worked on the lobster for a few seconds. "That sounds great for you two. But, you don't sound that thrilled about it," he said.

"Well, I am but it means that I'm officially moving out and leaving town and I thought that might bother you."

"Why would that bother me?" asked Jim and realized why even as he said it. He actually stopped chewing the lobster when he realized it. Dean was the only friend in town who really knew about the lottery and the money and the pre-ticket Jim vs. the post-ticket Jim. Jim had a number of friends from the sailing club and there was Sable and a few other friends but none of them knew the whole story. With the people he had known before and worked with at his old job, he had lost touch the last few months as their lives and his rapidly fell out of sync. Jim's family had been down a few times but he had never been close to them and money didn't seem to be changing that very much. Dean had been pretty much it, and even Dean had not been around much lately. It was then that Jim realized how much time he had been spending with Sable the last few months as well.

Dean looked over and realized that Jim was lost in thought, which made him a little uncomfortable. "Of course, you are welcome to come out and stay with us any time you want. I am thinking that in about five years I will have a real job as a doctor and we will have enough money to even get a little condo up by the ski areas and that would be fun. Heck, you could come out and we could ski for a few weeks every winter and hang out. It would be fun." After a long pause while he shoveled some lobster in his mouth, he hesitantly added, "We just felt like we had to get out of the Midwest plus the program there is really great."

At this point, Jim was able to focus again on what Dean was saying and started to follow along. "Yeah, skiing would be fun. And you should move. It will be good for both of you to get out of the Midwest for a while or longer. Don't worry about me. God knows that I can move somewhere else more easily than anyone else." With that, the moment passed and they were men again and strong. They talked about how best to move and Jim offered to help. They talked about how Dean was a little freaked out by moving in with Ellen officially when they moved to Denver but it seemed like the only logical way to arrange it. Jim even thought out loud that he might buy a place up in Vail or something to have as a retreat.

Before it got too late, Dean decided he needed to get back home as he had rounds at 6 AM the next morning. Jim said he would clean up the galley and told Dean to head on back to Madison. Dean was going over to Ellen's anyway, supposedly so he could walk to the hospital in the morning for exercise, so they wouldn't even see each other at home anyway. Dean walked off the boat and Jim went back down into the galley. He was down there for a few minutes when he heard footsteps on the decking outside and someone coming down the steps. Without looking up from the dishes, he yelled out, "Dean, did you forget something?"

And, suddenly, a very familiar but unexpected voice said, "I don't think I even look at all like Dean!!" Jim dropped the dish in the sink and luckily it was designed for a sailboat so it was plastic and it didn't break. His eyes shot up and came to rest in the eyes of Sable who was still standing in the stairwell with one foot on the lower level and one foot still perched on the lowest step as if to indicate that she would leave without question if he asked her to. She was dressed like a Ralph Lauren ad again with the perfect jeans and an oversized brown heavy cotton shirt open just enough to show that she had a tank top on underneath. There was some dazzling bauble hanging around her well-tanned neck. Jim was always amazed at how well she dressed and also amazed that she never put any conscious thought into it. Just years of practice. However, tonight something was definitely amiss. Her eyes were bloodshot and her nose looked raw. Jim slowly put it together that Sable had been crying and had driven over from Madison to find him because of it. As he looked at her, she realized what he realized and tears started to form on her face again and she just turned away to sit on the couch across the galley from him and put her face in her hands.

Jim set aside the remaining dishes, wiped his hands on the towel and crossed over to her in five short feet. She turned to him and buried her face in his shoulder and just started sobbing. Jim knew better than to try and get her to explain so he just waited for a few minutes. Finally, the crying slowed and he pushed her back from his shoulder enough to ask "What happened?" She started explaining, in half sentences, while still crying and gasping for air. "It's Cliff! He left this morning. He was supposed to be here through Thanksgiving and...now...he left!...He is going to be gone until December on...some new big f'ing ...project in

Australia!...I told him...I was...so...so...pissed off...and he just laughed..." And the crying started again...

"Why did he laugh?" asked Jim - not really sure if it was the right thing to say but he was really curious.

"He said...that...it seemed like I couldn't be too pissed considering how much money I spend while he's gone...Like a bunch of damn money is why I married him! Like a bunch of damn money is what I want!!! How are we supposed to have kids if he is never home? How are we supposed to..."

The crying and holding went on for another half hour until Sable just ran dry. And when her tear ducts dried out, she got thirsty. "What do you have to drink around here?" she asked.

"Well," said Jim, "Dean and I were just working on that bottle of champagne but maybe I can get you a glass of water too?"

"Sure, water would be great."

Jim walked over to the galley sink realizing he was grateful for a moment to collect himself. Silently, he got the water. As he turned back around, the sight of Sable chugging out of the champagne bottle and the bottle slowly emptying made Jim realize this was going to be a long evening. "Hey," he said trying to think quickly, "Aren't you going to share some of that with me?"

"Sure, are you having problems with your husband too?" she asked.

"No, but my roommate is moving to Denver, does that count?" he said.

"What?" While trying to drink more of the champagne so she couldn't slam the whole bottle, Jim told her quickly about Dean and Ellen's plan to move to Denver in a few months. Sable had spent some time with Dean and Ellen and between everything else and this news, she abruptly got up and said, "Dammit, everyone is leaving us. Denver, Australia, parts unknown. And, oddly, we are the ones on a boat!"

With that, she marched over to the fridge and grabbed out the Rose's lime juice and ice, marched over to the liquor cabinet to grab the tequila and triple-sec. Jim realized simultaneously that he was getting drunk on the champagne. He was in fact drunk already – and depressed that Dean was leaving and that he wanted Sable now more than ever. His half-drunk mind had them moved in together before Cliff's plane even reached Australia. So, he walked over to the galley and took the margarita that Sable had made for him. However, he was still sober enough to realize that she was going to get sick if she didn't eat something. Luckily, he had gotten the marina to load up the fridge with a broad array of food for the little trip he had planned for the next weekend (especially in case he got stuck somewhere with his new boat) and so he got out some frozen quesadillas, chips and guacamole and even some tiramisu. It turned out that Sable was really getting hungry as well and so he was able to get several plates of food in her. But, the alcohol didn't stop flowing either and pretty soon they were both totally blitzed, full and communally angry. They were sitting around the galley table with a spread of reheated food that looked like it had been attacked by a 2-year-old. Sable was cursing everything there was to curse about Cliff. She was really pissed off at him and was starting to get rather petty about the whole ordeal.

Finally, she said, "And you know what the worst is? The worst is that I have had little doubts about what he does when he is on the road - so every time he is on the road it drives me crazy." Jim was still sober enough to remember his conversation with Cliff's buddies at the car race about the hookers all over the world. He was also sober enough not to mention it, but he did ask, "Well...what...what...what makes you suspect him of being with a hooker?"

"Hooker?! I didn't say that! How disgusting!" Sable turned up her nose and wrinkled up her face in the cutest display of disgust in the world. "It is just that there are some charges on the credit card that seem exceedingly high. He always says that it is for entertaining clients but the stories don't really add up and...well...it just seems like he doesn't

101

really ever want to talk about what he has been doing. I assume he is just doing boring work but then he has a couple of receipts for a Cirque de Sol show in his jacket pocket or a receipt for a Pussycat club or something. God, sometimes I just think I am wasting my time with him. I really do love him but I just think he doesn't care! God, maybe I should just leave him!" And she stared at the table again and finally she looked up at him and said, "Well, I think it is time for an after-dinner drink, don't you think?" Despite Jim's protests that he was already drunk, she staggered over to the reservoir of broken-dream-juice also known as the liquor cabinet and came back with a bottle of cognac. Now, everyone knows that cognac should be sipped and taken in small country-club doses. Everyone except Sable, seemingly. She poured both of them a tall glass of cognac on the rocks and tossed hers back.

Jim started downing his drink not wanting to fall too far behind at this point. Sable put down her glass and shoved her fingers in the tiramisu and then shoved the pile of food into her mouth and started to squirm in her seat with delight. "My God! Tiramisu is incredible! It and cognac together are well too! You have to try it." And she moved around the table next to Jim, shoved her fingers into the tiramisu (obviously not realizing that Jim could have shoved his own fingers in it) pulled out a big chunk of the dessert and shoved her fingers and the dessert into Jim's mouth. Jim was shocked. He was shocked not at the thought of tiramisu but of having Sable's hot fingers shoved in his mouth. She started to pull her fingers out and said, "Isn't that great? Do you want some more?" and Jim just nodded his head because his mouth was full. And suddenly, there were her fingers again inside his mouth.

Jim shut his eyes so he could focus on getting the dessert off his fingers without gagging when suddenly, they were gone. And, before he could open his eyes, he realized that Sable's lips had found their way to his lips and in the smallest split second, her tongue had replaced her fingers in his mouth. Jim paused for just a split-second, a little bit surprised, and then he threw his arms around her and returned her kiss, hard. The tension that came from holding back for months and months was suddenly broken and they leapt at each other like arrows launched from a bow. The first time, they were still next to the galley table and Sable kept drinking and feeding Jim. By the second time, they had made it to the bed in the state room. Sable had started to feel a little more sober and the third time happened in the walk-in shower. It seemed that the world had shrunk to the size of the boat and a bottle of cognac that traveled with them.

Jim must have passed out around 11 PM but suddenly came to a start when he heard a loud crash on the deck above him. He was still drunk but no longer in a good way. He looked around, realized he was lying in the master bed and that Sable was not around. Suddenly, a second noise came from above and he recognized it as the riggings being raised. He jumped up and realized that jumping wasn't good and that he was naked. He quickly found some pants on the floor and threw those on and ran up on the deck.

If he had truly been sober, he would have thought it was funny. Sable was standing there trying to raise the main sail wearing only one of his polo shirts, clutching the mostly empty cognac bottle and pulling on the wrong rope. "Dammit," she said. "I want to leave my husband tonight, I want to leave him with this boat and dammit...the damn sail won't go up." And, as if this wasn't enough, she added, "Oh, and I love you and you're going to marry me but we can still live next to each other so that I can keep my house. OK?"

Before he could say anything, she continued as if he had. "Shh," she said, "Don't tell Cliff and we can be gone by the time he realizes."

Jim said, "Hey, let's go back downstairs and go to bed and you can leave Cliff when you're hungover in the morning. He already is on his way to Australia anyway, isn't he?"

"Dammit, he already left ME!" she said. "Can't you take me night sailing?" and she started to cry and the rope fell from her hand and she started to lean against the cabin crying. "Can't you take me sailing? I just want to go sailing

103

and feel the breeze. Can't you take me sailing?" Jim could
never stand a woman crying. Suddenly, he had the idea that
he could motor the sailboat just out of the marina a short
distance and take a few turns with the motor. So, he got
behind the big wheel and held on for support. "OK, ok, I'll
take you sailing...", he yelled up to her. It had cooled off a lot
but it was very humid so the air was still relatively warm for
this time of night and this time of year. Of course, the water
was cold no matter what time of year it was. He started up
the motor and threw the sailboat in reverse. Suddenly, the
lights came on in the marina office so he fumbled with the
radio until he got the watchman and told him he was trying
to see the stars and was just going offshore to do that for an
hour or so. The watchman started yelling that it was against
the rules to go out this late and that he thought the boat had
been stolen, etc. Finally, Jim managed to push enough
buttons to turn off the radio.

As Jim navigated towards the end of the marina,
Sable moved back to the cockpit and stood behind him,
wrapping her arms around him. She was holding on for
support when she wasn't running her hands all over him. As
they moved out into the darkness across the lake, they left
the lights of the city behind. The breeze made it seem like
they were moving quickly and she left Jim and worked her
way back up towards the front of the boat. Wordlessly, Jim
willed her to back off from the front of the sailboat but he
couldn't do anything except continue to steer the boat and
couldn't even yell over the motor under his feet. The waves
were really picking up and Jim wasn't sure what he should
do. At this point, Sable was out on the prow of the ship, the
waves were beating up on her bare feet and bare legs and
she seemingly didn't even notice. She started screaming and
crying. Worried, Jim throttled back the engine but the boat
still moved fairly quickly through the waves. Jim started
moving up the deck towards her. She was almost completely
incoherent at this point although Cliff's name and swear
words continued to spill forth from her mouth. Jim had put
the boat on a straight course as best he could but as soon as
he left the tiller, the boat started to rock to the side in the

waves. He was picking his way along the deck and calling for Sable to come back to where he was in the middle of the boat. "It isn't safe," he yelled.

Finally, she turned around and looked at him. Now, it's an unfortunate thing that was about to happen but Jim couldn't have known that his timing could not be worse. Months later, he would still be going over those actions in his mind. Just as she turned back to look at him, the boat had turned just enough out of the wind and a very large swell hit the boat at a right angle. Her legs were numb from the cold water that had been beating against her for the last hour. Her balance was gone because she was hammered. Her numb and drunk legs flew out from under her. Her head slammed onto the white deck, knocking her out. Her limp body slid overboard, leaving a red streak as her head must have started to bleed, with the cognac bottle still clutched in her hand. Jim actually thought he heard the bottle bang against the bottom of the sailboat.

Jim's body reacted before he did. His eyes widened, his jaw dropped open and he suddenly was hit with so much adrenaline that he just about leapt into the water. Within a second, he raced ahead and immediately got caught up in the lines which Sable had splayed all over the deck in her attempt to raise the mainsail. It only took Jim a few more seconds to untangle his ankles but by the time he reached the bow, Sable's limp body had sunk under the surface and the momentum of the ship meant she had probably already slipped astern of the boat.

All the time Jim had spent sailing had not prepared him at all for this. He scurried to the back of the boat, still not really quick on his feet. He grabbed the life ring but he couldn't see any sign of Sable in the darkness. He started fumbling for the spot light and pointed it out across the water. Nothing. He saw nothing. He fired up the engine and started running the boat in reverse until he started moving backwards towards where he felt that she might be. It was an almost impossible task however because there were no lights to orient him and the waves were coming in all different directions.

After what seemed like hours but was probably only minutes, Jim managed to get the radio turned on again and started yelling "Mayday! Mayday!" until someone finally answered. The guy at the marina had wandered away from his station or fallen asleep it seemed. Anyway, Jim got the Lake Michigan rescue crew on the horn finally. "Man overboard. Man overboard!" he yelled at them.

"OK, sir, settle down. We are here to help but you must tell us where you are and who you are."

"OK, this is the sailboat Lucky Ticket. My name's Jim Wells and I just lost someone overboard. I'm sitting off the Royal City Marina with my sails down. My sails are down. I've activated my lights. I can't locate my man overboard. She's a woman. Blond hair. I think she received a concussion when she went over. I need help finding her."

"Sir, we are sending out a chopper. They will be there soon. Can you send up a flare?"

"No! I don't have flares. Damn! I'll turn on all the lights and I'm sending you my GPS coordinates, I think."

"Very good, sir. We will do what we can. Keep looking in the water as she might surface."

Jim kept looking and shining the light and tried to keep the boat floating with the current. He stopped the engine and started yelling for Sable. He saw nothing. He heard nothing. He started to realize what was happening. Sable was dying. She had come here, cheated on her husband with him and fallen overboard. "This isn't happening! This is not happening," he kept repeating and repeating over and over.

Jim sat there in the short calm before what he knew would be an incredible storm in his life. He started to cry very quietly while still trying to hold the boat steady and watch for any sign of Sable. Meanwhile, he continued to have to respond to the rescue squad on the radio. He cried for Sable and he cried for himself as he was faced with the fact that she was probably dead and that he was partly responsible. He really didn't care about his own future, he realized. And finally, like a rose opening to reveal its beauty in the middle of a rain storm, he realized that Sable was

106

probably the only true relationship he had been in, in his life. The fact that she was married to someone else somehow made it more unique and special rather than wrong and illegitimate.

And then, almost like God turned on the light above his head, the sky broke open with incredible light and noise. The helicopter must have been flying high above until it spotted the "Lucky Ticket" and then had rapidly descended upon him. The chopper circled his area twice and lowered themselves down til almost touching the water in order to look in pretty close at Jim. Then, after giving him the obligatory thumbs up, they started flying a rescue pattern out from where Jim was located. With their help, he communicated via the radio his GPS readout of where he had been. Luckily, the GPS unit had been turned on the entire time.

Within probably fifteen minutes of the helicopter arriving, the Rescue Squad cutter pulled up alongside the sailboat and several crewmen tied up alongside while the obvious man-in-charge jumped aboard the "Lucky Ticket." He got right into Jim's face and was going to start giving him hell about being reckless when he saw the look on his face. Jim's face told the entire story to the captain, who had been doing rescue work on the lake for over 20 years and had probably seen similar stories etched on other faces. Captain Oleson had grown up either next to or on the lake and hated the rich old drunks up from Chicago who were constantly getting in trouble on the lake through sheer stupidity. But, he saw the fear and panic and guilt and growing cloud of doom on Jim's face and he stopped short of lambasting him.

"Let me guess," he said. "Your "plan", if we can call it that, was to motor out and see the stars away from the lights of the lakeshore. Then, the "plan" went horribly wrong." Jim just nodded affirmatively. Captain Oleson then asked the million dollar question, "Your friend wasn't wearing a life jacket, was she?"

Jim looked him in the eye but said in a strong voice, "Yes, that's correct. She wasn't wearing a life jacket." With that statement, Jim collapsed on the deck and started crying again. The captain looked out to the horizon which was his habit when he was thinking. He slowly watched the helicopter retracing the boat's path and said over his shoulder, "Well, let's hope that the chopper guys find her. Those guys can sometimes even see the bottom of the lake from up there with those lights."

The rescue crew took over motoring Jim's sailboat back to shore. They would moor it at the Coast Guard station - standard protocol in a missing person situation. If the person remains missing or is dead, then the boat would be evidence. Jim asked to stay out on the Lake with the search team. Both the Coast Guard cutter and the chopper kept searching and searching. In a few hours, the dawn approached from the other side of the lake, over where Michigan rose out of the water. The dawn raced across the water to them as if to be a cruel reminder that Sable had now been in the water for several hours. A second chopper had also joined the search at some point but when both choppers got low on fuel and they had searched the entire extended grid area of the lake several times, the Captain called of the rescue search and converted it to a recovery mission. He called for the dredging team to come out to this part of the lake. Then, the Captain went down to the galley where Jim had finally passed out despite several large cups of coffee. His feet now had thermal socks on them but were most probably frostbitten as he'd been standing barefoot in or close to the almost frozen lake water most of the night. The captain hesitated before waking him up but finally roused him and gave him the bad news. Jim was past crying for the moment and just absorbed what he already knew in his heart as truth. He simply nodded and silently looked out the window as the cutter headed back to the dock.

Chapter 9: High Adventure

At the MGM Grand Hotel and Casino on the Las Vegas strip, off to the side of the main casino is a three story, 40,000 square feet glass habitat enclosure. When they are taking a break from losing their life savings, gamblers can view the lions inside the cage. The tourists can walk around and even underneath the lions as the lions like to lie down on top of the glass ceilings of the hallway that passes through the habitat. To the untrained eye, the lions appear to be very large, domesticated cats. However, when one considers the relative scale of a 400-pound female lion and a 10-pound mid-size cat, one starts to understand the power contained in that cage. However, as the lions look out at the rows of walking dead feeding their money into one-armed bandits, perhaps they wonder who's really in the cage.

Jim suddenly said, "Damn! I forgot to pick up any snacks." He said it to no one in particular because he was alone in the hotel room staring into the little fridge that came with the suite."Dammit!" he said again slapping his hand on top of the TV. He thought about heading down to the bar to get a drink and something to eat but then nixed that because of what had happened the other day when a couple reporters had heard he was in the hotel bar. Suddenly, the whole hotel was being staked out by the legions of TV vans that had been following him around. The vans seemed to nest outside his house (and Cliff and Sable's house too) but were ready to go as soon as someone saw him out and about.

109

Jim's stable little life of relative anonymity had been blown out of the water as if by someone fishing with dynamite. Jim had never endured anything like it before. On top of his grief and guilt about Sable, his entire life was being flashed on the TV screen. "Entertainment Tonight" even had a guy calling him and looking for an interview. Jim had tried to hold a press conference, at the advice of his lawyer, a couple of days after the accident. Suddenly, Cliff had shown up looking completely unlike his normal dapper self. He started shouting at Jim in the middle of the press conference saying that Jim had killed his wife, that Jim would pay, that Cliff would make sure Jim would pay, etc., etc. The only thing that Jim could do (which partly saved him in the eyes of the public) was to break down and start bawling in front of the entire press corps. He mumbled something about how Sable had been a good friend of his and that she had not been cheating on Cliff but that was all the information he had gotten out. The local Madison papers were having a field day, especially when they pieced together that Jim was also the mystery lottery winner from the previous year.

Due to Sable's death, Cliff had done the one thing that she had wanted him to do while she was alive - get on a plane and fly home and stay with her. Suddenly, Cliff was home all the time and not traveling and there was no mention of his impending promotion that would keep him away even more. The police and his lawyer told Jim not to leave town either. He had almost daily meetings with his lawyer at various locations around town or at police headquarters. So, Jim did what any wealthy man trying to hide would do. He checked into the fortress known as the Madison Hilton where he was guarded night and day by the highly effective concierge staff. Jim spent most of his time talking with lawyers and police and reading about himself in the paper and watching about himself on TV. He cried a lot about Sable. He talked with the shrink that the police had "strongly recommended." He had told her most of the story but not anything too specific about that night because he

110

didn't really trust her. He had even been visited by a minister from a church he had never attended in town. The pastor wanted to encourage him to start going to his church. Jim wondered what the mix of altruism and desire for his tithe was in motivating the visit. Luckily, his lawyer was fairly effective at screening access to him so that not everyone got through to him. He had a new cell phone and had rented an SUV which he changed every few days so that he could at least get around town without being followed. Dean stopped by frequently but he was busy at the hospital and getting ready to move to Denver.

Jim was looking for a beer because he couldn't sleep. Tomorrow morning, he was meeting with a judge and the state prosecutor who were deciding if there was enough evidence to go to a grand jury and try to indict him on criminal charges. They had found Sable's body a few days after the accident. It had washed ashore a few miles from the marina. A random guy walking his dog along the shore stumbled upon the body which would have been almost unrecognizable. Of course, this gave Cliff and his family another opportunity to skewer Jim in the press and on TV again. Finally, Jim ordered two $10 beers from room service which arrived in the hands of Jim's new best friend, Vincent. Vincent worked for the hotel and was seemingly one of the only black men in Madison. Vincent was an odd combination of James Earl Jones and BB King. Jim felt really grounded when he talked to Vincent. They had developed a little routine over the last few weeks in which Vincent just came in with the beers, sat down, opened both beers and handed one to Jim.

Tonight, Jim said, "Well, Vincent, tomorrow is the big day. I either find out that I'm free to go about my life or that I'm going to go through a big trial and perhaps to jail. God, what would I do if I had to go to trial?"

Vincent looked at his beer not really sure if he should answer but finally said, "Well, seems you'd have to go to trial then."

Jim looked at him and then looked out at the lights of the State Capital outside the window, smiled and replied, "Yeap, that's what would happen." Vincent looked at Jim and watched Jim watch out the window.

Vincent said, "So, did you watch the Packers game?"

It took Jim two seconds to come back to reality. "Yeah, I watched most of it. It was a pretty good game. Favre is getting old though, don't you think?"

"Yeah, but he still has a strong arm and he has so much experience. I expect you're right, though. If he gets hurt, they won't hesitate to replace him with Manning. The offense is all built round Favre. So, they need another good quarterback so it doesn't come crashing down, right?"

Jim said, "Yeah, although some big Packers' news might drive my story from the front page."

Vincent started to laugh a little. "No sir. Ain't nothing driving you from the front page."

Jim shot him a stern glance, then his face relaxed and he was able to laugh at his life too. "Yeah, not even another 9/11 could drive me from the front of the paper in this town. Here's to me!" and they clinked their beer bottles together. They continued to chatter about the Packers until Vincent noticed Jim yawn, his beer empty. The wise old Vincent knew that the beer and the company had done their job and Jim would be asleep shortly after he left. So, he got up and made his usual excuse about needing to get back to the kitchen, Jim gave him a couple $20's for his tip and Vincent was gone. It would be a long time before Jim ever thought of Vincent again, let alone saw him.

The next morning Jim climbed into one of his suits, which Sable had helped him pick out a month or so ago when she saw one of his other suits. "Dreadful", she had said, "Let's take you shopping for some clothes." The suit was a little too hip for the judge's office but Jim would rather look flashy than drive by his house again to pick up something more serious. Jim took the hotel elevator down to the basement just before his lawyer pulled up. Jim climbed into the passenger's seat. They drove directly across town to the guarded underground parking lot in the justice building that they had been in many times over the last few weeks. The press was camped outside the parking lot entrance and snapped a bunch of footage of them driving into the building. The press, of course, knew what was special about today. As Jim's lawyer, Mr. Weiss, was wont to say, "It's like they just opened the hunting season on Jim and there's no limit."

Soon, they were sitting in the Judge's chambers. The Judge was across the desk, Jim was sitting in front with Mr. Weiss who looked like he was there for a funeral and was more than serious enough for both of them. Judge Peterson started talking in his almost-too-stereotypical Wisconsin accent, "So, then, Jim Wells, how are you doing then?"

Jim nodded and replied, "As well as can be expected, your Honor, considering the circumstances."

"Yeap, must be rough on you with this media circus on top of the situation. "Well, then," said Judge Peterson, "As you know, the report from the State Patrol and from the Coast Guard is finished. I got it right here, in front of me. You can get a copy pretty quick here as it will be public tomorrow." Jim found himself trying to read the page that the judge had open even though it was upside down. Judge Peterson continued, "Well, you see, Jim, it seems that the story is a wee bit confused. It seems that the evidence shows a bunch of alcohol spilled all over the galley and food spilled all over everywhere. However, the Coast Guard Capt., whom you met that night, claims that could all be due to the high waves during that storm that came up and while you were up top through the night. The report also details a bunch of ...How should I say this delicately? ...a bunch of evidence of several sexual encounters on the boat. Of course, the body of Sable Wainwright was too decomposed to either do a blood alcohol test on nor could any reliable evidence of sexual activity be determined. The testimony of your friend Dean helped establish your alibi because he said hello to her as he was leaving and she was arriving of her own free will. And the marina log tells a similar tale of when the cars checked in and out of the parking lot. So, there seems to be no conclusive evidence that your story of events is in error."

113

When the Judge failed to continue, Mr. Weiss said, " And, so you are saying…?"

Judge Peterson looked up and laid his hands down with an air of finality, " So, my judgement is that there isn't enough evidence to indict you, Mr. Wells. All we have here is some circumstantial evidence. Of course, more evidence could come out in the future and the situation would have changed but for now, we are not going to charge you."

Jim let out a long slow breath which just about whistled through his teeth.

The judge paused for a minute and then added "There is something ya should know though, there, Mr. Relieved. The chief prosecutor for the State did officially hypothesize in the report that the two of you had been having an affair, that something went bad and that you two fought. You accidentally killed her, threw her overboard and then called the shore patrol. The A.G.'s office is also quite upset with the Coast Guard for not breathalizing you immediately as well. However," and he looked Jim directly in the eye as if to say that he believed that Jim was getting away with something "However, there is no proof of that."

Jim could feel the anger welling up and blurted out, "I would never have harmed a hair on her head and I", before Jim's lawyer could get out, "Jim! Don't say another word." Jim glanced sideways at Carl and then back at the Judge but stopped talking.

And with that, the Judge reached for another pile of papers and his voice started to increase in tempo. "OK, so today we are charging you with several boating tickets for not wearing life jackets while boating and for failing to have your running lights on at all times. That total is $400 which you can pay the clerk on your way out. I assume from what I read in the papers that it will not be a problem for you to pay it, correct? You are free to go, sir. Hopefully, we'll never see each other again."

Jim walked out of the Judge's chambers feeling very light on his feet. Jim's lawyer grabbed him by the elbow and turned him out of the hallway and into a meeting room. The two of them sat down. Jim started "Carl, I cannot thank you enough! You have been a real rock in this storm. Thank God! Thank God!" Carl had been doing this for twenty-five years which made him wise enough to let Jim sit there feeling relieved for a few minutes. Finally, Jim said "What is it?" after reading Carl's silence for a few seconds.

Carl Weiss said, 'Jim, I don't know for sure what happened on that boat but I believe you when you say that she came over to complain about her husband, that the two of you made love, that she got upset, you went for a quick motor into the lake, the waves came up and she slipped and you could not get there in time. Both of you were fairly tipsy which you already admitted. I believe you when you say it was a terrible accident and that she meant a lot to you. Anyone who has been with you the last two months has seen that. But, and I tell you this as a friend and your lawyer, this outcome is almost worse than if you could tell your story in court. Because, when the A.G.'s report hits the streets in a few days, you are going to be indicted, tried and convicted in the papers. Cliff Wainwright will pull every string he can get his hands on to make sure that you come off looking like the evil villain. God forbid anyone question his love for his dead wife! You think these last few weeks have been bad? You won't be able to come out from under a rock in this town for the next decade. Normally, I'd tell my clients to stay and defend themselves in the press and on TV if they want to ever rebuild their lives. However, in your case, with your money, my strongest advice is to get the hell out of this town. You need to heal, you need to build a new life and you have enough money to do that anywhere. Find yourself another sailboat somewhere and sail into the sunset, Jim."

For what seemed like eternity, Jim sat and looked at the cherry wood table in the conference room which his hands rested upon. He couldn't talk or think. He was just contemplating the fact that one wrong move for just a few seconds, to impress Sable and get her to stop crying...had cost him everything – the woman he loved, his anonymity, his reputation and almost his freedom. Jim resolved not to make any more wrong moves...and then a single tear ran down his face.

Carl Weiss's heart went out to Jim again and he said, "You know Jim, my Mom once gave me a piece of advice that I am going to give to you. When I was a little boy, the world was pretty tough and overwhelming for me and you know what she said? She said, "Carl, there isn't any problem in life so big that you cannot run away from it.""

Jim looked up at Carl and stood up and walked out without saying anything. When he got into the hallway, he dialed Dean on his cell phone. Like some kind of secret agent, Dean had been waiting to pick him up in the garage after the meeting. Jim said into the phone, "Good news. I'm free. No grand jury, no indictment. It is all over." He paused looking down the hallway, and said to Dean, "Pull around to the front steps. I am coming out the front door like a free man who didn't do a damn thing wrong."

Dean wasn't sure this was a great idea but he just said "Yes."

Jim turned to Carl and said, "Dammit, Carl. I did a lot of wrong things here but I'm done hiding in the hotel and parking garage." And with that, Jim pushed his way through the front door with Carl by his side and marched up to the stunned reporters who started fumbling over themselves trying to record his words and take his picture all at the same time. Jim said simply, "Well, the Judge has informed me that I could go free because they have determined this situation has been a terrible accident. Sable Wainwright was my best friend. I miss her very much. If I could change places with her, I would do that. I would also like to express my sympathy to Cliff and the rest of Sable's family. I am going to try and disappear now and I would like to encourage you all in the press to put this story to rest now." And with that, Jim walked away from all the questions leaving Carl to spin the details.

In the car, Jim and Dean just sat without speaking as Dean drove away from the courthouse. Finally, Jim told him the jist of what had happened with the Judge and told him about the report and how tough things were going to be for awhile. Finally, Jim noticed that there were several very large suitcases in the back seat. Jim said, "So, are those for your move to Denver?"

Dean said, "Nope, those are for a surprise. I hope you don't get mad, and I can pay you back eventually if you are, but here is what I was thinking...Ellen and I were going to take a vacation at her parent's timeshare in Florida before I start in Denver. But, four days ago, we were talking about you and she told me that she wanted me to take you away for a week or so instead. That you needed it and that she wanted some time to see friends and pack up anyway. She is such a great woman. Anyway, I took the liberty with your credit card number and we will have to rent equipment and everything when we get there but... you and I are going skiing in the Alps!"

"What? What?" said Jim. "That's awesome, Dean! Thanks you! Wow, this is really exactly what I need. Getting out of the hotel!" Jim started to cry again as they drove out to the airport. Jim just stared out the window and cried for the town he was being forced to leave and the woman that he had loved and the mistakes he had made. On the short drive to the airport, Jim called Carl and told him that he was going on vacation and thanked him again for everything. Carl told him a little about the questions the reporters had asked. Jim also asked Carl to alert the Madison airport security that he and Dean would like to not have the TV crews with them at the airport. They currently were leading a small pack of vans heading out of town.

When they arrived at the airport, they parked in long-term parking. At such a small airport, long-term parking consisted of a four-level parking garage next to the terminal. The TV vans followed them into the parking ramp and parked close to Dean's Honda. Their crews leapt out to converge on the car. The TV crew started to ask Jim questions even before he got out of the car:

"What's your reaction to the Judge's decision?"

"Did you feel like you got away with something?"

"Were you having an affair with Sable Wainwright?"

"Did you kill her before throwing her overboard?"

As they had discussed, Dean grabbed all the luggage and started walking towards the terminal. The TV crews stayed with Jim who still had not said anything at all to them. Suddenly, Jim said, "Follow me" and he started walking through the garage and away from the terminal. There were now two TV crews following and peppering him with questions including Melissa Sanchez and her cameraman Tom from Channel 4 and Tom McDowell and his cameraman from Channel 9. They all trailed behind Jim as he walked briskly across the garage and kept pestering him with questions, although he said nothing more.

Jim walked quickly and deliberately over to the railing. Melissa Sanchez asked him "Mr. Wells, you're not thinking about jumping are you?" It wasn't very high so it would probably just hurt badly. Jim laughed a little and said "Not today and it isn't very high either." Jim looked over the Wisconsin countryside from the edge of a parking garage on the edge of the only town he had known for over a decade. After a few minutes, saying nothing to the camera crews, he turned back suddenly and hustled back to the terminal. He walked across the parking garage with his entourage in tow, walked in the front door and straight through the security checkpoint, thereby shedding the camera crews. He met Dean on the other side. Dean had checked them both in, checked the luggage and gotten the boarding passes (with the help of Jim's lawyer calling the airport manager). And very soon, with one stop in Detroit, they were sitting in first class and winging their way across the ocean on their way to Switzerland and Jim was still staring out the window at the darkening ocean below thinking, "Well, perhaps one can run away from even the biggest problems..."

Chapter 10: Lost in Translation

In the summer, a mountain forest is a mass of fallen trees, rocks and dozens of species of underbrush. Flowers and weeds and saplings compete for the light falling through the trees while the deer and squirrels and bears pass through looking for food. But, this world is hidden in the wintertime under a thick and almost impenetrable blanket of snow and ice. Only the pine trees bridge these two worlds and give an indication to the winter world that life continues below. The snowshoe hare is a highly adaptable creature – so much so that it can change the color of its pelt in the winter to match the snow and then in the summer to match the grasses below.The hare lives in both worlds and seeks to simply blend in for it's own protection.

Jim and Dean landed in Geneva and then took one of those incredible European first-class trains to Zermatt. Dean had not really known where to go skiing, especially at the last minute, but had gone to the Barnes and Noble bookstore close to the Madison hospital and looked quickly at a few guide books. He picked Zermatt because it was small and a little remote and because he read it was the very best. The skiing would be good early in the season, and one guidebook had stated that "Zermatt will make you forget that the rest of the world even exists." Zermatt was a very international town considering there are only 5500 permanent residents and it was crammed into one skinny valley. It sat at the border of Switzerland and Italy with much of the ski area crossing between countries. The sun rose long before the rays reached down into the valley and set long after the town fell into shadows. There were more than 8800 skiable acres (plus what is out of bounds) 62 lifts on the Swiss side, plus 30 lifts on the Italian side. This acreage all sat on a slope with 7520 feet of vertical drop. The town of Zermatt was down at 5300 feet surrounded by the densest cluster of 13,000 foot peaks in the Alps. Above the entire landscape, towering down over the entire area was the Matterhorn itself at 14,692 feet. Down below in the town, the residents knew that tourism was the economic lifeblood of the community. Therefore, they continued to work hard to maintain the old world charm the tourists stepped off the train expecting.

Jim and Dean checked into the legendary Grand Hotel Zermatterhof which towered over the square in the heart of the downtown district. Not large by international hotel standards, the Zermatterhof was the "place to stay". When politicians, singers and the uber-rich came to town, they stayed here. The hotel was also close to several of the ski lifts; although, not many places were far away in town. It was an idyllic town that had just enough imperfection so that you knew it wasn't designed by Walt Disney. The town was small enough that most people walked around and they didn't allow cars anywhere in Zermatt, except for some horse-drawn carriages and electric taxis.

By the time they were checking into the hotel, the guys were really starting to relax and were even joking around with the hotel staff behind the counter. Jim was relaxing from his ordeal simply due to the fact that it wasn't facing him at every turn. Dean was actually and unexpectedly overjoyed at the prospect of being away from the hospital and wedding planning with Ellen and everything else that was hanging around his neck. Dean also felt like he was finally able to give back a little to his friend Jim, who had given him so much. Dean had started to feel like a bit of a leech around him. They checked into a suite with a room for each of them and a big common room with a bar, fireplace and large, new flat-panel TV. The big excitement was brought on by the hot tub on the patio. They were both dead tired from traveling but didn't want to wait and started to rush out to find rental equipment and hit the slopes for the afternoon.

Jim actually paused before he went outside the hotel the very first time. At the rotating door on his way to rent skiing equipment, he hesitated. Dean had been walking in front and was already through the revolving door. But Jim stopped. He stopped long enough for Dean to look back at him and saw Jim looking both ways on the street from inside the lobby. Suddenly, Jim realized that he wasn't in Wisconsin any more and that he would be completely anonymous here. With a strong shove, he pushed through the revolving door from the gilded, carpeted safety of the hotel lobby into the cold, clear winter air. He looked to the left and the right at a bellhop who looked back to see if he needed something. Jim smiled. "I like not being known," he said to Dean as they started walking down the street, "It's nice to go back to being a nobody."

They started the afternoon by going to the Matterhorn Sports store just around the corner from the hotel. Hans, a young ski bum in his twenties who spoke English, German and Italian, was incredibly helpful and Jim and Dean ended up buying brand new Voelkl skis, boots and bindings along with appropriately matching ski clothes. Jim was feeling so great that no one knew him that he got all excited about spending money and splurging on the best equipment that they could buy in that store.. Plus, here in Zermatt, no one blinked an eye at an outlay of cash for all new equipment. A little different than Wisconsin. After buying equipment and getting some very strong Italian coffees, Jim and Dean got in line and rode in the gondola up and up, out of the valley and onto the peaks that cradled the valley below.The view from the top of the mountain was so magnificent and expansive and sunny that Jim and Dean simply stood at the edge of the hill looking out across the mountaintops for what seemed like an eternity, in silence.

They soaked in the view and then closed their eyes to face the sun and soak in a little of its energy.

Jim finally said, "Dean, thank you so much for taking me away from everything and taking me here. My God, this is just incredible. I feel like a real honest-to-goodness human being again."

Dean turned and looked at him, "Well, no problem Jim. That's what friends are for. Besides, you're paying for everything."

"Oh, that isn't the point anymore, is it?" replied Jim.

"No," said Dean as he stared back out at the mountains, "It certainly hasn't seemed all that important lately, has it? You miss her, don't you?"

Jim stared out at the mountains silently while the wind ruffled across their newly acquired ski clothing. Finally, he said, "Yeah, I miss her. I also just miss having someone to talk to though. It got really lonely holed up in the hotel the last weeks. She was always much more of a friend than a lover, until the last night, of course. Hopefully, someday I can find that again."

Dean didn't want him getting too morose, so he said, "Well, all the ski bunnies are a couple miles straight down from here. Last one there goes home single." And he launched off the side of the mountain down the hill and immediately "yard saled". His poles, skis, hat and gloves went in different directions away from his body as he fell. The end effect did look something like a yard sale as his stuff was scattered all around the hill.

Jim started laughing and skied down to Dean, a little more in control. 'Yeah, well... it is a damn good thing that you're already engaged because you're not going to get to the ski bunnies at this rate!" With that, Dean threw some snow at Jim and eventually made it back on to his feet. Dean said, "Yeah, so I forgot to mention that I'm not much more than a beginner skier." Jim said, "Well, no one from Wisconsin is much more than a beginner on this hill. Let's take a lesson tomorrow."

Within just two days, Jim and Dean were making serious progress toward being better skiers. Of course, they couldn't have gotten much worse. They had taken a few private lessons which had worked out well on several fronts. Their first ski instructor, Henri, was the quintessential ski instructor who worked when he needed to and skied the rest of the time with a permanent seat at the bar once the sun went down. Dean envied his freedom and Jim was completely entertained by him. Henri led them up the Klein Matterhorn tram and then up and up the lifts to the top of the Klein Matterhorn. The town was just a small spot far below.

As they started to ski down a very shallow and wide ski run, Henri was yelling at them, "No, no," said Henri, "You're both skiing like silly Catholic nuns! You need to make love to the mountain. You need to move like you are caressing the hill. You need to massage the curves and explode over the jumps! Explode! Caress! Now dig in! You, Sir, are no lover, are you!?"

Jim and Dean could barely ski because they were laughing so hard. But, they got better in spite of themselves. Henri knew what he was doing. They eventually could make it down at a relatively normal rate of speed. At the end of the lesson, once the mountain and town were hidden in shadow, at Jim's insistence, Henri came to dinner with them. He took them to a favorite authentic Swiss restaurant of his that was on a back street away from most of the tourists. They had Swiss Raclette, which was something neither Jim nor Dean had tasted before. Raclette is both the name of a cheese and a slow process in which you put the cheese on your food and then heat the whole thing under a small flame at the table. This process heats the food while melting the cheese on top. This is a slow way to eat dinner but allows plenty of time to drink. Combined with the jet lag and the altitude, Jim and Dean were quite drunk and a little sleepy by the time their Raclette dinner (and the other couple of courses included on the fixed price menu) was finished. Jim and Dean had such a great time that they begged Henri to be their instructor the next day - for the whole day this time.

Jim said, " Henri, I'll douple yer free - I mean fee - for tomorrow."

Henri said, "Oh, you're quite the drunken sailor, aren't you?! Noo, I cannot. I already promised the company I take out these fat Americans tomorrow and if I don't the company gets mad and stops to give me reservations. So, I cannot. However, for you, drunken sailor, I will send over Gabrielle tomorrow."

"Humm, a female instructor?" said Jim.

"Yeah sure, my friend." replied Henri as he stood to walk out.

"Well, OK then, but she better be as funny as you are." Jim called after him.

So, the morning of the second day (Jim and Dean were actually up pretty early due to the time change), the phone rang in the morning and the front desk said that a woman had called to say she would be over in an hour to take them skiing. Jim and Dean came downstairs an hour later looking like beginners in their brand new ski clothes and equipment and came out of the elevator only to be confronted by a woman who looked like she had just finished shooting a Warren Miller ski movie. She looked like a supermodel who just happened to sleep in her ski clothes the night before. Even through several layers of Thinsulate and under a helmet, Jim and Dean could both see that she had the well-built body resulting from genetics, constant exercise and good mountain living. She had piercing blue eyes, stood about 5' 9" tall and obviously would never be mistaken for a man on the hill, either from in front or behind. She spoke with a strong French accent which caused the boys to drool even more. "Good morning. I'm Gabrielle. I assume you are Jim and Dean? Henri was a little drunk last night when he called me but he seemed pretty clear that you would want another lesson today. Is that true?" At this point, Jim would have taken a ski lesson in a blizzard with a broken leg and pneumonia if it meant hanging out with this vision.

124

Dean was suddenly in his own inner turmoil as the engaged man. As a result, his course of action was to simply stare at his ski boots as if enraptured by the fact that plastic could form so well to his feet.

Jim finally spoke for both of them. "Yes, YES! I mean...Yes, we would like a lesson. Henri was very good yesterday and if he recommends you then that is fine with us. We definitely could use more...training." Jim was suddenly thinking that if this woman told them to caress the hill, he might just explode.

Gabrielle's skills kept up with her looks all day. Jim and Dean were huffing and puffing from the effort while Gabrielle was skiing circles around them. She drilled them over and over to boredom about weight placement through their turns and incessantly worked on their ability to stop. In the afternoon, she even started teaching them to ski moguls, which caused severe bruising on both Jim and Dean until they gave up. Jim was in pretty good shape from sailing all summer and fall although he had been basically sitting in a hotel room for the last weeks. Dean, however, suffered the ironically poor health of many health care providers. They survived and actually got even better than they had with Henri the day before. Gabrielle was an incredible motivation.

Over lunch, they found out that this beautiful woman with bronze hair (they had almost dropped their lunch trays when she took off her helmet at lunch and unleashed her long hair and exposed the perfect cheekbones underneath) was actually taking a break from University for a year or so while she figured out what she wanted to do with her life in the future. Jim told her that he had inherited a little money recently to pay for this trip and Dean told her he was a doctor. She didn't seem to care too much nor was she impressed. It was probably a completely typical story for her here in Zermatt. Doctors, lawyers, people who "came into money" somewhere and all other manner of rich guys trying to impress them for a few days before they left. She was a little more impressed when Jim said that he was a sailor. She had spent a few summers at the coast in the south of France and learned to sail down there. Jim was suddenly struck with a vision of her on the front of one of those huge Mediterranean yachts.

At the end of the day, neither Dean nor Jim really wanted to part company with their new best friend Gabrielle. So, like all the rich men before him, Jim asked her to have dinner with them. " It would be great to talk to you more about your life of sailing and skiing" he coaxed.

"Oh, uhh, no, but thank you," she said. "I have some other plans."

However, just as they were walking toward the hotel so that Jim could pay her, a huge man with a body made in an Italian sculptors eye came up to them. "Gabrielle," he started and then launched into French so fast that, even if they spoke a little broken French, they would never have been able to keep up. However, facial expressions require no translation and Jim could tell that Gabrielle didn't like what this guy was saying. She muttered some stuff back at him that was pretty negative in tone. She crossed her arms in front. Obviously, this big oaf was upsetting the beautiful Gabrielle. Jim and Dean looked at each other as if wondering what brand of moron would upset this woman. Finally, the mystery man just shrugged his shoulders and walked away.

By this point, Jim and Dean had backed off a few yards and resumed the process of staring at their boots and looking around without really looking at anything other than Gabrielle and the other speaker. After the mystery man walked away, Jim slid closer to her and asked, "What was that all about?"

She stared after him while stating in a clipped voice, "Well, nothing...That was my boyfriend and he has to "work" with some buddies of his tonight so he cannot take to me dinner."

Jim latched onto that like a dog on a bone. "Well, our dinner offer is still available. We'll go wherever you want."

She turned and Jim realized she was steaming mad at her boyfriend. "Yes, yes, I have dinner with you tonight.

126

How do you feel about Italian food? There is a great gnocchi at El Maggiore just a few blocks from here."

Jim looked at Dean who nodded agreement. Jim made a mental note to check if Dean had actually lost his tongue or simply ran out of things to say in front of Gabrielle.

El Maggiore was a classic darkly lit Italian restaurant a few blocks from the main square on which the hotel sat where Jim and Dean were staying. They felt a little uncomfortable greeting the well-dressed host in their ski clothes but then they realized that a lot of people were similarly dressed. It was a very expensive restaurant due to its reputation. Jim noticed most all of the clientele were still wearing ski clothes which made for an interesting contrast to the white table clothes and fine china.

They started with a mug of 'vin chao" or hot mulled red wine. Jim and Dean explained that people would always have a beer after skiing in the States but that they agreed with Gabrielle that a glass of hot wine definitely put the heat back in the cheeks. The fixed price menu actually had 5 courses during which they were able to drink 4 bottles of wine between them. Gabrielle's English actually got faster and better when she was drinking and the whole story of her ski-town boyfriend came pouring out with Jim there to be the incredibly mature and understanding recipient. It turned out that Gabrielle had met this guy when she had first left University and was traveling around. They decided together to move to Zermatt but once they got here they drifted apart toward being more acquaintances than lovers. Gabrielle claimed that her boyfriend had changed once they arrived in Zermatt. She said, "You know, it's almost like he fell out of love with me as he fell in love with the mountain. Seems that he can't have both me and the mountain as lovers." She went on to say that she had talked with other women who claimed to have had the same thing happen to them.

By the time they left the restaurant, the three white candles on the table had burned to the bottom of their wicks and most of the other tables had already turned over so that a whole new group of people were seated around them. In fact, these were the people who had gone home after skiing to change and perhaps sit in the hot tub to warm up before flocking back to the restaurants. They looked far more respectable than Jim, Dean and Gabrielle. Gabrielle almost fell over three times on the way to the door. Dean would later try to recall how it happened that Gabrielle ended up back in their suite. But, there she was and the three of them raided the mini-bar looking for something to mix and drink before they sobered up even a little. Pretty soon they were sitting in front of the little fireplace. Gabrielle kept bitching about her boyfriend but, through a pretty drunken haze, Dean realized that for all the talk about her boyfriend she was now practically lying across Jim. Jim almost seemed to be ignoring her, either on purpose or through sheer drunkenness. He stared into the fire – transfixed by the flames.

The amazing thing about being drunk is the illusion of teleportation. H.G. Wells must have done a lot of drinking before writing the "Time Machine" because the feeling is very similar to how Wells made it seem in his book. Dean woke up and realized that light was coming in the window. For a moment, he felt like he had been teleported through time AND space because he had no idea where he was. Finally, he realized that he was laying on a couch in the living room of the suite in Switzerland and that it was morning, after a very short night. He was lying on his belly with his body half under the couch cushion and half above it. He realized that alcohol, elevation and jet lag had all combined into a cerebral "perfect storm" resulting in an incredible pain somewhere between his eyes, his hair and his neck. The more he woke up, the more the pain focused into a distinct place in his neck, the back of his head and his sinuses above his eyes.. He wandered into his bedroom and his bathroom and started searching for some kind of painkiller. "Being a doctor has some advantages", he thought as he threw back a few sample prescription pain killers he'd thrown in his bag in case he or Jim had been injured skiing. He then wandered back out to the living room looking for a soda. It was at that point that he realized

128

that Gabrielle's ski boots were still scattered along the floor of the room along with his and Jim's. Dean's head hurt too much to give it much thought but he just shook his head - worried just a little, in passing, about Jim and a strange foreign woman. Slamming down a sparkling water from the minibar, he put out the "Do Not Disturb" sign to the suite, went back in his bedroom and shut the door. He slowly lay down on the bed and turned on CNN but immediately went back to sleep once the pain killers removed the throbbing from his brain.

Sometime later, Dean got a knock on his bedroom door which woke him up again. "Dean, you in there? Gabrielle took off and I was wondering if you want to get some food with me. I think it's probably lunchtime about now," Jim's very quiet and slow voice came through the door.
"Yeah, yeah, don't talk so loud and I'll come out," said Dean.
When Dean got out in the living room, Jim was cleaning up the spilled bottles and ski boots and everything else. "Did you put out the Do Not Disturb sign?" he asked Dean who nodded. Jim continued, "Good call. A vacuum this morning would make my brain leak out my ears, the way I feel. What happened last night? I thought we were just going to get some dinner."
"I don't know! Why are you asking me? You're the one with a girl in his room last night! Why don't you tell me what happened while I watch you clean from this couch" Dean said as he sat down on the couch?
Jim stopped cleaning and turned to Dean. "Hey, we didn't actually have sex if that's what you mean. Sure, we ended up making out a little bit and then I –or maybe it was she – put a stop to that. God, do you think that after everything I have been through that I would really just jump in the sack with some ski instructor? Sable meant a lot to me." By now, Jim was standing and looking out the window onto the city square below. As Dean looked at Jim and listened to his words, it struck him that, sometimes, when

129

you are thrust into a new world completely unlike your normal world, it is easy to forget where you are and who you are. Amazingly, Dean had completely forgotten the situation that Jim had just gone through. Jim looked back at Dean seemingly a little surprised by his own reaction.

"Well, Dean said, "Good to see that you haven't lost all sense of control. I just made an assumption and you were both pretty drunk and...well...perhaps you need a bit of comforting from a beautiful woman at the moment."

Still holding two empty beer cans in his hands, Jim looked over at him, " So, you think I should have slept with her? "

"Humm, no. Not yet, I guess."

"Well, when do you think I'll be ready to do the horizontal mambo again then, my esteemed doctor friend?"

Dean looked at the ceiling for a minute and said, "Well, not sure but it's at least some time after breakfast." And with that, the two hobbled and hung-over Americans organized to get outside and perhaps even find a breakfast that they could stomach. Luckily, at the little café around the corner (so they didn't have to walk too far) they found some muesli and yogurt and fruit which went down pretty easily with an Orangina and a cup of coffee. They collapsed into a couple of chairs, ate their breakfast, squinted into the sun and waited for the recovery to begin.

Dean sat partly slumped in his chair, trying to finish his food and finally said, "Hey, about this Gabrielle this morning, you know I wasn't trying to imply anything about the way you felt about Sable or anything, right?"

Jim shifted in his own chair and said, "Yeah, I know. Don't worry about it. I'm just really sensitive to it. I'm more sensitive than I realized, I guess. The whole thing with Sable is just so bizarre. I mean, not really a Tom Hanks-Meg Ryan type of romance. Just so crazy..." And he sat up in his chair as if he really had something important to say to Dean. "You know what though, I did learn a lot. I really did. I learned a lot about what I could really feel for someone and that I still could feel after all these years and after winning the money and everything."

130

Just as they were sitting there waiting for their bodies to stop complaining, their old ski instructor friend Henri came by the café and their little table. "Hey, my favorite ugly Americans!" he called out coming closer. He took one look at them and said, "Seems that you are both not skiing today because of the bottle flu, ehh? How did things work out with Gabrielle? Was she a good instructor or...?"

Jim and Dean looked at each other and grinned. Finally, Dean said fairly straight-faced, "Actually, she was really excellent and put us through a lot of drills and if we weren't so hung-over, we'd be much better skiers today."

Henri said, "That's excellent. That's really great. I am really happy for you. By the way, if you're feeling up to it, they're having a mogul competition today. In fact, I think Gabrielle is working at it."

"Oh, that explains it," said Jim.

"Explains what?" said Henri .Exhibiting some quick thinking in spite of his cerebral deficit this morning, Jim said, " Well, like you, we convinced her to come to dinner with us but she had to go home early because of something she had to do this morning so that must be it."

Henri started to leave and then turned back to say, "So, you guys need a lesson tomorrow?"

To which Jim and Dean replied together, "No!" They could not even think about skiing at the moment.

A few hours later, after some more painkillers and some bad European TV, Jim and Dean wander up to the last part of the mogul competition. Gabrielle was indeed working at it because they could see her on the monitor which was showing the start box. She was helping the competitors get in the box and ready to go. They found out that she probably had been up there most of the day and they just wondered how she was able to do that considering the night they had all had. Dean reminded Jim that she was used to the altitude and was probably used to drinking hard. "I don't know" said Jim "she seemed pretty hammered last night." Even if they had been up for it, they couldn't get up to where she was even to say hi so they started looking around for somewhere to sit.

They ended up having to buy tickets for the reserved bleacher area in order to get a decent view with all the tall mountain people blocking the view of the course. Most of the spectators had made a special trip to see this and had not just happened on it by accident. They ended up sitting between a couple with the type of ski clothes that look incredibly expensive but never had been used on an actual mountain for more than one run. The moguls on the run were tightly packed and the competitors were incredibly skilled. Jim and Dean actually started to enjoy their day (although it was now late afternoon).

They didn't see the Neibaums. John and Judy Neibaum had a nephew in the competition, Jimmy Neibaum, from Michigan. John and Judy had flown over to vacation in Switzerland and combined that vacation with the opportunity to see Jimmy compete in Zermatt. John and Judy were wearing matching ski suits which they had bought at the Marshall Fields store on the west side of Madison, Wisconsin. They lived in Middleton, which is one of the tonier suburbs on the west side of Madison. They had yet to ski in their new ski suits and John was secretly hoping to return them to the store after this trip as he realized they had no cause to ski in Wisconsin. They were sitting a few rows behind Jim and Dean and were intently watching to see Jimmy come down the hill. However, they were not really ski-competition fans and John's eyes started to wander around the crowd when the other skiers were racing down the hill. Just at that moment, Jim had to stand up to let some fur coat festooned older Swiss woman pass through the row and John saw just enough of his ragged, hung-over face to recognize him from all the news coverage the previous month back in Madison. John stared at Jim for a minute as if he had just seen Bruce Willis or Bruce Springsteen. Finally, he elbowed Judy in the ribs. Judy shot him a look of surprise because she had been busy worrying if their "Wisconsin clothes" were fitting in appropriately in Zermatt or not. She too was secretly considering bringing back her ski clothes if they didn't get them very dirty here in Switzerland.

"Oh, what is it?" she fired back at him.

"Look, look over there, " he whispered. "I swear that's Jim Wells from Madison. The guy who killed Sable Wainwright on the sailboat. Remember?"

Immediately, Judy shot to her feet salivating at the thought of getting the first look at a brewing story. Her head was bobbing around like a prairie dog looking through the crowd and trying to see Jim. In the few days since Jim and Dean had flown to Zermatt, the story had gotten bigger instead of smaller with the national news having covered it and the Wisconsin papers were reporting a movie-of-the-week being developed as well. "Where? Where?" she said.

"Down over there about four rows up from the front and right there at one o'clock", he said. They had both now completely lost interest in the ski competition. She watched until Jim turned to say something to Dean and she just about squealed. She whispered at the top of her voice, "Yes, that is him. That is definitely him. Wait until I tell the ladies back home." Instinctively, she reached for her cell phone at her waist before realizing that her Sprint phone had not been working in Europe anyway.

John said, "Well, this is where he disappeared to then. Everyone said he was in South America or Africa or something." In reality, the Neibaums were just repeating rumors because it hadn't been reported where they had flown to.

The Neibaum's were in Europe for the rest of the week. However, thanks to the wonders of the Zermatt Internet Café and Judy's addiction to checking her email, within hours of seeing Jim and Dean at the mogul competition, Sable's grieving, bitter, wealthy and fundamentally amoral husband knew that Jim was in Zermatt.

After the ski competition, Jim and Dean tried to meet up with Gabrielle again to no avail. She had seemingly

133

resolved things with her boyfriend magically while she was stuck up in the starter's box all day. They waited around at the bottom of the hill until she descended from the top. She did say hello, as she went by, but she excused herself quickly, mumbling something about needing sleep and a hot shower because she was freezing. So, Jim and Dean finally went to the bar by themselves which soon turned into a conversation with the entire Voikl men's mogul team. A few of the guys were Americans from Telluride and Aspen but were spending the competitive season in Europe skiing for the sponsor. Jim and Dean both lusted after their carefree life involving skiing all day, eating and drinking all evening and exercising with the women's team until dawn. They didn't have a care in the world and the team manager made sure that no big issues bothered them at all. They basically had to show up and be incredibly talented skiers.

These guys took Jim and Dean to yet another excellent restaurant filled with solid, heavy German food with spaetzle and wurst and kraut and all things good for you, especially if you're a professional skier burning thousands of calories every day. Jim and Dean had an incredible evening even without much alcohol and felt very welcomed by their countrymen and vice-versa, especially as Dean was about to move to Denver. They told him about all the skiing in Colorado and argued at length over the merits of Telluride and Aspen.

A few days later, their week was up. Jim and Dean spent the last day shopping through the small but expensive shops in the back streets of Zermatt. Each of them bought (actually Jim bought...but who was counting) a very nice Tag Heuer watch, a few sweaters, and a literal cart-load of presents for Ellen. Jim had really appreciated Ellen giving up Dean for an entire week while they gallivanted around the Swiss mountains. They packed up their bags and took the train back to Geneva. They headed directly to the airport. They checked in for their flight and after a short wait at the airport bar, they stood in line together talking about Ellen and Colorado and laughing about the skiing guys they had met. They got to the front of the line to board the plane –

first class, of course. At the front of the line, a tall, blond, very attractive Swiss woman in a crisp looking Swissair uniform stood between them and the gangway to take their tickets. As each person walked up, she smiles, holds out her hand for their ticket and asks them, "Are you sure you want to go home?". Dean walked up, she asked him the question and he replied "Unfortunately, my fiancé is back there and not here or I'd definitely stay." She smiled in return and processed his ticket through the machine saying, "Well, I hope you both come back soon." She never expected anyone to say anything else but that they would love to stay except for …

Jim came next. Suddenly, Jim started to get a knot in his stomach, a pain in his temple and he started to feel very warm. When the kind woman from Swissair asked him, "Are you sure you want to go home?" he didn't say anything. He stood motionless looking at her outstretched hand.

She said, "Sir, are you ok?" and Jim said nothing. Dean had paused in the gangway and turned back towards Jim.

Jim looked at Dean and just started shaking his head. "I don't want to leave!" he said, more to Dean than to the woman in front of him. She suddenly realized that something abnormal was happening. Dean came up and said to her, "Don't worry. I'm his doctor. Why don't you board some other passengers and we will be right over here?"

Looking out at the remaining 1st class passengers not to mention the 400 normal people waiting to board the flight, the woman turned to them and said, "Well, it's unusual to let you back out but I guess it's OK. Just don't leave my sight."

Jim and Dean stepped around the corner out of ear shot and Dean said, "What is going on?"

Jim replied, "I really don't want to go back. The press will still be hounding me. Cliff will still hate me. My friends, other than you, have deserted me either for drowning Sable or not telling them about the lottery in the first place. You're my best friend and you're leaving. It's not like I'm going to get my pay docked if I don't go back."

Dean just looked at him for a minute realizing that everything Jim was saying was correct but at the same time not sure if hiding in Europe was a good long-term strategy for Jim. "Who are you going to hang out with? How long are you going to stay?"

"I can hang out with the Colorado guys until they leave and maybe I can get Gabrielle to give me more lessons. Maybe I'll visit some other parts of Europe. Some other ski areas, perhaps. I don't want to stay forever. Just until things settle down and maybe I can work through what to do next and where I want to live."

Suddenly, Jim stopped talking, looked Dean in the eye, squared his shoulders and said in a firm voice, "Look, I appreciate everything that you have done for me but I need to do some of this myself. You can't sit here with me until I get completely well. Go, go back to your wife, and go back to your life. I will be fine here in the mountains."

Dean leaned over and gave Jim a hug and whispered in his ear, "It isn't your fault, you know that, right? It was an accident – a horrible accident."

When he backed up, Jim was starting to tear up and he just said, "I know. Thanks. Now, get on your plane and get the hell out of here. Oh, and don't forget to make them give you my drinks too 'cuz I paid for that seat."

With that, Dean disappeared back down the jet way, Jim told the attractive Swissair woman that thanks to her, he had decided to stay and asked her if he could buy her a drink when she finished her shift.

She smiled and replied, "Actually, sir, I live in New York and am getting on the plane with your friend."

To which Jim replied, "Humm, damn unfortunate. Well, if I give you $50, will you give him some extra drinks or something?"

She seemed a little surprised, "But, he's in first class so the drinks are all free."

"Oh, right you are," said Jim and he started to head back away from the gate and the crowd and picked up his luggage again and went down two levels to the train station, took the next train back to Zermatt, and walked back down to the Grand Hotel Zermatterhof. They were more than happy to give him back the same suite again. The first thing that Jim did was go and lie down in the hot tub on the deck for a good long soak.

Chapter 11: Rewind and Fast Forward

Every year, robins and other city birds build nests under the eves of homes and office buildings all across the world. Every year, they build these nests. Most humane people are kind enough to leave the nests alone until the eggs are hatched and the chicks are gone. Then, the robins leave and the nest deteriorates through the winter and often completely collapses and falls from the perch. The next year, they are back to build the nest again. If they could build a permanent nest, would they? Or, does the building of the nest serve some greater biological purpose for the nesting, expectant parents?

The elevators at the hospital were ungodly slow in the consensus of everyone who worked there. Something about their size and the safety requirements made them unnecessarily slow. On the other hand, it could be due to the fact that all the people that Dean rode the elevators with in the hospital were always doped up on coffee, not enough sleep, were overworked and that any kind of real or perceived delay irritated them. Dean realized that he had started to get used to the altitude in Denver as he was able to make it up the stairwell in the hospital without almost passing out. He thought that a week in the Swiss mountains would help with moving to Denver but whatever he had gained by being at altitude was negated by eating and drinking with Jim for the week. He had put on five pounds before he got back, not counting the junk food that he had started eating in the intervening three months. Ellen was starting to get after him to eat more healthily but so far he just had been overwhelmed with being a resident and the "about-to-be-a-husband" role and so on and so forth. Dean's days started at 5 AM with a quick commute to the hospital for morning rounds and that was followed by non-stop action until the end of the day around 6 PM, after which he wrote all the charts for everyone whom he had worked up that day. When he did get a free day, it was generally when Ellen had to work so he didn't get much time to explore their new town with her at all.

After dealing with a toddler who had somehow managed to cut his thumb half off with safety scissors, Dean got a call from Ellen who was at home that day. "Dean, I just got a call from Jim. He's flying in tonight and wondered if he could stay with us and take us out to dinner. He says that unfortunately he will probably leave tomorrow. I said that'd be fine but that I needed to check your schedule. What do you think?"

Dean slumped against the wall and looked down at the little boy's drying blood on his scrubs and pondered this news for a second. It had been just about three months since he left Zermatt and he had not really heard anything of Jim in the meantime. When he remembered to do it (which wasn't often, unfortunately), Dean looked up the Wisconsin papers online and checked on Google to see if anything more was coming out about Jim. However, the early blizzard in Madison had overtaken all other news. Of course, the local gossip might be completely different. And, there was still talk that Jim and Sable's neighbors were still upset with all the people driving by. Jim's lawyer had hired a security firm to watch Jim's house for him as everyone knew he was gone.

Dean replied, "Did he say why he's coming?"

Ellen replied, "I asked him what brings him out here and if he could stay longer. He said he didn't want to say on the phone why he was coming – he'd rather tell us in person."

Dean was very curious to hear what Jim couldn't say on the phone and had to fly out here to tell them. Probably

139

he was buying a place in Aspen after all like they had discussed. Realizing that Ellen was still on the other end, he said, "Well, I guess that's his perogative which is good for us. Yeah, today seems like the normal level of carnage so far. I can be home about 6:30, if that works. Did he leave you a number? Should I try to call him?"

She said, "Yeah, I got a number out of him and he said to call collect so I'll just buzz him back to confirm. Where should I make a reservation?"

Dean replied, "Well, hum, we haven't been here that long have we…How about that place in Lodo called Josephina's? That's supposed to be good and plenty of variety for whatever he wants."

Ellen finished up by saying, "Okay, dokey, cutey. I will handle all the communiqués and reservations, doctor." Dean smiled and realized again why he loved this woman.

Dean got home at around 7 PM. He and Ellen had followed the advice of all doctors before him and gotten an apartment close to the hospital to reduce commuting fairly dramatically. They had actually rented half a duplex which must have been a real rage at some point in Denver history because they were everywhere. They got a small two bedroom, one bath but it was laid out well and Dean promised Ellen a house in the mountains when it was all done – if they even stayed in Denver. He walked back from the hospital most evenings to try and get at least a little exercise. He was in the shower when the doorbell rang. He heard Ellen greeting Jim out in the tiny living room. Like a good Wisconsin wife, the first thing she did was ask him if he wanted a beer which he wholeheartedly agreed to. They'd found a huge liquor warehouse called AppleJacks on the west side of Denver that carried several Wisconsin beers so they had just recently stocked up.

Dean came out looking more like a person and less like a doctor and was immediately captured in a big hug by Jim. Stepping back, Dean sized up Jim again. The last time he had seen him, his nose was a little sunburnt from skiing but otherwise the month after Sable's death had left him completely wrecked. He had put on some weight and looked

140

awful. But, the last three months had really improved Jim in both disposition and appearance. He looked tan from head to foot and looked like he had just walked off a beach. His hair was on its way to being bleached out and his belly had completely disappeared.

Dean was so surprised he blurted out, "Hey, you really look different. What happened to you?"

Jim replied, "What didn't happen to me?! What happened to you? You look like you haven't been outside since Zermatt!"

With that, Ellen walked back into the room from the kitchen balancing three beers and a platter with chips, salsa and hummus on it. She chimed in, "Yeah, he's going through the ringer over there. I just go to work occasionally compared to this guy. Of course, I still get in my 40 hours a week."

They sat down on the mismatched furniture that Ellen and Dean had collected. Some of it actually had been a hand-me-down from Jim. Jim took the individual comfy chair which had been his favorite about a year before – before the winning ticket. Dean and Ellen sat kitty-corner from him on the couch which Ellen had rejuvenated with a khaki slipcover.

After a few minutes of chit-chat about the new apartment and its location, Dean finally said, "So, again, what happened to you?" stating it very bluntly. Jim sat back in his comfy chair and ran his hand down the arm of the comfy chair and then, as if deciding to share his deepest secrets, leaned forward and started the following soliloquy:

"Well, I guess I'll start at the beginning. After you flew home Dean, I took the train back to Zermatt and checked back into the hotel and the same suite even. I spent a day just sleeping, hot tubbing, and thinking about Sable. Then, I started skiing. I skied alone or with a guide all over the mountain for six days. Remember Henri? I hired him for fun one day. I kept trying to reach Gabrielle to have her go out with me for another day. But, she seemed to have disappeared along with you. I hung out a few more times in the evening with the Colorado mogul guys before they moved on to the next stop on their tour. I was very pleased just with the skiing though as I really started to get much better. And you know what? Skiing is a lot more fun when you're good at it!"

Jim stopped to take a drink of his beer and then leaned forward and lowered his voice a little as if he was telling a great secret story. "So, anyway, about a week or so after you left, I was hanging out in that same skier/local bar, Elsie's, that we had been going to when you were there. I was sitting there with Henri and a few of the local mogul women"

Dean wondered at this point if the story would be different if Ellen wasn't here but Jim suddenly got more excited.

Jim leaned forward and gestured with his hands, "OK, Ok, so picture this. Me, Henri,, a few female mogul skiers and mostly other locals hanging out at this big bar.

Suddenly, guess who comes through the door? Cliff Wainwright! Cliff walked in the door with three of his fellow hockey players behind him. I found out later that someone from Madison had recognized me in Zermatt and told him that I was there. He and his goons had very quickly organized a trip and had been looking around Zermatt to try and find me for a few days before they stumbled into this bar. So, they walked in and, of course, I was paying attention to the people at my table ["I'll bet", thought Dean] and suddenly, these huge hands fell on my shoulders, slammed my head into the table, and then pulled me to my feet. Cliff spun me around and laid me out with a quick shot to the jaw. I flew across the table in front of Henri and managed to ask him for some help. Cliff pulled me back up off the table only to hit me again. I couldn't do anything. But, luckily for me, I had probably bought a drink for almost every ski bum in the bar, by this point in my visit, and Henri got together six guys who started circling to rescue me from these whackos who had come from nowhere. So, it was about six ski bums against four hockey players. The hockey guys held their ground against the skiers and Cliff just focused on beating the crap out of me. Along the way, I

142

recall him holding me up and yelling at the crowd, "This man stole my wife and then he killed her! He killed my wife!"

I could barely talk but croaked out "No, it was an accident, Cliff. An accident! And she was leaving you anyway, you heartless prick!" Jim suddenly stopped and looked at Ellen realizing he had said prick in front of her.

Ellen said, "Well, he is a prick! Keep going! What happened?"

Jim continued, "So, Cliff has probably gotten in about eight or ten good shots at this point compared to my one or two when suddenly, a shot rang out and we all stopped. The bartender is standing on the bar with a shotgun pointed at us. He is yelling in broken English, "You American bums leaving now, you are! Rous, Rous." That didn't bother Cliff as he just grabbed me by the arm and was about to carry me out of the bar to finish me off in the street.

Luckily, all the ski bums blocked the door in front of him. There was the great bum Henri in the front. "Yeah, Msr. Jim is our ami. You leave but he stays with us." The bartender nodded agreement. Again, it helps that I had bought about half of what the bartender had sold during the previous week. Cliff said, "Fine. This man killed my wife and ruined my life. We are not leaving town without finishing this."

And with that he dropped me on the floor and leaned down to whisper in my ear, "Jim, the cops wouldn't take you down back in Wisconsin because of all your money but I'll hunt you down no matter where you go. We'll be waiting outside if you want to just submit now." And with that, they walked out the door.

Suddenly, Gabrielle appeared out of the fog in front of my face. She and Henri helped me into a chair and started looking at my face. "You need a doctor! Did you really kill that man's wife?" I couldn't decide if killing someone's wife was appealing to her, disgusting or if she was just morbidly interested. I told her that I had definitely not killed his wife but that she'd fallen off my sailboat in the middle of the night when she was drunk. I told Gabrielle that Sable's

143

death had been a terrible accident, at least I tried to say that but my lip was rapidly expanding at the time and so I was probably pretty unintelligible by the end.

Anyway, Henri and Gabrielle got me out of the bar through a back door and had already ordered a horse-drawn carriage owned by their friend to come to the back door. Actually, it seemed like they had done something like this before which made me wonder a little but…anyway. They got me to the local hospital without running into the pack of wild Wisconsin killers again. They explained roughly what happened to the local doctors who put a few stitches in me and put me in a bed to wait and see if I had a concussion as well. The staff put me in a locked room to which only they had the key and I even used a fake name for the register.

Henri and Gabrielle came to the hospital in the morning. They said that they'd seen Cliff and his little gang hanging out around my hotel. So, I called the hotel and told them that I was worried about my safety there. The nice thing about staying in the suite of one of the most prestigious hotels in town was that they immediately sent two electric cars full of security guys over to the hospital to fetch me, take me back to the hotel and kept security guys on my floor and by the front door. If anyone even attempted to get in who looked like an American, they stopped them and asked what they were doing, etc. So, I hung out in the hotel room for a day or two to recover from the thrashing that they gave me. Pretty soon, I realized that I was basically trapped in the hotel suite, JUST like I'd been here in Madison only a few weeks before. Then, it got worse. Cliff got the local Swiss press to interview him and told the local papers all about how I'd killed his wife. "

Ellen interrupted Jim's story with, "Holy Crap! Didn't the paper want to get your side of the story or did they just print Cliff's side. Before you answer that, do you want another beer?"

Jim handed over his empty bottle and continued," Sure, another beer would be great. Well, once he told the

144

paper about it, they looked up all the articles from the Wisconsin papers and the national papers over here and ran that as the rest of the story. They called me to get my side but I hung up. By that time, I decided to just get the hell out of there. But, I didn't know where to go. I didn't want to come back to Madison; Cliff would surely follow me back here. I didn't want to just be a bum all over Europe waiting for Cliff to walk into a restaurant and mug me again. So, one night I was sitting in my room and I opened a copy of Forbes magazine that I had gotten in the lobby bookstore and there happened to be this ad" and with that Jim pulled out from his pocket, a slightly worn folded page, ripped from a magazine. He unfolded it and said, "Amazingly, this Beefeater gin ad has been guiding my actions for the last six weeks or so since I left Switzerland. It was a picture-perfect couple lying in a hammock with a couple of drinks propped up on their bellies. They were tan and relaxed and looking like they didn't have a care in the world. The hammock was hanging from a palm tree at the edge of a beach with a bottle of Beefeater sitting in the sand underneath the hammock. Pretty typical ad. But, it was the tag line that attracted one's eye. Somewhere, some ad copy person should be probably losing their jobs because the ad wasn't selling gin, it was selling location. The tagline read. "There are 15 private islands for sale in the Caribbean. Or, for the rest of us, there is Beefeater."

Dean looks at the ad and looks at Ellen who is still transfixed by the ad as if by looking hard enough, the hammock and people might start to sway in the breeze. Finally, his brain puts it together and he shouts at Jim, "Oh my God, did you buy an island somewhere? Did you?" His voice got louder as he got more and more excited.

With that question hanging in the air, Jim leaned back into the couch, simply smiled, held his arms out in the air beside him and said, "You, my friends, are looking at the new owner of Mago Island in the area of Fiji."

Ellen, who had barely sat down from getting another round of beers, kind of did this coughing, gasping thing as if trying to catch her breath and scream at the same time.

Jim continued, "It's a big island but still has no airport and few roads which means that Cliff and his boys can't reach me there without my knowing about it immediately. Frankly, I felt like I had to go somewhere that he could neither find me nor find anyone else who knew me. They say that when you own the island, you make the rules and my Number One rule is:

NO CRAZY GUYS TRYING TO KILL JIM ALLOWED ON JIM'S ISLAND"

Jim walked over to his bag, talking the whole time. "Actually, that rule seems like it should go without saying, don't you think? So, after I saw this Beefeater ad, I did some research online and on the phone from the hotel in Zermatt about what was available and what the prices were and where they were. I looked at areas all over the globe. I wanted something far, far away from a big tourist island and big enough to perhaps build a resort on or something eventually. So, the Caribbean seemed frankly too close to the US and too darn accessible. So, I flew down and looked at several different islands around Fiji and a few around New Zealand. The islands around New Zealand and south of there get too cold in the winter and the days get really short. Therefore, I started looking quite a bit north of there in the Fijian chain. After some more searching around, I ended up with this."

With a flourish, Jim unrolled a large map of Mago Island across the coffee table. It was really a topographic map with overlays indicating the location of all the buildings, hills, forested areas and the depth of the water. In fact, in addition to the main inhabited island, Dean and Ellen could see three or four tiny uninhabited islands off the shore as well.

146

Jim gave them a second to look at it and then started spewing forth details. "It has 5,411 acres and has these three small islands. As you can see, the main island is roughly oval-shaped. See how the south end is much higher and then it flattens out more or less before rising up to the Northern point although that is still only about half as high as the southern point. There's a protected lagoon here," he pointed to the map, "coming off the southern tip of the island, and the snorkeling is good even from the beach. There are several natural springs on the island; they are marked with those blue triangles. So, the island is self-sufficient except for the diesel for the generators and vehicles and the food that cannot be grown locally. There are about 40 employees and their families that live in the village on the eastern side of the island along with the tiny harbor. Heck, there's even a two-room schoolhouse. And see here? This big plain in the center used to be the largest sugar farm in the South Pacific. Now, it's basically a defunct operation. The company that owned it was trying to make it as a specialty rum producer. They got killed on shipping and delivery though as they had to charter their own boat or else get some passing fisherman to deliver a shipment to a larger island serviced by FedEx. Not to mention that the price of rum has really dropped. Anyway, I'm getting off track. I spent several days on the island in the owner's residence. It's a nice, although old, plantation house that sits up on the hill on the southern mountain (well, they call it a mountain). It needs a little updating. Anyway, I met the villagers, the island manager, went for a run on the beach, drank some of the local rum, went snorkeling, and, frankly, just felt so safe and free to be myself there. It was so relaxing! I can have my sailboat shipped down and sail to the neighboring islands, if I want, with friends or even tourists. Anyway, according to the realtor, they were having trouble selling it because of the size, the existing population and the location, so I got them to knock off a million from the asking price. So, it was only fourteen."

To which Ellen spurted out, "14 MILLION? …
Dollars?" as if Jim was perhaps speaking of Italian lira or
Monopoly money perhaps. Something that would give her a
grip on reality.

Finally, Dean looked up. He had been looking at the
blueprint of this island the entire time that Jim was speaking.
He simply said, "Well, when you get away, you really get
the hell away! Jim, this is incredible. But, we're never going
to see you anymore!"

Jim just stopped in the middle of sipping his beer
and stood there looking dumbfounded at Dean until he
started to smirk and said "Hey, I won't be down there all the
time, especially once I get settled in. And, whenever you
guys can get away, I'd be happy to fly you down. You know
that, right? Anyway, buying this island is just something
that I need to do right now."

Ellen finally regained her composure, stood up and
gave Jim a big hug. She said, "Well, Jim, I think it is a
splendid idea! As soon as you get hot running water and a
masseuse down there, I will arrive on the next plane for
pampering! Now, shall we get some dinner? I think we
missed our reservation at Josephina's but we can probably
find something!"

They ended up at Ted's Montana Grill which is one
of a small western chain of restaurants started by Ted
Turner. The story goes that because no restaurants were
buying his buffalo meat from his many buffalo ranches in
the west, he started a restaurant chain that would use the
buffalo meat. They ended up there because Jim had read
about it in the United Airlines in-flight magazine on the way
in from Wisconsin.

Jim explained that he had just come from Wisconsin
where he had paid someone to sell his house and arranged
for his furniture and everything else to go into storage. He
had also arranged to get his sailboat shipped down (about
half the cost of the sailboat) to the new island. The sailboat
had been released by the police and Jim wanted to keep it
from being some talking piece for the Cheeseheads for years

148

to come. He figured that if it was too emotional for him to sail it after everything with Sable that he'd just sell it in New Zealand or somewhere down there. What was amazing to Ellen and Dean was that he had pre-arranged almost all of these logistics, had flown into Milwaukee early in the morning, met with everyone in Milwaukee and Madison during the day, drove down to Chicago and stayed in a hotel under another name before flying here. Dean realized that Jim was really scared of Cliff and his guys. That pummeling in Zermatt had really shaken him up, unfortunately. Dean didn't think it was a good idea for him to be running away like this but he did know Jim well enough to know that talking, at this point, would be pretty futile. Not to mention that he had already taken out the mortgage on the island.

After the buffalo steaks had come and gone, Jim finally said, "So, I have a favor to ask you guys, which is partly why I'm here."

Dean said, "Sure, what is it?"

Jim elaborated, "Well, I need to have someone in the States that I can trust to oversee certain financial matters because the delay in getting mail and everything down there can be tremendous. I'd be happy to pay you for your time but don't think it'll be endless hours. I don't think it will be too much time really. I got the name of a lawyer and my old financial company has an office here so I'm going to meet them in the morning and set up everything. If you agree, I'd give you some limited power of attorney to sign things in my absence. Speaking of communication, I'm hoping to get a satellite phone and satellite internet access but it won't be installed for a little while. What do you think?"

Dean wrinkled his brow and said, "Well, I don't know. I don't want to have too much responsibility for all your money?"

Jim said, "Oh, no. The key they explained to me was to split the money between several organizations. You pay more fees but it keeps you from being totally open to fraud. Anyway, I only have a few million in that account, which will handle all the fees and other bills that you would be responsible for. Essentially, what would happen is that you

149

would need to go in once a month for an hour or so and sign a bunch of checks and authorizations. The rest I can handle from down there – like most major purchases. Most of the money is locked up in more long-term financial institutions and funds. I'm also opening accounts in New Zealand and Fiji. Not that you want to know, but where I officially live has a big bearing on my tax burden so we're still trying to figure out where I should officially live. Heck, it might be over in Monaco but I'm hoping that the Fiji taxes and so forth are the best option. I can still be a US citizen but just take up residence over there from now on."

And Jim continued and continued down this discourse on financial alleyways until , eventually, Ellen just butted in and said, "Jim, we'd be happy to help you. If it gets to be too big a problem, we will let you know. On the condition that you always stop and see us when you're in the country."

Jim said, "Sure. And, everything might change in awhile if I get too bored or something grabs my fancy. "

Dean chimed in, "Yeah, so, do they have Match.com on your island down there? Cuz otherwise, it's a long way for a first date from the States."

Jim looked at him. "Very funny. Yeah, the owner gets to take over the harem from the previous owner. Plus, there are lots of passing mermaids!"

Chapter 12: It's My Island

If the African savannah is a study in subtle variations of the color brown, then the area around a coral reef is modern art. Colors everywhere. Movement everywhere. The water applies various filters of blue on everything but still the brilliant reds, oranges, yellows and greens moving in all three dimensions are enchanting. As a scuba diver or snorkeler, the experience is almost completely visual with one addition. The water is warm and welcoming to the air-breathing intruder. The feeling of floating and warmth leading to serenity is hard to capture anywhere else.

There was something about the water inside the reef that Jim felt like he could never take for granted. The color of blue that shimmered beneath him on this warm, sunny day had a similarly captivating effect as a campfire in the north woods of Wisconsin. The inherent movement of light under the surface and the natural rhythm lulled him to a slow stop. He was piloting his kayak across his lagoon next to his island when suddenly he had one of those "Oh my god, how did I get here?" moments. The kind of moment that makes your eyes pop open wide and you look around trying to really "absorb" where you are in an attempt to regain your sense of place. Jim had had many of these moments starting with when he was awakened by Dean to the fact that he had won the lottery – until now. But, instead of lying down, Jim started paddling harder and harder. He had started doing this every day to get in shape – paddle out to the reef in the sea kayak and along the inside edge of the reef and eventually back to shore. It took him about half an hour typically now, although it had taken over an hour the first time. Jim could feel the pounds coming off slowly and the muscles in his arms getting stronger. His skin was turning brown from the sun. A few weeks ago when he had arrived on the island, he had felt completely out of place with the other islanders with his pasty white Wisconsin skin and his winter belly.

After the comment by Dean about what he would do on the island, Jim had been worried on the flights down that he would be bored. However, that hadn't been the case. If Jim had ever even had the thought of being bored, immediately something or someone would interrupt him. He had started scheduling these kayak trips every day to give himself a break from the demands of being "the new owner man" or "Mr. Jim Sir". He received special deference from everyone because he actually owned it himself. Previously, the island had been owned by a nameless, faceless, relatively meaningless corporation and the person who had occupied the owner's house had been just an emissary of the corporation. The previous guy had constantly been hampered by the need to take many decisions to the corporate board and CEO before initiating any projects. This had resulted in huge delays because the communication alone had taken hours if not days and the CEO and board were busy with many items other than this little island and its little rum business. The downside of globalization, it seemed. All of this remote control was probably a large part of the reason that the business hadn't succeeded, Jim came to realize.

The owner's house was, at one time, a very classic tropical plantation house. It was two stories tall with high ceilings and almost boxy looking. It had large windows facing the sea on one side and looking down on the village from the other side. Inside, a large hallway ran through the core of the house. The main floor had a large kitchen, large formal dining room, sitting room, library with a pool table and a small office. The second floor had one master bedroom with a small bathroom, three smaller bedrooms and another main bathroom. The nicest feature of the house, as far as Jim was concerned, was the huge porch which wrapped completely around the house. The previous owner essentially lived out on the porch with a dining table on one end of the house and a nice outdoor sitting and reading area at the other end. Now, Jim realized that in addition to the allure of being outside, the other reason was that the interior was falling apart. In addition to being a poor mid-level manager, the previous occupant was terrible at home maintenance. Either that or the previous owner couldn't convince the corporate penny-pinchers of the need to renovate. Finally, the forest had almost swallowed the house entirely.

So, the first thing Jim did was initiate a project to renovate the house. First step was to fix the structural problems, put on a new roof and upgrade the electrical service so the whole thing was at least safe and dry. Next, clean and paint all the surfaces. Third, rip out the master bathroom and some closet space and put in a much larger bathroom with steam bath and a soaking tub. He ordered the staff to completely relandscape the area around the house. Finally, via a few catalogs he picked up while in the states, he ordered a large flat-panel TV for the library and converted one of the upstairs bedrooms into something of a home theater.

The full-time house staff had a small cottage where they could live but most lived in town with family as that building was decrepit as well. Jim initiated improvements on that building too.

Anyway, as the new owner, tradition dictated that Jim be invited to everyone's home for dinner. Jim could have refused but having dinner by himself – especially with the owner's house under renovation – would have been rude. So, Jim would go to people's homes for dinner. He would bring a gift based on whatever Nixon suggested for him and he usually brought Nixon along for company.

Nixon was the island manager. At thirty years of age, he was younger than he seemed and far wiser and filled with infinitely more integrity than his namesake had been.

153

He had a small goatee and short hair with a few gray hairs already, which made him seem much older. He was about six feet tall and matched up well against Jim but was probably twice as strong even with a thin, wiry frame. He had a bright smile which was normally hidden by his all-business demeanor. The previous owner's rep could not say enough good stuff about Nixon. They said that there wasn't much that they had to do because Nixon was so efficient, smart and reliable. Nixon had his own home in which he lived with his wife and several children but he spent many of his days and evenings at Jim's house since Jim's arrival, which Jim appreciated. Nixon also was the direct supervisor for the servants who worked in Jim's house. At the moment, they were primarily helping with the remodeling going on in the house but still had time to make meals for Jim and keep the inhabitable parts more tidy.

So, between making a house call to every home on the island for dinner in the evenings, Jim spent his days with Nixon and the visiting off-island construction foreman making plans for the improvements to the owner's house These improvements required more electrical power that required a new generator addition in town and new lines to be run out to the house. In addition, Jim's sailboat was enroute to the island from Milwaukee (just a few months to get it there) and so he'd been outfitting improvements to the tiny harbor, making sure that there was enough underwater clearance for The Lucky Ticket and any other sailboats or other boats that might come to visit. Finally, he was getting the satellite TV, radio and also the long-range phone transmitter system installed and running. When he had a break from that, he tried to learn more about the rum business and the history of the island. And, by the time he sat down to breakfast, lunch, and high tea – all prepared for him- the days had flown by. So, Jim was incredibly busy and didn't have much time to think – except when he was out on his kayak or running along the beach or in the quiet times in the evening after everyone had gone home. During those quiet times, Jim wondered if he had done the right thing but he felt really good about it so far. He finally had the time

154

and distance to process everything that had happened with Sable. He still felt partly responsible for her death, of course, but he slowly started to accept that guilt as his own. He slowly was realizing that he needed to face it and transcend it so that he could live the rest of his own life. There weren't any shrinks on the island but perhaps the island itself served as the best therapy possible - plenty to keep him busy, beauty at every turn and a tight-knit little community for company.

Jim pulled up his kayak on the beach and magically two young boys came down to the beach to help him carry the kayak up the beach and to the equipment shack which was below his house many, many steps up the hill. The view from the top was incredible but Jim just longed for an escalator from the beach on most days. Jim started hustling up the steps to find Nixon waiting for him at the top. Nixon said, "Sir, there is a community meeting and party tonight. Can you go? The elders have invited you."

Jim thought for a second while catching his breath, "Did Pendelton go when he was the owner?"

Nixon shook his head, "No, sir. Pendleton asked for a verbal report the next day."

Jim looked out at the lagoon, thinking for a second, "Will it be in English?"

Nixon started to smile, sensing that Jim might come. "Yes, sir. For you, everyone will speak in their goodest English."

To which, Jim looked at Nixon and laughed, "Very funny. Yeah, I'll go. I'd like to talk about my rough ideas for the resort too and see what people think."

Nixon nodded his head smiling and said, "Very good. I'll come at dinnertime to get you. I am going down to the dock to check on improvements there for today. Seems I need to check on them every day or it doesn't move forward very fast."

Jim left to meet with the contractor about the progress on the house and Nixon went off to check on the dock workers.

Nixon came to get him about 6 PM and they rode on Nixon's dirt bike down to the village – an experience that always made Jim wonder what a good road or, to dream really big, a subway would cost on the island.

The village consisted of just over two dozen buildings with other people living a short distance outside the village. Most of the buildings were the permanent homes of the villagers. They were oddly laid out on strangely shaped streets but a rough "main road" ran through them. In addition, close to the harbor were the general store, the bar and the community center that also included a small office. The small office was really just a big square with a door and a window. Previously, it had been used by the rum company. However, like the production facilities out in the center of the island, it had been abandoned. Nixon used the office now to manage the island although that job had little value until Jim had arrived on the island. Some of the villagers did make some money making weavings and other craftworks that were sold or traded to the trading ships and fishermen that plied the ocean in the area. Jim, of course, received samples of all of it during his home visits and very quickly had amassed quite a collection of island jewelry.

Away from the harbor was the church, a source of inspiration if not actual activity. The schoolhouse was also located at the end of the "main road" across from the church. Most of the children did spend parts of their days in school while the mothers took turns trying to teach the students. Jim thought that he better find a schoolteacher quickly if he wanted these kids to contribute eventually to his planned resort. He also wanted them to learn more English as he wasn't getting anywhere at picking up the local dialect.

Jim and Nixon walked into the bar and not into the community center, to Jim's surprise. Nixon explained that the village elders felt that a few beers made it easier to discuss difficult issues. Of course, Nixon said, "Too many beers can be a problem too." In the back area of the bar, one of the pool tables had been converted into a table and decorated with beers, sodas (a real luxury for the average islander) and plates of fruit and barbequed beef kabobs.

156

There were several other people already seated but they had left some seats open. To Jim's surprise, Nixon took the seat at the obvious head of the table and motioned Jim to sit next to him around the corner. A few more people came in, all of whom Jim had met previously. They all asked how the improvements to the house and dock and everything were going. Soon, Nixon (again, surprising to Jim) started the meeting by going through the agenda with everyone. He wanted to devote most of the meeting to allowing Jim to speak, which was nice, Jim thought. In addition, he wanted to talk about the school and the problem with some items from the community garden shed which had disappeared and a few other matters. Jim didn't know anything about any of the issues on the agenda or, even more troubling, when they were discussed later.

At this point, Nixon allowed Jim to speak. Jim realized that the beer was a good idea and was glad he didn't have to stand up to speak. "First, thank you all for inviting me. I will be happy to come as long as I am still able to contribute to the meeting and am on the island. What I really want to talk about tonight are some of the plans that I have for the island both immediately and long-term. In the short term, I am working on the owner's house," He counted off on his fingers. "The generator site, the communications both from the satellite dish and the shortwave telephone and the dock facilities. These three just need to be done to make things hospitable for me primarily and also for some visitors which might be coming. Oh, and just as an aside, as I think Nixon told you, I want to be immediately informed if any strange Americans show up on the island. I have invited lots of sailing people to "stop by" and want to make sure that I know about it." What Jim was really thinking about was Cliff Wainwright and his yuppie posse although he wasn't really worried about them very much any more. "Oh, and we're preparing for my boat which is being very, very slowly shipped down from the States. The current improvements should all be done in another few weeks, hopefully." To which everyone started to chuckle quietly. Jim continued with a smile on his face "Yeah, at the current

157

rate of progress, it'll take longer than that, which is one reason why I'm here tonight. I hope to get your ideas about how to get the work done faster. After everything is back in working order and useable, I'm interested in starting a business."

To which someone at the other end of the table said, "You're going to restart the rum business?"

And Jim replied, "No, I wasn't thinking about doing that. It didn't work for the last guys and they know a lot more about rum than I do. No, I am thinking about a very exclusive, very small and very expensive resort. The island isn't big enough to handle a large resort and it is a little too far from a major airport to keep a big resort full. However, it is big enough to handle a small, exclusive resort. Obviously, to do this, we're going to need somewhere for the guests to stay and things for them to do. So, we would need to convert part of the old rum facility into a spa with hot tubs, massage rooms, pools and a fitness area. We would need to clear an area on the other side of the hill from my house for a series of bungalows. I'm thinking that a number of bungalows separated from each other but still accessible to the central spa area and able to be serviced by the staff is probably the best layout. I'm also going to visit a few of the other exclusive resorts in this region to get ideas. Any information that you all hear about them, please let me know. Anyway, this plan is still in development, but I just wanted to let you know what my plans were at this point. Let me continue…"

And so Jim continued talking about some of his brainstorm ideas for the island, not realizing that they were absorbing every idea as if he already had the blueprints drawn and the contractors hired. They might have been upset at some of the ideas but didn't voice their displeasure. Jim was having a good time. Of course, he had another reason for creating an exclusive resort instead of a rum factory or something else. He realized that there was no surplus of attractive women on the island and he did know that exclusive resorts attracted their fair share of exclusive women. If he marketed to groups of executive women…well, things could only get better.

Suddenly, three guys with big beer guts burst through the door to the bar. They looked like the modern day equivalent of the Mongol horde. Chubby Japanese guys dressed a little too warmly for the island in flannel shirts and heavy jeans. The obvious leader barked out, "Hey, what's with this sign that the bar is closed! We came all this way to this stinking backwater island to deliver your diesel and you thank us by closing the only bar!"

One of the islanders, Jack, jumped up and yelled, "Shaku, quit your yelling, you all know we have meetings here sometimes in the evenings. I'll get you some beers if you just sit outside until we are done."

Meanwhile, while Jack was moving behind the bar to fetch them the usual, Shaku approached the pool table quickly, looking directly at Jim. He kept approaching to the point where Jim took a step back. Jim leaned back until Shaku stopped in front of him and said, "So, you're the new American owner, I guess?"

Jim stammered, "Uh, Yeap. And, who might you be?"

As he said this, Shaku leaned in to shake Jim's hand and Jim realized what Shaku's profession is from the scent. Shaku confirmed Jim's suspicion by saying, "Deepsea fishers, that's what we are! We're out here chasing the tuna around the ocean. In addition, we are about the only regular boat coming by to refill your diesel generators. According to what I hear, you're going to need a lot more diesel and power for your big plans."

Jim glanced over at Nixon who kept his normal blank look on his face. Jim said, "Probably. At the moment we are fine but we're looking at starting a resort, maybe, in a few years."

Shaku said, "Well, good! Better than the damn rum business. That never seemed to work with these guys drinking all the profits."

To which Nixon added, "Yes, and the rum business meant there were a lot of boats coming through for pick up and delivery so we didn't need you to bring the diesel."

159

Shaku looked indignant, if that is possible for a man smelling like fish, and said, "We bring the diesel and other stuff really cheaply for you all!"

Nixon counterargued, "Yes, but we also let you dock for free unlike the other islands and the tuna sit outside the reef all the time."

The argument was abruptly ended by Jack the barkeeper, who shouted (loudly for such a small bar), "Your drinks are ready!"

Shaku glared at Nixon but walked over to the bar casting a "Nice to meet you, owner!" over his shoulder.

Nixon said to Jim, "Don't worry. Those guys are pretty harmless. They come to the island to recover and drink. They do bring us diesel for the generators and they also bring mail and some supplies. The big, regional supply ship comes every few months, as you know, but they won't bring diesel because they think it contaminates all the produce and everything else. Anyway, their bark is worse than their bite. Shall we get back to the meeting?"

Jack the barkeeper came back and sat down in his place. The remaining orders of business were dealt with pretty quickly. Jim was amazed at how many issues there were. The most pressing issue was getting a teacher for the school. Jim found himself volunteering to advertise the teaching job to other islands and on the internet. "Who knows," he said, "Some disgruntled teacher from Detroit might want to move here for awhile."

Ezekiel turned to him and asked, "What does it mean if they are disgruntled? Can they still walk?"

Jim leaned back and smiled and said, "No, disgruntled only means they don't like their life and want a change." As the meeting progressed, Jim found himself getting more and more involved in the needs and activities of this little community on this island. He had not expected to do that but he just kept seeing opportunities for him to easily contribute as they went through the agenda. By the end, he had quite a little to-do list (studiously recorded by Nixon who, Jim was sure, would hold him to it later). Jim stayed relaxed though because he didn't really have anything else to do but to-do lists so they might as well be long.

The meeting ended a little later than expected (which is expected on the island) and pretty soon, it seemed like most of the village showed up at the bar. The fishermen were allowed back inside but few people talked to them. Everyone was talking about the new opportunities that might come with a resort including the jobs, the money, the visitors, and the option for new things to do. Everyone seemed really happy that Jim wasn't starting the rum factory up again. None of them had really liked working there (which was probably another reason that it was such a dismal failure). Jim was a little overwhelmed. He had come down to this island to get away from the guys trying to put him in the hospital and running from his past. He hadn't expected to find much more than a rum drink and a beach. He finally realized that, without his knowledge, he had become part of the community on this island and, in fact, responsible for its future in many ways. He would have never asked for it, but now that it was upon him, he felt quite empowered by it. He realized slowly that a sense of community had been missing from his life almost as long as he could remember. Sure, he had all the money in the world and he had good friends like Dean and Ellen but community was a different beast requiring trust and responsibility and the acceptance of the fact that one cannot just walk away from the community without consequences. Back in the States, moving out of a community had been reduced to calling a realtor, changing a phone number and finding a new Starbucks to go to...but not here. Literally, on this island, there was nowhere else to go. Jim got a little anxious as he realized all this but he came to feel that it was something he could handle, at least for right now.

Chapter 13: Between a rock and a hard place

When an animal is large and powerful and possibly dangerous, it doesn't seem like it can be fragile as well. But, birds cannot fly away from the bird flu, the white tail deer cannot leap away from chronic wasting disease and the polar bear cannot escape from the impact of global warming on the length of winter. Like David and Goliath, the smallest and seemingly insignificant threat can bring down the giants. These are the most difficult threats to protect against as their attack is insidious and it's not obvious how to fit the problem.

The party at the bar had lasted until midnight after which Nixon took him home on a speedy and bracing ride through the night on his motorcycle. Jim made a mental note to only get really drunk in the safety of his own house. Of course, the fact that he was out later than usual had no impact on the workmen who were at the house at their normal 7 AM start time. Whoever said that islanders were lazy had never met the contract carpenters who were staying up by the house in a makeshift camp. Of course, they were paid by the project and not the hour so that might make it go a little quicker (as long as the foreman, Nixon and Jim kept them from getting sloppy by watching them like hawks). So, Jim attempted to bury his head under the pillows for an hour and finally gave up and got up.

He spent an hour or so monitoring the laborers but they were just doing the same thing they were doing yesterday and finally he had had enough coffee and breakfast fruits that he felt awake enough to do something else. A run might be good before he started trying to work on his to-do list from the night before, he thought. He'd been kayaking every day for a week in the morning and wanted something different. Going on a run on the beach was something that he had been expecting to do frequently, when he arrived, and had only gone twice since arriving. Since then, he had lost fifteen pounds and was in better shape so he wanted to try it again. He got out his running shoes and set off down the path to the beach and then along the beach towards the tip that faced the reef. It was a lonely part of the beach on a typically lonely island which suited him fine. The islanders didn't make much sense out of seeing him exercise because they had never seen much point to it. Of course, they didn't get a lot of French fries on the island either, Jim thought.

Jim had never been a really great runner. In high school, he had run cross-country but mostly because his best friend had and Jim didn't want to come home early after school. But, Jim had learned the basics and over the years had run off and on. Of course, there were always excuses in Wisconsin not to run – from the hot humid days in the summer to the icy roads and bitter cold in the winter. Everyone crammed in their running during the spring and fall plus some late summer nights and some sunny Saturday afternoons in the winter. Jim said a little prayer of thanks that none of that was a problem down here on Mago Island. After the party last night, Jim was feeling a little lousy this morning. He started off pretty slow on his run and then did a few sprints to really warm up before settling into a pretty good jog. He ran on the sand just on the ocean side of where the seaweed piled up. The sand there was firm and clean. A little further left and he would be in the surf and the sand would be soft underfoot and hard to run in. A few feet to the right, past the seaweed, he would be in the very dry sand that is also soft and filled with sticks. So, he ran along on this optimal little pathway at the junction between ocean and land. On the edge.

He was feeling strong as he rounded the point and realized that he was getting in pretty good shape in spite of staying up too late partying the night before. At this point, he was running in the direction of the sun and the glare off the ocean made him squint and look at the ground. So, he didn't really see it until he was upon it. In fact, he stepped on a few of the filaments before he even realized there was something lying across his path ahead. An issue that he was going to have to stop and deal with. He stopped running and looked down and then, to confirm his suspicions, he looked up the beach ahead of himself. As it dawned on him what he was seeing, he got that instant nausea that comes with the discovery of death and decay. He was able to avoid throwing up but he did have to double-over and close his eyes for several seconds to let the shockwave pass. Jim didn't know it at the time but this moment would forever change his conception of the border between the ocean and the land.

Arrayed out in front of Jim for several hundred yards was a hopelessly tangled mass of tuna net. It spread out into the water as well as all around him. The net however, was not what caught Jim's eye or what brought him to the point of physical revulsion. Woven within the net and trapped so tightly that it seemed as if it must have been done on purpose were at least a dozen sea turtles. They were contorted in various painful-looking positions several even with their heads yanked up onto the top of their shells. Many of their flippers were compressed right against their bodies and obviously broken. Most were bleeding or, unfortunately, done bleeding. They were all going to die if something wasn't done immediately. As Jim raced back and forth across the beach surveying the carnage, without thinking he started trying to untangle the turtles that seemed to be potentially alive. He didn't have a good understanding for how strong these nets are though. The nets were well-constructed of hemp that was designed to stand up to the brutal ocean environment let alone Jim's soft hands. He found a turtle that was still squirming. The net was wrapped around the shell itself, leaving the head and flippers free. Jim tried to squeeze the turtle out from between the netting – trying desperately to simply move a single strand away from the turtle's shoulder in an attempt to ease it out of the larger mass. He was soon sweating and breathing hard and straining against this very solid netting. He stopped for a moment to catch his breath and wiped his hand across his forehead only to realize his hands were bloody – his own blood unfortunately. After a few short minutes, Jim's hands were bleeding worse and the netting hadn't budged. Of course, he had no knife and there were too many tangles to loosen the net's unrelenting grip. Jim had seen these turtles swimming in the lagoon while he'd been kayaking\. They had been swimming gracefully and effortlessly through the water, easily keeping up with the kayak – when they weren't diving for fish or investigating the coral. This turtle realized some new torture was happening while Jim was struggling to free him. He tried vainly to nip at Jim but was so weak and confined he couldn't move any faster than Jim could move out of the way.

Finally, after far too short a time, Jim's hands were in so much pain he had to stop working on the turtle. He sank into the sand and watched the turtle for a second. The turtle's eye turned toward Jim, watching him. The eye was bloodshot and within a minute or two his head sank into the sand and the eye closed for good. Jim began screaming for help. He was quite a distance from his house – the workmen wouldn't find him here. He screamed and ran up the beach looking for a path deeper into the island. By now, he knew the inner island roads but still didn't have a mental map of many sections of the beach. He hoped he could find someone, get a sharp knife and get word to Nixon to bring help.

Soon, two little boys came running in response to his cries. They'd must have been playing in the trees close to the beach. They ran up saying "Mr. Jim, Mr. Jim, what's the problem?" When they saw that his hands were bleeding, their eyes got huge and they started to walk backwards.

Jim cried out, "Wait! There are a bunch of turtles trapped in a net and washed up on the beach. I need a knife to cut them free and I need someone to run and get more help. Do you see them?" and Jim turned back to look over his shoulder and point the boys towards the spot on the beach.

One of the boys said, "We have no knife but we do have these that we pretend are knives." And, they both held out their most prized possessions – sharpened oyster shells which they had worked into the shape of a knife. "We were playing soldier" said one of them.

Jim collected himself, smiled at the boys and took their prized possessions and said, "OK, I thank you and will give these back to you when we are done. Now, which of you is faster and braver?" Both of them raised their hands. Jim smiled and said, "Great, you're both brave. Now, I promise each of you some ice cream or whatever you want if you both go and get as much help as possible. Try very hard to find Nixon too. Tell them that Mr. Jim wants everyone to come to this beach and help save the turtles."

Wanting to make sure they really went, Jim watched the boys until they rounded the first corner and were out of sight. They were both running fast. Jim turned and raced back down the beach. The turtle he'd been working to free had taken this break to seemingly ensconce himself even more in the net. Jim started cutting the net with the sharpened shells. Tenaciously, he made progress and slowly cut through one of the filaments. Between his cut hands and the fact that the shells were not really very sharp, it was slow going. He had cut through about six of the strands when several more men from the village came racing down the shore each with several different knives. As Jim started to rise to greet them, the first one raced up, grasped a turtle's head just down the beach from where Jim was standing and, before Jim could say a word, lopped the head off with a large machete.

"Ahhhh! NO! Stop! Stop! Stop! Don't kill them!" cried Jim and the man stopped dead staring at Jim.

"I thought we were called here to help you with the turtles" asked the man. Now, all the men were standing around Jim and puzzling over him, looking him up and down. Jim hung his head for a moment of resignation and looked at his bleeding hands. However, when he lifted up his head again, Jim's eyes were clear and there was a look of conviction on his face that told these men that the owner of the island had truly arrived. Jim said (far too loudly for these three men standing here), "We are not here to kill the turtles. We're here to rescue every turtle we can. This is atrocious and disgusting and these turtles were not meant to die today. This net is meant for catching fish in the deep ocean not catching everything else. You all start cutting the net and helping these turtles get out of the net. Any of them that are dead, you can take home to eat but we are not going to allow this net to kill more of our lagoon than necessary today."

The men stared at Jim for a second and slowly it all started to fit together for them. Jim had called it "our" lagoon – not "my" lagoon or "your" lagoon or even "the" lagoon and they realized that he felt that he belonged here and was one of them. Suddenly, like good soldiers following a great general, they jumped into action. They searched through the turtles on the beach and started working on the three that seemed to have the most life left. Jim moved back and forth between them – pulling and helping were he could - though, as the crisis wore on, his hands hurt more and more, especially with the sea salt working its way into the cuts. They worked and worked and got those turtles freed. Two of them promptly tried to bite them and so the men tried to herd them away from the net and back towards the water. The third turtle tried to move away from them only to realize that its back right flipper was obviously broken resulting in sort of a sliding hobble across the sand. Manuel, one of the men, turned to Jim and said, "It doesn't look good for that one."

Jim shook his head while staring after the turtle as it tried to make it to the sea. He replied, "It doesn't look good for any of them."

By this time, they were all covered with sand and the afternoon sun was making the dead turtles give off a terrible smell. They all paused on the sand while Jim continued his turtle triage and selected the next most likely turtle to survive. As he did this, Nixon drove up on his motorcycle and several more men came up behind him. Nixon had brought more knives and some snorkel gear. Nixon hopped off and looked at the carnage and the four bloody and dirty men in front of him. By this point, Jim's fresh running shorts and tank top bore the story of what had happened. Nixon walked up, "So, you want to save the turtles caught in the net, I hear?"

Jim nodded and explained, "The turtles weren't supposed to die today."

Nixon looked Jim over and spotted his hands, "Let me look at your hands."

Jim hid his hands behind his back and barked, "No! Just start cutting the netting and helping. My hands aren't important." To which Nixon wordlessly replied by handing him a pair of gloves. Jim stopped and calmed himself down before saying,"Oh, thanks. Sorry, I just don't think we have much time left." Jim slipped on the gloves with a grimace and said, "OK, I'm having these guys cut the turtles free in order of the most likely to survive. What do you think?"

Nixon said, "I think that seems like a good plan. I am going to look out in the water to see if any more are trapped out there. They can't survive as long trapped underwater but we should check and they might not be as tangled as onshore." Jim looked out at the net dragging off into the water and realized he hadn't thought at all about the unseen cost under the waves.

He said, "Oh my God! I didn't even think…Of course. Of course. Good idea, Nixon. I cannot explain why exactly but I'm very determined to save as many of these turtles today as possible."

Nixon replied, "You don't have to explain, we all understand now."

Jim selected the next several turtles to be saved and the men started back at their job. Nixon stripped down to his underwear, grabbed the snorkeling gear and headed into the surf following the edge of the netting. He stayed out for a long time with his knife. Jim was so focused on the turtles he was helping with – especially now that he had gloves to

169

wear – that he didn't notice how far out that Nixon was going or his thrashing about in the water. Just as they were finishing extracting this next group of turtles, Nixon came back up to the beach and collapsed on the sand.

Jim ran up to him and said, "Have you been checking it out this whole time? What's it like?"

Nixon was out of breath – obviously having spent as much time out in the water as his body would allow. Without saying a word, he handed Jim the mask and snorkel. Jim ripped off his gloves now panicking about what was under the surface of the lagoon. He grabbed the mask and snorkel and dove 20 yards out in to the water.

Jim swam out following the same edge of netting that Nixon had. What he saw made his heart sink and tears fill his mask. The good visibility in the lagoon was something that Jim cherished about the island but today he could have done without it. The dozen or so turtles on the beach were the tip of the problem under the sea. Arrayed before him, as far as he could see, there were schools of angelfish, dozens of parrot fish, immature dolphins and more sea turtles. Jim could see where Nixon had tried to cut some of the turtles free, as he had asked. However, Jim could immediately see the futility in this effort as the turtles which Nixon had cut free were either floating to the surface or sinking due only to the weight of the netting still wrapped around them. Nothing was moving and Jim was oddly reminded of every battlefield in every movie he had ever seen from "Glory" to "Braveheart". Jim realized that, in the war of man's immediate need for fresh seafood versus the oceans need to survive - man had won the battle here today.

Jim headed back to the beach and strode out of the water to face his hearty assistants. He said, "It seems that everything out there is dead or almost dead. How are we doing here?" Manuel piped up to represent the group "The rest of the turtles are dead" and then they stood there silently, waiting. Jim turned and looked out at the lagoon and the carnage and the horizon for a long time. He turned back to them and said, "Thank you all very much for your help."

Manuel said, "Thank you for working so hard for our lagoon, Mr. Jim."

Jim nodded and slowly turned to Nixon. "What should happen next?"

Nixon had recovered by this point enough to speak. He said, "The afternoon waves will push the rest of the net and fish up to the shore but all of this will bring sharks and others to feed. We should have everyone stay out of the water but perhaps send the women down to get what they can use for food. They would like to use the shells for decorations and to make crafts to sell."

Jim was still transfixed, looking at the carnage on the beach, but said, "OK, sounds like a good plan. Please get word to the women but warn them and the children not to go out in the water very far. I don't want to lose any people today too." He paused and then turned to look at Nixon. "Where do you think this net came from?"
Uncharacteristically, Nixon didn't say anything and tried to look preoccupied with getting himself cleaned off. Suddenly, Jim started to put it all together. He remembered the crazy fishermen, who were so obnoxious at the bar. He remembered the fact that they were fishing for tuna and that they had just arrived the day before. He looked at Nixon for a long while and his exhaustion turned to rage. Nixon looked back at him silently. Jim finally asked the obvious question, "It was those obnoxious fishermen, wasn't it? Shaku and his men, right?"

Nixon seemed a little conflicted but finally stopped what he was doing and said, "Please don't make any trouble, Mr. Jim. They bring the diesel and they were the only ones we could find to bring it. But, I did hear them saying that they had less work to do because they had been forced to cut loose one of their big nets on the way in."

"Why would they do that? Why would they cut the net loose?"

"If the net gets caught on something or maybe they got too close to the reef trying to get the tuna...Usually, they

171

cut the net as close to the area where it is caught as possible but the water gets so shallow that sometimes they cannot salvage much and just cut most of it loose. Of course, they are always walking the fine line between getting close enough to the shore for a big catch and too close and getting snagged. Anyway, a new net doesn't cost too much really."

Jim sat down at the edge of the surf and stared at the dead turtles. Now, the women were coming down to butcher the dead turtles and other fish and shells which were washing ashore. They made busy trying to make the most of this carnage. Jim turned to Nixon. "How much control do I have over the water around the island?"

Nixon just looked at his hands but answered honestly, "You officially own the reef and everything up to 2 miles out to sea. But, what are you thinking?"

Jim replied, "I don't want this to happen again, Nixon. It cannot happen again. It's morally unacceptable and wasteful. Even financially, it's a bad idea for the island. If we open up a resort, this kind of incident would be terrible for business not to mention that it's bad for the long-term ecology of the reef and the lagoon. I want to kick those damn fishermen off the island, not allow them back and keep all fishing boats more than one mile offshore. Obviously, we don't have a Navy but, if we don't allow them to land here, they won't come. What do you think?"

Nixon sat for a long time and realized that he had to say something. His voice was slow but strong. "Well, the fishermen bring lots of money to the bar and store. They bring our mail and supplies between the main deliveries. The big delivery ship only comes every three months or so. Most importantly, they're the only ones who will bring barrels of diesel because they have an onboard generator for their ice maker."

Jim stood up and said, "Good. The money I can take care of. The deliveries we can fly in or special order for awhile. That will all change with a new resort anyway. And, as for the diesel, well…there are lots of ways to make electricity. Hell, we'll use the wind and the sun. I won't be held hostage to these killers over a few barrels of diesel fuel!

Nixon, we need to be in control here. Damn, let's go kick them off my island. Sorry, I meant, let's go kick them off of our island, Nixon."

They gathered together all the villagers who were down at the beach and Jim explained to them that this disaster could not happen again for the good of the island and the good of the future resort. He told them that he was going to make it illegal for net fishing to occur in the waters off the island, and promised to figure out solutions for everything that the fishermen supplied – especially the diesel fuel. The villagers were very quiet but they also seemed a little apprehensive and even confused as they were not sure that this huge haul of food was such a bad thing. They did see that Mr. Jim was not taking any more suggestions about it, though, and that he was incredibly determined. Several of the men started walking over to the village to be ready to help when Jim arrived to kick out the fishermen.

Jim walked over to Maria, who was one of the women butchering the turtles. She was in the middle of sawing the lower shell off the turtle to get at the meat within. She would try to save the upper shell for decoration or to sell off-island. She stopped when Jim approached. He asked her, "Do you use the head for anything?"

She replied, "No. Some of the older women used to make soup with it but I think it tastes terrible so I usually just throw it away."

Jim asked, "So, can I have the head?" She nodded agreement; Jim grabbed the head and stood up. Soon, he and Nixon left for the village on Nixon's motorcycle with several knives and a sack hanging off the back. Behind them, the sun continued to bake down on the carnage of the beach and the women worked quickly to finish before the meat started to go bad.

Once everyone was in place, Jim and Nixon headed directly for the bar as the fishermen were normally there as soon as the sun made it too hot to work on the boat in the harbor. Manuel, one of the villagers who had been first at

173

the beach, was standing outside. He came up and said, "They are inside at a table in the back. They are a little drunk, as usual. The others are inside waiting for you."

"Thank you." Jim and Nixon got off the motorcycle. Jim walked in, carrying his sack from the beach. He looked bizarre. He was still wearing his running gear from the morning but it was now literally caked in blood all down the front - even after his snorkeling should have washed the initial blood away. His lower legs had been washed in the ocean but the blood had stained his new running shoes. He was sunburnt and he still was wearing the blood-soaked gloves he had been given earlier in the day. Taking them off would be a painful process later, when his work here was done.

Jim entered the bar with Nixon behind him and stopped to allow his eyes to adjust to the dim interior. His entrance brought the world inside to a sudden halt. The bartender saw him and stopped talking to the five village men at the bar. They had all been at the beach. A man from the village was sitting in a corner reading a book and drinking a beer, but looked up and stopped reading. This was Jonas, who had been out in the gardens all day and had not heard anything about the scene at the beach. Jonas would later be happy to see that his wife had gotten a lot of good meat and fish to cook. Jonas looked absolutely shocked at the sight of Mr. Jim covered in blood and mud, followed by Nixon who looked just as strange.

And finally, through the dim haze, the four fishermen in the back noticed Mr. Jim. They stopped talking and drinking and simply stared at him. Quickly, they realized that he was looking back at them. They started to sit upright and vigorously shake their heads as if to get the alcoholic cobwebs shook loose allowing sobriety to return. Jim started walking slowly and deliberately across the room toward them. It didn't take sobriety but rather lots of experience in bar fights to realize that the five guys at the bar were on Jim's side and were now standing at the ready, instead of sitting at the bar.

Finally, Shaku said, "Mr. Jim, what happened to you?" Jim didn't say anything but walked over to the table and with a flick of his arm, dumped 10 turtle heads on the table in front of them – sending beer pitchers flying and beer flowing and glasses tipped over. Beer started mixing with blood on the surface of the table. Simultaneously, all four fishermen tried to jump back from the table, scattering their chairs in the process. Jack, the bartender, tried to rush over with several towels but Nixon motioned him to stop.

Shaku finally wiped his now wet pants and anger started to well up inside him. "What the hell is this? Where do you get off dumping those turtles heads on our table?! For Christ sake, you spilled ALL the beer!"

Using one of his gloved hands, Jim grabbed one of the heads off the table and held it in Shaku's face.

With a voice as hard as steel and quietly demanding of everyone's attention, Jim said, "This morning, I was running on the beach when I discovered over two dozen turtles trapped in a driftnet. We spent the day trying to free them from the net. These heads are from some of the many that didn't make it. Did you lose a drift net off the west side of the lagoon on your way here?" Silence from Shaku as he realized that the truth would bring the wrath of this man. Like a small child, he looked at his feet.

Jim, like an angry parent, said, "Dammit! I know you did, as you told someone in the village that you had less net fixing to do. Dammit, Shaku. I am holding you, and your men, responsible for this disaster today. The deaths of these turtles and all the other wildlife caught in the net are on your heads! "

Shaku chuckled. He said to Jim, "Let me get this straight. You just spent the whole day trying to save a few dozen turtles and whatever else got caught in the net? Damn, we probably dump more dead turtles overboard in one day of drift netting even out in the deep water!"

Jim hadn't felt such intense emotions since Sable had died. He realized that Shaku didn't value anything that he couldn't sell for money in order to sit in this dingy bar, watch the dingy TV and drink the crappy beer that Jack sells.

175

Jim's move was so unplanned and happened so fast that he surprised himself. As his arm with the turtlehead, hanging like a mace as Jim held it by the neck, came flying up from his side and across Shaku's head, it was as if his arm had suddenly taken to improvising its own actions. The beak of the turtle ripped a gash in Shaku's skull sending more blood around the room, leaving wet blood on top of the dried blood on Jim and Nixon. Shaku fell against the back wall of the bar and, in the split-second that it took for the turtle head to fall on Shaku's head, the other four fishermen and the five village men from the bar converged on the same spot. The fishermen tried to get at Jim and one of them got in a punch to his face. Quickly, the villagers pulled all the fishermen off of him. The fishermen were drunk to begin with, which slowed them down anyway. Shaku struggled to his feet, clutching his bleeding head. Jim said to him, "You, and all fishermen, are banned from the island and the waters that we control – which go out four miles. You all need to be gone by dawn. We will sell you whatever you need to get to Wantau Island or further. These men will be watching you throughout the night. Don't come back. Ever."

Shaku stood there dumbly for five seconds before finally saying slowly through his pained and scrunched up face, "You just wait. No one else will bring you supplies and fuel like we do. When that diesel runs out in a few weeks, you're going to be calling us up and begging us to come back here with more diesel. You're really going to do this for a few turtles?"

Jim backed up a few steps, casually swinging the turtle head at his waist. "No," he said, "Like you, we are doing this for ourselves! We need fish and turtles in the lagoon. The tourists we are going to bring here expect wildlife, not carnage. We don't want to risk this destruction again. Doing it for the turtles? If anything, we're just as selfish as you but we value this island for more than a few dollars and some warm beer in this bar! We choose the path that values our land and the ocean. We choose to make money by sharing the beauty we have with others. You can

176

choose to live any way you want - just not here. Now, get the hell out!"

As they shuffled towards the door, Jim turned to Jack and said, "Get him some first aid for that cut on his head if he wants it. Also, give them three days food and provisions from the store." Jim and Nixon organized several shifts of men to watch them and their boat throughout the night and until they left. The villagers were given several guns and radios but no one was expecting much from the fishermen once they were back on their boat getting ready to leave.

Jim headed back to his house with Nixon. Several of the women had left Jim a lot of turtle and fish for him to eat in the big freezer at his house. Because of the random nature of when deliveries arrived at the island and the timing of any slaughtering on the island, the previous owners had installed a very large freezer down in the basement of the big house. He woke up Monica, the maid, who helped him cut the gloves off his hands and clean and bandage the cuts in his hands. As she worked, Jim wondered what he had done. He stared at his running shoes, realizing how long ago it seemed that he had left to go running. Jim started thinking about all the ramifications of his actions today and how he was now responsible for providing power for the island, for getting supplies to the island, and bringing in money to the store and the bar. Jim had a lot to do and only weeks until the diesel would run out and the lights would go off. He couldn't let that happen. First thing in the morning, he would start rationing the power for night time and then he would have to find someone who could help build a power system for the island....

His hands relaxed and went limp. Monica looked up from her work on his hands and realized that Mr. Jim had fallen asleep. Monica spoke only a little English but the women had explained to her in the island dialect what had happened at the beach today. How Mr. Jim had tried to save all the turtles and fish. How Mr. Jim had been so upset to see the dead wildlife in the net. How he had explained about kicking the fishermen off the island, etc. Monica had never

177

liked the fishermen because they always tried to get the island women to sleep with them when they were on the island. She was glad to see them go. She had been watching Mr. Jim these past weeks and was confident that he would take care of them. Right now though, he needed caretaking. She delicately finished bandaging his hands and stirred him just enough to go to his room and help him out of his running clothes. Then, she left him sleeping on his bed and went to her room to try and sleep because she knew that tomorrow many people would be coming to visit.

Chapter 14: Lonely but not Alone

While courting seems to occupy the waking thoughts of everyone between the ages of 14 and 64, it is even worse in the animal kingdom. Take the Australian bower bird for example. The male bower bird constructs a bower, a raised platform structure, on the rainforest floor. He then spends 50 -70% of his time decorating the bower with flowers, pebbles, feathers, baubles if humans are nearby, and even painting the walls with berry juice. When a female visits, he struts around and sings to her. If his decorations are wonderful, his singing divine and his effort substantial, she relents to mate with him. She then flies off nearby to build a nest and care for the children while the male continues to beautify his bower and wait for another female to seduce into his bachelor pad.

Kelli Nelson wondered briefly if they were courting, as she watched the two squirrels run across her path. Unfortunately for Kelli, her yellow lab – Sundance – didn't think twice about the nature of community but only thought "Game On!" and took off across the walking path and after the squirrels. Sundance jerked the leash out of Kelli's left hand, which was also trying to manage a Diet Coke and a cellphone, and charged off after the squirrel.

"Stop! Wait! Sundance, wait!" she screamed, knowing that it was pretty much a lost cause when squirrels were concerned. She thought, "I really need to get her out into the mountains this weekend for a long hike where she can chase whatever she wants". Meanwhile, she was running across Washington Park after Sundance who had treed the smart squirrels just a short 200 yards away. When

Kelli walked up, she was sitting patiently with her tail wagging slightly as if to say, "Look, look I have the squirrels cornered. They can't get away now!" Sundance was understandable confused when Kelli grabbed her snout and expounded loudly on the merits of listening to Mom when Mom wants one to stop, wait, come, etc.

Kelli Nelson was 29 years and 18 months old as she liked to say. She lived in downtown Denver and had bought a little bungalow in the trendy, yuppie, older neighborhood that sits around Washington Park. Water is hard to come by in the high-desert environment of Denver but the little lakes and extensive grounds within Wash Park made it a real crown jewel for the city of Denver. It was common to see joggers and walkers, and especially dog walkers, in the park at all times of the day. Special events were held in the park almost every weekend.

Kelli had gotten Sundance through some friends and the dog was now about three years old. She was a cute and easy-to-tolerate dog and was typically (when there were no squirrels) a good companion. Between their daily walks and running through the park almost every day, they kept each other in shape.

Not only that, but the dog was about the only thing about Kelli's life that was keeping her extended family off her case for still being single. She knew when her Dad built Sundance a dog house that the dog had become a pacifier for the grandchildren that they didn't have. It wasn't like she wasn't trying to get herself carried across the threshold. There was Bill who loved her but didn't realize that love came with decisions and responsibility. He was still rock-climbing - somewhere in Brazil now. There had been John who had been perfect for her, absolutely perfect, on paper. She tried really hard to love him until she realized she shouldn't have to work so hard.

It didn't help that she traveled quite a bit for work. She had gotten an environmental science degree because she really couldn't decide between biology, engineering and economics so she combined all three. She had worked on a few environmental projects back in Ohio as a contractor to the state but joined the Peace Corps when she realized that the Midwest was not the only place she wanted to live in her life. She ended up being assigned to manage a project installing solar photovoltaic lighting systems for villagers in western Kenya and working with the communities to maximize the value of they lighting at night to do work on micro-businesses and education. When she got back from Africa after almost three years, she was lucky enough to continue this type of work at the National Renewable Energy Lab (NREL), just on the west side of Denver. She worked in the international group trying to facilitate the use of renewables throughout the world. She did a lot of work with the UN Environmental Program and USAID also partly funded her efforts. So far, it was a wonderful job and very rewarding. It also paid much better than the Peace Corps.

"OK, Sunny. I gotta get home now so that I can go to that thing with Julie," she said as she grabbed the leash, yanked hard and headed for home. Sundance trotted along now more concerned about being yelled at than the squirrels anyway. Even though she was only talking to her dog, she couldn't say "8-minute Dating" out loud. Her friend Julie, who also worked at NREL, had talked her into going to this "thing" the week before. Basically, Julie wanted to go but didn't have the courage to go alone. Kelli couldn't say "No" in general and she thought she would give it a try anyway. She had promised herself a year ago that she would really start working hard at trying to find someone new. Of course, she had gone on three different month-long trips to Haiti since then as she attempted to get a community wind project off the ground.

Julie pulled up in her new Toyota Prius hybrid in front of Kelli's little bungalow. Like Kelli, Julie was blonde, in good shape, had a great job at NREL, and had trouble finding a "keeper". There were not many people at the office that were even single, let alone that they would want to date. Julie jumped out of the car, talking already, "So, I'm so sorry I'm late! Bob called me at the very end of the day and wanted to discuss the UNDP initiative. I finally had to tell him I was going on a date, so I will definitely hear about that tomorrow."

Kelli ran out to the car, waved at Sundance sitting in the yard behind the fence and jumped in the car. She said, "Well, if nothing else, this will be an interesting experience, right?"

Julie nodded, "Yes, yes, I think you are probably right. Interesting experience is the most likely outcome. I guess finding the perfect man is less likely. What are the odds of finding someone among eight strangers when there seems to be no one among the dozens of people that I already know?"

Kelli nodded agreement, "Yeap, and sometime in the future we can look back at all these dating fads and say that we tried them all!"

Julie chuckled, "I also had the terrible thought on the way over – what if one of the geeks from work is there?"

Kelli smiled, "Julie, we are the geeks at work."

Julie retorted, "Well, we don't use lasers or Petri dishes, at least."

They drove down to Wahoo's Fish Taco's, a very fun and hip little restaurant in the LoDo (lower downtown) section of Denver. At one time, this area was one of the most run-down and neglected parts of Denver. The city and developers had spent most of the 1990's redeveloping the entire area and now it was a very lively section of town filled with restaurants, clubs, office space and overpriced condos. Fish tacos were not the reason that Julie and Kelli were here, however. They walked in and a very attractive looking woman greeted them. Her name was Janeen and she was very excited to see all these people "connect". Janeen started by explaining rapid-fire, "As you know, you each have eight different dates tonight with each date being eight minutes in length. There will be a 15 minute intermission but otherwise there won't be any breaks and we'll just ring this little bell when it's time to move to the next date. Here are your nametags and your numbers. If you meet someone that you would like to ask out, you write down their name and number on this pad and enter it into the website. If the person you select also selects you, then the website lets both of you know how to reach the other person. For now, help yourself to some appetizers or the cash bar and we will start as soon as everyone is here."

They had signed up for a session with ages 25 to 35 which was about the only filter that was applied, unfortunately. The rule was that no one could ask you for your number or even your last name at the session. As Kelli looked around the room at the men with nametags on, she decided she was grateful for that rule. She thought, "Is this a good cross-section of the men that are available in this whole city?" She realized it wasn't. Some guy named Tom, who was a chemist for a pharmaceutical company in Boulder, came up and started chatting their ears off. She was determined to have a good time, she told herself, even if this would just be an exercise in human interaction.

Somewhat like musical chairs, Janeen the host asked them to take a seat according to the list they had been given upon entering. Kelli sat down across from Rodney. Rodney was in decent shape and was not unattractive.

Kelli shook his hand and said, "Hello, I'm Kelli. Pleased to meet you."

Rodney said, "Pleased to meet you too. Have you done this before?"

"No, this is my first time. My friend Julie over there invited me to come."

Rodney said, "Me neither. But, it's so hard to meet people, especially with a job and the kids."

He looked down as he took a sip from his beer and missed the slight twitch that went over Kelli's face.

She said, "Oh, I love kids. How old?"

Rodney continued as if what he was about to say was typical for a man under 35. "Well, I have two kids in high school and another in junior high so just a few more years and they're off to the real world and out of my hair," he said smiling.

Kelli smiled back but inside her head stamped Rodney with a "Return to Sender" stamp. Kids in high school? He must have started when he was 12! He doesn't have kids; he has adults that live with him. These will be a long eight minutes, she thought. But she continued, "Where do you live? I live in the Wash Park neighborhood."

Rodney looked a little surprised. "Wow. I heard that area was quite expensive! I live down in Parker, which is close to my ex-wife and my job."

Kelli pressed on, "What do you do for work, Rodney?"

"I work two jobs actually. I do construction and then pull some shifts at Home Depot too in order to pay all the bills."

She continued to press onward through this conversation, "Hum, I could certainly use a person with construction skills at my place. Lots of things to fix."

Rodney didn't ask what needed to be fixed. Instead he went in a direction that interested him more. "So, and what do you do?"

She replied, "I work at the National Renewable Energy Lab out on the west side of town. We do research on solar and wind power and I do a lot of international development."

As if she hadn't known about it, Rodney said, "I drove through Wyoming last month. Did you know they have a TON of windmills up there? Is that what you do? Build them? Aren't you afraid of heights?"

Before Kelli got a chance to say that she didn't actually build anything the hostess Janeen clanged her little bell and thankfully, the moment ended.

Rodney held out his hand, " Kelli, it was very nice to meet you. I really enjoyed our time together. Hopefully, I can finish our conversation at some future time."

She smiled. "It was very nice to meet you too."

And she was off. She moved from table 12 to table 3 and was greeted by Karl. It was really amazing how much more immediately relaxed she was with him. "Karl, very nice to meet you." She looked down to write down his name and number and put a slash through Rodney's name above it. Karl did the same and then leaned into the table. "Have you done this before? Is this pretty typical?"

She replied, "No! I haven't. In fact, my friend Julie is around here somewhere and she convinced me to go."

He said, "My situation exactly. My buddy Nate is desperate to find a new girlfriend but, for no good reason, gets a little nervous so he asked me to come along."

Kelli thought for a second and inquired, "But, are you not really single then? Or..."

"Oh, no, I'm single and if I meet someone - that would be great but, left up to my own devices, I probably would just take my dog for a walk and work on my house."

"What? Me too! What kind of dog do you have?"

"German Shepard and black lab mix. She was however seemingly blue-black as a puppy, so I named her Indigo. She's great and really loves to run. How about you? What is your dog's name?"

Kelli leaned back and looked at the ceiling smiling just a little thinking of her dog and said, "Well, my dog's name is Sundance. She's some kind of yellow lab and golden mix. She's a little smaller – only 60 pounds – but she loves the mountains. I take her hiking and camping in the summer and snowshoeing in the winter because she loves to play in the snow in the winter. Really a great dog for Colorado. So, what is it that you do?"

"I'm a pediatrician at Children's hospital downtown. I really love it and have been here for about two years since finishing my residency."

"Where were you before you came here?"

"I did my residency up in Seattle for four years. That was a great place but I couldn't deal with all the rain forever. I grew up in Virginia but wasn't really fired up to go back to the East coast so I tried to find something in the sunny mountains. And, what do you do?"

"I work at the National Renewable Energy Laboratory which is out on the west side of town. "

Karl interjected, "Hey, I know that place! I toured the visitor's center when I first was out here looking around."

186

She almost couldn't contain her shock, "Really, you know about us? That's surprising! I work in the international group and do a lot of traveling and work with groups in developing countries that are trying to promote the use of renewable energy in their countries."

Karl said, "Wow. Sounds very interesting and exciting. Must be a little hard on your dog if you're gone a lot. Right?"

BING! Before she could answer, the bell rang and she realized that these second eight minutes had gone by incredibly fast compared to the first eight. This time, she put out her hand and said, "Karl, it was really great to meet you! Hopefully we can get Sundance and Indigo to meet at some point."

Karl said, "It was nice to meet you as well. I would like to hear more about your work later too."

Next, Kelli sat down at Table 4 with Vincent. She talked to Vincent but was still really focused on Karl and put a big circle around his name. Vincent was very handsome but had that kind of detached stare of the criminally insane, she thought. She tried to talk to him about activities and what he liked to do. He didn't mention anything involving the mountains. When she talked about snowshoeing, he didn't really know what it is. "That's with those racquet things on your feet, right?" Vincent left her unimpressed, unfortunately. The façade was great but the interior was empty, she thought.

After Vincent came Joe, the database administrator, whose idea of fun was renting five or six movies and just holing up in his apartment for the weekend to quote "get away from it all". Kelli wondered, "You're a database administrator. Aren't you already away from it all most of the day?"

Joe was followed by Phil, whose first question was, "So, do you happen to like martial arts? I'm really into martial arts."

"Well, I haven't actually gotten into it before but it does seem interesting..."

"Yeah, most people are kind of ignorant about the subject. It is so great though once you try it."

"Really, I'm sure it is. What do you do for work? | "

"Well, right now I sell Farmer's insurance but I'm getting pretty close to opening my own Karate academy. I'm really excited about it."

By this time, Kelli wasn't even listening to Mr. Miagi anymore.

In the end, she was left with just a circle around Karl's name, which she planned to enter into the website the next day. She and Julie stuck around for a drink afterwards but found that mostly it was the people they didn't want to talk to who came up to them afterwards. Julie reported that she hadn't met anyone that she wanted to enter in the database.

Riding home, Julie said "God, where are the good men?"

Kelli tried to cheer her up, "I met someone that I'm going to put down, Karl. Did you talk to him?"

Julie said, "Yeah, he kept talking about his dog and I think he asked me if I minded that he was divorced."

"Divorced?" Kelli said, "We didn't talk about that."

"Well, are you still going to put him down? I didn't really get a good vibe from him."

"Yeah, I'll put him down. What do I have to lose? Lots of nice guys are divorced, anyway. Of course, he has to put me down too and he probably has his pick of women at the hospital. Although...maybe it was just in comparison to those other guys that he seemed so great."

They started to laugh when Kelli described her conversation with Rodney with the four teenage kids. "I think he must have lied about his age," Julie said between chuckles. Julie told her about Chavez who basically said that he writes down every woman's name just to see who picked him. Julie apologized but it was so pathetic it was funny. They concluded that it was an interesting experience but that they probably wouldn't be doing it anytime again soon.

Kelli was happy to get home to Sundance, who was waiting patiently behind the fence. Kelli was always so happy to see her (and the tail wagging indicated the feeling was mutual) and relaxed by hanging out with her. She loved her dog, loved her life but just was waiting for Mr. Right to walk through the door …or even walk by on the sidewalk…

Chapter 15: A Hard Row to Hoe

In the 60's, it was about Saving the Whales. In the 70's, it was about Clean Air and Clean Water. The 80's got more international trying to save the elephants. The 90's brought us the spotted owl in the northeast and the manatee in Florida. The new millennium takes this all to the next level. Global warming, population growth and economic development are combining to put pressure on all species and ecosystems simultaneously. From polar bears dying due to a lack of sea ice in the Arctic to the imminent death of coral reefs due to the oceans heating up to people dying from changing weather patterns in slow (melting glacier slow) and fast (stronger and more frequent hurricanes) ways, existence was getting more difficult.

It wasn't often, lately, that Dean came home early. Being a resident was more of a marathon than a sprint, everyone said. But, to Ellen, it seemed that Dean had been sprinting forever. Luckily, she had made a few friends through her work and had been able to find things to do and keep busy in the evenings and on the weekends. She made every effort to be home when Dean was planning to be home but, often, he had little energy left to do anything more than eat some food and go to bed. Ellen knew that it was not going to last forever but that was little comfort when he was at the hospital for 32 hour shifts.

But, tonight, Dean had promised to come home at a decent hour because Jim had emailed a few days before and said he was coming to town on "business" for a few days and wanted to take them out to dinner. He had said in his email (the fact that he now has email on that island really amazed Ellen) that he was really in need of a good Midwest meal so, Ellen had made reservations at the Brown Palace – one of Denver's premier restaurants and the hotel where the famous and rich stay when they are in town. When well-known bands play out at the Red Rocks Amphitheater or presidents come to town, they typically stay at the Brown Palace. About two blocks from Coors Stadium where the Colorado Rockies play baseball in the summertime, the Brown Palace was a place that Dean and Ellen couldn't afford even on their anniversary, which is why Ellen thought it was perfect for when Jim came to town. As Ellen said, "God knows he isn't spending money on restaurants on that island. Supposedly, it only has a bar and no real restaurants…"

Dean arrived early but still late. He had hoped to be home at five (instead of the usually eight or nine PM) and got home about 5:30 having obviously run the whole way home. He was still in the shower when the doorbell rang. Ellen walked over and opened the door, expecting to see the typically affable Jim – all suntan and relaxation. She was surprised by what stood on the other side of the screen door. Jim was still lean and smiling but the tan was fading and there were shadows of fatigue and effort under his eyes. But the thing that really surprised Ellen was the look in his eyes. The face was still smiling but there was something subtle about the look of his eyes. It would take Ellen until dessert that evening to realize that his eyes were filled with excitement, conviction, purpose and passion. As long as she had known Jim, he had been a man seemingly without much direction, disengaged. His look had always been one of slight withdrawal.

She stood there mute for a split-second until Jim chimed in, "Ellen, it is great to see you! You're looking wonderful as always." And with that, he opened the screen, walked in and gave her a great big hug – something else that he didn't do ever.

The only thing that Ellen could say is, "Dean's still in the shower."

192

Jim said, "Well, I still have the limo from the airport outside so I was thinking that we could just take that to dinner. Is that ok? Did you think of a place to go or should we ask the driver?" Ellen told him about the Brown Palace and also mentioned a few other places like the Chop House if he wanted something else. Jim said, "No, No! Anything but Monica's cooking would be music to my mouth. She's an excellent cook but she only has so many things to work with on the island at this point."

Ellen said, "Oh, I thought you could get lots of stuff brought in?"

Jim shrugged. "Well, not as much lately but that's my fault."

Just then, Dean yelled down from upstairs that he was almost ready and interrupted their conversation. Jim asked Ellen how things were going and she replied, "Well, at the moment, Dean is on an oncology surgical residency rotation which means endless hours at the hospital and he loses a lot of patients to cancer which is difficult for him. Only another few weeks, though, and then he will switch to cardiology surgery which has better hours and greater success stories."

Jim just looked at her a little sideways and said, "Well, I'm sure you two can get through it together. It is hard though, I'll bet. Perhaps, sometime soon, you can have a little vacation down on the island?"

Ellen nodded vigorously – "That would be exactly what we need!" She was starting to absorb some of Jim's energy now too and soon Dean had bounced down the hallway and they had all bounced out the door into the limo. Jim had a bottle of champagne in the limo. They shared it on the way to loosen up Dean and Ellen and prepare them to get out of the rut of their life for a few hours.

The Brown Palace was a somewhat formal place which made the entrance of Jim, Dean and Ellen somewhat grand. Denver was not very formal but most of the people here were quite well-dressed, with jackets, ties and dresses the rule of the day. Jim, of course, had no idea that this was what was going to happen although he was wearing a

193

button-down shirt and pants at least. The maître d' tried to get him to put on a tie but Jim slid him a few twenties and he ignored the lack of a tie. As a result, they were seated close to the window, which suited them fine.

Everything on the menu looked incredible and Jim was dying to order absolutely everything. He ordered them three different appetizers, several salads, five entrees and several different desserts to try. He also ordered two different expensive bottles of wine.

But, in spite of the succulent food and the incredible service (which got better every time Jim ordered something more); Dean and Ellen almost forgot to taste their food because they were hanging on every word of the story that Jim was spinning for them. It shocked them for its content and surprised them due to the storyteller. They just couldn't believe that Jim had done these things. Jim was changed, as Ellen was realizing. He was passionate, fired up and fully committed to this project.

In his best Garrison Keillor impression, Jim told them the story of the turtles and the fishermen in exquisite detail. He showed them the little scars on his hands from the cuts due to the net. He demonstrated swinging the turtle head and hitting the Korean fisherman, Shaku. By the time the salads arrived, he had explained how he had kicked the fishermen off the island completely and, hopefully, for good. Then, Jim slouched in his chair and said, "That is when the real work began. These fishermen brought a great deal of essentials to the island, the most important of which was the diesel for the generators on the island. The only other source was the supply vessel from Fiji which is supposed to come by every two months but is unreliable even by island standards. So, I decided that we had to do something other than diesel and we needed to move quickly on it. Plus! Plus, I was still trying to move ahead with the plans for the resort to get jobs for everyone and bring tourists to the island. Luckily, I'd finally gotten the satellite working to communicate from the island for the internet. It's a little slow but I was able to get a hold of some people in Australia who were renewable energy developers. I also stumbled across some free software, which was very helpful. A program called "Homer" that comes out of the National Renewable Energy Lab right here in the Denver area. Anyway, working with this software and talking to these developers, I figured out a system that combines wind power, solar power and batteries for electricity and solar thermal collectors for hot water."

Ellen broke in, "What in the world are solar thermal collectors?"

Jim paused long enough to drink some wine and relaunched into his story. "Well, it's really simple, in theory. You have a large flat metal box that usually lies on the roof with a big sheet of glass on the top. Inside are black-painted, copper tubes snaking through the box that carry water. The sun shines on the box and through the glass, hits the copper tubing and heats up the water inside. A small pump moves the water around and into a hot water tank where it waits for you to use it. These systems are the cheapest way to use solar energy and we are going to need a lot of hot water for ourselves and the resort. You can also use these to heat pools and sterilize water, if necessary. Anyway, between the solar collectors for hot water, the wind and PV panels for electricity and trying to be smart about using less energy to begin with, we should never need to run the generators again and just have enough diesel for the few vehicles we have but we are also working on getting electric golf carts too. Now…"

"Wait," interrupted Dean," I'm a little drunk but what are P.V. panels?"

Jim said, "They're just big versions of the little panel on your solar calculator. They're expensive but lightweight and easy to install, which is really important for getting them to the island and installed. Actually, the world market for both wind power and solar power is growing by leaps and bounds, over twenty percent per year, and even though the wind is not blowing hard on the island, it is quite consistent and the amount of sunshine we get is very consistent every day so we can get away with a cheaper

195

system. I mean, we don't get as much sun as the Mojave Desert but we're right up there."

Ellen had been focused on her food for the first time realizing that, due to Jim's story, she was going to walk away not knowing how the food really tasted here. Hopefully, Jim would come back again so they could eat here again. Suddenly, she broke in," Wow, that sounds amazing. Is your business in town related to that project?"

Jim paused to pour more wine for everyone and said, "I've been emailing back and forth with some of the researchers here in Denver that work on this "Homer" tool for designing village renewable power systems. Anyway, I asked them if I could visit to discuss the details of the system and to double-check what the Australian developer is telling me. They were very kind and invited me to talk about my plan for the island. It seems that even though they made this tool, there are not thousands of completely renewable systems on islands and, needless to say, most of the people involved cannot just fly up to Denver at the drop of a hat. In fact, they said that they are interested in maybe sending some people down to monitor the system for awhile and take some measurements of how the system performs. Anyway, I'm totally looking forward to talking to them. I think you guys might enjoy it. Do you think you could come with me?"

Dean looked at Ellen and said, "No, Jim, I'm actually on call again tomorrow and so I can't go. Maybe Ellen would like to go?"

Ellen put her head back in the air to laugh out loud. "HA! No, I think that I'd be asleep in a matter of minutes. But, I think it is really, really great that you are doing this. I'm totally behind it even if I can't understand it. Now, if we bought a house, how much would it cost to do a wind and solar system for it? We have plenty of sun here in Denver, of course."

Jim said, "Well, too bad you cannot come because you could definitely get the answer from these people. For my system, I'm looking at probably about $ 2.6 million dollars to do the whole system and make it big enough to

196

handle the future resort hopefully. Of course, if I ever sell the island, it'll still be a good investment. It will increase the property value by at least that much because they'll not have to buy diesel anymore. But, whether or not it makes sense for you to do it for your house is a different question.

The cost of having diesel hauled out to the island is much, much higher than the cost of the natural gas pumped up to the edge of your house. The cost of natural gas and electricity in general is really cheap for a home. However, the prices have all gone up a lot in the last year. Oil has been increasing in price for a while, especially with the Iraq war and all the people in China that now want to drive cars, etc. In the near future, it may be much cheaper to install renewable power on your house here in Denver and not just in the middle of nowhere. "

Dean interrupted, noticing that Ellen was getting distracted by the next table over, "So, is that what we should do then? But we're only renting?"

Jim continued on just as fast with the answer, "The way I understand it, the best thing for a homeowner to do is to buy what they call "green power" .That means you pay a little extra every month in your normal utility bill – probably less than twenty bucks – to help the utility company cover the cost of big wind or solar power plants. Big central wind farms or solar power plants are much cheaper than having one at your own house typically. Plus, you're just writing a check – what could be simpler? Anyway, that'll be what I'm trying to verify tomorrow. It will hopefully be really worthwhile. OK, who is ready for the next course...is it dessert now?"

****

The National Renewable Energy Laboratory was originally established by Pres. Carter in the mid-1970's as a reaction to the first oil energy crisis. It is the same type of government research facility as Los Alamos or Sandia, famous for making nuclear bombs during the cold war, with one distinction. NREL only works on energy efficiency and renewable energy and doesn't do any nuclear weapons R&D like the other laboratories. NREL is comprised of about eight large laboratory buildings and several office buildings located just west of Denver on the edge of the Rocky Mountain foothills. It has a Golden CO address but isn't really in Golden. NREL employs roughly 1000 people and does research in building energy efficiency, wind power, solar energy, geothermal power, hydrogen and other transportation research. NREL conducts the cutting-edge, unprofitable work that industry won't or can't do. They get the vast majority (over 95%) of the 250 million that flows through the lab every year from the U.S. Department of Energy. Some money, especially for international projects, comes from other government agencies or large corporations.

The conference room at NREL was packed to overflowing. It was an ordinary conference room in an ordinary looking office building. The international team, who organized Jim's presentation and was responsible for the Homer village power software that Jim had used, had made the well-intentioned mistake of advertising to the entire laboratory of 1000 people and spelling out a little of Jim's background including his minor celebrity status. Other than the occasional visit from environmentally-conscious celebrities like Leonardo DiCaprio, not many celebrities visit national laboratories. Therefore, the room was absolutely packed with a combination of people interested in Jim's island power project and Jim's lottery-winning-girlfriend-death-accident notoriety.

The international group at NREL contains the staff that work to promote renewables around the world. They bring NREL's expertise to countries ranging from Russia to Zimbabwe to Brazil. They follow international energy and climate treaties for the laboratory and, in the past, have done a great deal of work on village energy development which is exactly what Jim had stumbled upon on their website. The author of the HOMER software tool, Paul Lindseth, was also in the room. About 20 to 30 people from the international team were sitting down in the middle of the room around tables – those who got to the presentation a little early or were meeting with Jim beforehand. About 100 more people stood against the walls and in the back just to get a glimpse of one of the super-rich who happened to be supportive of renewable energy.

As he began speaking, Jim realized that he was a little out of his element. Luckily, he'd worked with the Australian system developer to put together slides that talked about the current and future power needs of the island and the system combination that they had settled on. Jim had included several slides of output from the HOMER program and explained how this information had helped guide the design process for the system. But, Jim started his presentation with several pictures.

"Ladies and Gentlemen, thank you very much for this opportunity to meet with all of you today. I certainly do appreciate it and hopefully we can gain some information from each other." As the first aerial view of the island appeared, Jim continued, "I would like to introduce you to Mago Island. It is located many miles from nowhere but is a little closer than that to Australia. Officially, I bought the island almost two years ago but, in reality, it belongs to me and these people [forward to slide of the entire village population standing in the middle of the village]. The village has existed for one hundred years and currently is home to about one hundred people. Several more people have moved to the island recently because of my plans and the construction activity. I feel very responsible for these people - to provide for them. I also now feel responsible for the land of the island [as he shows a picture of the island] but also [forward to the underwater slide of the reef] for this - one of the largest lagoon ecosystems in our area of the world."

Next, Jim forwarded to a picture of the women cleaning up the carnage of the net incident and then a picture of him standing stone-faced next to a turtle carcass completely entangled in net fibers. And then, another picture, pointing down the beach in which the audience can see fish and small dolphins and more turtles stretching to the edge of the picture.

199

Jim said nothing as he slowly advanced forward through these slides but stopped on the last one only. He turned to the now completely silent room and said somewhat somberly, "I apologize for the graphic nature of the slides but I felt it necessary to convey to you the motivation for the project that we are pursuing. For many years, our island was a safe harbor and common stop for tuna fishermen. They spent money at our grocery and even more at our bar and paid us docking fees. More importantly, because they came so frequently to the island, they brought the diesel that the island needed for the few vehicles we have and the electric generators.

However, we, and by we I mean myself, the island, and the villagers, paid a terrible price on this day. The fishermen were chasing tuna into the shallow waters around the lagoon when their net got hooked on the coral. When they couldn't free it, they cut it loose. Tragically, the net floated across the lagoon. We think that the fish trapped within the net initially attracted more fish and the turtles to feed upon them and they were subsequently trapped. Fighting only made the net wrap tighter around them. The net with its trapped and dying cargo drifted to shore on the tide where I discovered it on my morning run. We attempted to rescue the wildlife that we could and that evening, I kicked the tuna fishermen off the island.

The island no longer allows fishermen to dock on the island. The only boat allowed to dock in the harbor is mine."

Jim forwarded the display to a happier picture of Jim standing on the deck of his sailboat.

"Therefore, without the fishermen, we had no good source of diesel fuel. We can get occasional shipments from Australia but it increases the cost dramatically and the shipments are not reliable. That is why I, and the rest of the island, began this project to use only energy we can generate on the island. I'm going to talk about the specifics of the project now but I want to emphasize that we're not doing this because we are hippies or just think it is cool. I am indeed starting a resort but we are not doing this to sell the

200

resort as an eco-resort. The fundamental truth is that we are doing this solely because it is the smart thing to do for our island.

I would like to get your feedback about the future cost of diesel but I think it's going to continue to increase. The developer and I figure that if the cost of diesel were to double in the next twenty years, this project will be the cheapest option. And, because we're using wind turbines and PV primarily, we can stage the project development and installation, as the load for the island grows, so we don't have to buy it all now. Combined with a lot of energy efficiency projects, we're very excited about the prospects for this project being:

the ecologically right thing to do,
the ethically right thing to do,
and the economically right thing to do.

OK, let's get into the details of the project and I'd like to start by giving some statistics about our resource followed by how we came up with the mix between wind and solar and storage. I would be happy to answer questions at the end."

And so Jim continued describing the system that he and the developer had come up with for the island. He went through the general design of the system and then the specific reasoning for selecting Bergey wind towers instead of something else and so forth. He explained the real problem issues that he and the developer had figured out and talked about the areas where he felt NREL or others could help the island-power developer.

"Specifically", Jim said, "What we, island owners and resort developers need, are more pre-designed systems - kits. In looking at the resource data, a lot of us are dealing with roughly similar weather patterns. I have an engineering background but most people don't and what we need are systems off the shelf that we can just put in an order for. People buy diesel generators because they only have to order one big item and have electricians come out for a few days to wire them up and lay out a basic grid and then the islanders can do the rest. These renewable systems require a lot more expertise especially with a hybrid system and the maintenance requires a lot of special knowledge that my staff doesn't have."

Jim concluded his presentation with another picture. This one was of a view from the cliff and what looked like a concrete slab. He said, "This is the first step towards the future of our island. This is the slab for our first bungalow. All you can see now is the layout for the radiant floor heating for the cool nights or stormy weather we occasionally have. Eventually, we will have fifteen to twenty bungalows large enough for a couple or a small family to get away from everything.

Our future is not making rum like the previous owners tried to do.

Our future is not pandering to fishermen.

Our future is using our resources in a profitable and sustainable way. That is our future.

Thank you."

As Jim stopped talking, there was a moment of silence. Suddenly, someone tucked into the crowd in the back started to clap. Within moments, the entire room was clapping. And soon, even the people who had chairs were standing and applauding. Jim stood in the front and to his surprise he started to get a little choked up. He looked back at the picture behind him and the faces in front of him and it suddenly amazed him at how far he had come. From the man who spent his evenings watching sports and eating pizza to a man responsible for the wellbeing of an entire community and attempting projects on a scale that he would have never dreamed of back then.

Finally, Dr. Bill Weston, the director of the international team and typically a reserved manager, stepped forward still clapping and looking very impressed by the presentation. He attempted to quiet the crowd. Jim took a deep breath and bowed to the crowd who started cheering again. Finally, Bill was able to say to Jim in front of everyone, "Jim, I think it's evident that everyone here is very, very excited about your presentation and your project. I think that we have gained more than you out of this exchange. It isn't often that we get such a visual and objective reminder of the progress we are trying to facilitate. Thank you for reminding us that real people get real results out of the work that we do."

Dr. Weston turned to the crowd and said, "We're now going to have some more detailed discussions about the project and we'll be trying to tweak the whole design a little bit based on the collective experience of the international team. Anyone is welcome to stay and listen and participate. We'll also be having a reception at 5:30 for Mr. Wells over in the Visitor Center."

With that, most of the audience filed out of the room and went back to their own research. Many of them stopped to say hello to Jim and thank him for his speech. They seemed very impressed and Jim really appreciated their kind words and support.

The rest of the afternoon wound up being a very detailed discussion of Jim's system and how to optimize it further. In the end, Jim left feeling like his design had been pretty good initially and realized why his designer in Australia was world-renowned; he knew his stuff. Jim also impressed himself that he knew his system so well. He thought momentarily about how he used to sit in his mansion on Lake Mendota in Madison and watch movies all day long. Now, he lived on an island and hadn't watched TV for months. He realized that he had replaced all that wasted time with learning about how to make this island system work. Because he had to do it.

The afternoon consisted of several technical presentations and discussions. Jim was reminded he lived on an island when Kelli Nelson stood up to give her presentation. While she went through PowerPoint describing a variety of village projects in Central America and Eastern Africa, Jim realized he was just staring at her legs which extended intriguingly from underneath her skirt and became fixated on the fact that her professional blue button-down blouse was still revealing enough to show there was more that could be revealed – creating an incredibly attractive "known unknown".

Jim shook his head a little to clear these unprofessional thoughts from his brain but the desire to speak with her alone remained. And, as he tuned back into what she was saying, he realized that it was important. She was speaking about all these other villages which had also installed these systems. NREL had gone in and done several studies about the ups and downs of all the villages and how their systems performed over time. Kelli herself had been onsite with many of these systems. Considering Jim's immediately preceding series of thoughts about her body, his following comment may not have been completely focused on the betterment of the village. He said, "So, how do I get you to come down and study our system on an ongoing basis?"

She smiled at him and responded, "We were hoping you would ask. The Department of Energy has some money for this but they would like to cost-share this with the hosting village, if possible. And, as soon as you finish your exclusive resort, I'd make a point of putting your island on the schedule."

Jim smiled broadly. "Well, we can definitely put you up for free in the resort whenever you would like to come down, and I can pay part of your labor time as well. The data and advertising via publications alone would be worth the cost." And so it begins, Jim thought. And he smiled, realizing that another pathway through life had opened for him to explore.

The reception at the end of the day was packed. It was at the NREL Visitor Center, which is the only part of the laboratory normally open to the public. It sits at the edge of the Laboratory campus and is a good example of green buildings that use a lot of natural light during the day. It contains a variety of demonstration and educational displays both for school kids and visiting politicians and dignitaries. It was a very inviting building with a large open space for

204

receptions right in the middle. Jim had funded a thank you spread of food and beverages for everyone. He had made sure that the organizers had invited the entire laboratory to this and it seemed that many of them were stopping by to see and meet him. He actually had an impromptu question and answer period and quickly recapped his presentation again and a further discussion about the island and the project. Someone asked him about the whole matter with Sable but he declined to say anything more than, "Well, there was an accident and my very good friend died as a result. Other than that, it's a personal issue."

Dean and Ellen stumbled in about 6:30 or so to say hello. They hadn't ever visited NREL so several staff members showed them around the Visitor's Center while Jim answered more questions about his life and his project. Jim paid particular attention to any questions asked by Ms. Nelson and, not being able to stop himself, asked her a few questions of his own including what her husband thought of all her traveling (to which she replied, "I'm not married but my neighbor is really great about watching my dog.").

The reception started to end around 7:30 and so Dean and Ellen and Jim decided to get some dinner. They invited the remaining half dozen people to come along across the road to the largest mall in Colorado. A mall isn't normally very interesting but this one had a great brewpub called the "Yard House" with over 100 beers on tap and good food to go along with the beer. Jim thought later that the dinner conversation was probably the most interesting because the NREL people seemed less constrained by their official position and the beer lubricated their attitudes. The discussion was wide-ranging especially with the presence of Dean and Ellen who knew almost nothing about renewables. They spoke about how important renewables were going to be in the future as natural gas and oil were getting ever more expensive. Jim didn't realize it but the general consensus was that the world was moving quickly to a future in which the cheap-to-extract oil and gas were going to run low and thereby get more and more expensive. If fossil fuels get even twice as expensive, then renewables need to be ready to be used extensively throughout the country and the world. As Dr. Weston leaned over and told him while they waited for the onion rings, "Most people think we're working to change the country's energy picture here at NREL. And, we are … in many ways. But, our larger role is working for change management. Because, as you're a prime example, change is coming. It's just a question of how fast, and if we have alternatives that are ready to switch to when it happens."

Jim was able to sit next to Kelli, who filled his ear full of more information. He hung on every word like a rockclimber. He asked her, "Why do you think the United States is so far behind Europe and Asia in valuing renewables?"

She said, "Good question, Jim. I think that the US is unique in its policies that emphasize low prices and economic growth over a higher price on pollution and a greater value on sustainability and a long-term view. In Europe, the average citizen could easily see the impact of pollution. In the US, it's easier to keep pollution somewhere else, especially if one has money. The communities immediately downstream of the northeastern coal-burning power plants are poor communities. Robust businesses left these towns long ago, leaving low-paying jobs. Not to mention that much of the renewable power is going to be wind which is the most economical option and is even the cheapest power option on a straight cost basis. And, much of the best wind locations are in rural areas that have been losing agricultural jobs for a long time. The positive side of the American system is that the technologies really need to stand on their own economic feet when they are finally implemented. People are coming around though, I think."

Jim asked Kelli, "So, do you guys think that the climate-disaster movie, "The Day After Tomorrow" is really possible? Big, sudden climate shifts?"

She replied, "Well, that's just a movie, of course. I guess it could happen. But, what are worse are the things that are happening that we don't even know about until it's too late. Carbon dioxide has been building up in the atmosphere for years and the real concern is that what we have already set in motion cannot be reversed and we just have to sit and try to survive whatever changes happen."

And it went on and on. The pitchers of beer seemingly emptied themselves. People slowly drifted off to bed while others continued talking, explaining and educating. Dean and Ellen were both converted to being big supporters of renewable energy.

Chapter 16: Good Conversation

Marine mammals cannot communicate visually underwater except at shallow depths. Therefore, they communicate via sounds – which travel five times faster in water than air. Dolphins make clicking noises for determine where they are and whistle to each other for communication. Humpback whales sing hours-long songs. Killer whale pods can be indentified by their dialects. But, most impressively, the Blue and Fin whales create low-frequency (sub audible) booms that can be picked up as far as 2000 miles away. If one could listen to the sounds under the ocean as easily as above, one would hear a thousand conversations from near and far.

Jim awoke with a nasty headache and it took him a few minutes to realize that he was sleeping on Dean and Ellen's couch. The evening before came back to him like something of a dream. As he walked it through in his mind, he realized that the evening had ended rather abruptly with Dean and Ellen hauling him out of the Yard House brewpub and into their car. He had been talking to Kelli when he suddenly just fell asleep in his chair. Damn altitude. Always gets in the way when one is trying to talk to the first non-islander woman that one has met in over a year. Oh well, Jim thought, "I have a lot to do and I am not planning to be in Denver more than a few days."

Jim realized that he had never really looked around before in the few times that he had been at Ellen and Dean's house. As he laid there trying not to be awake, Jim realized first that Ellen had patched and slip-covered the furniture pieces that were left over from when Jim and Dean had lived together but the old fabric from underneath still peeked out from the bottom. Then, Jim noticed that there were some cracks in the plaster and some stains on the carpet, not to mention a couple cracks in the windows. He wondered how he hadn't noticed any of this stuff before. Suddenly, he realized something and sat straight up on the couch which immediately gave him a headache and so he lay back down again and closed his eyes. He laid there with his eyes closed and contemplated the fact that he had just realized: whenever he got together with Ellen and Dean, the conversation and really the whole visit revolved around him, his winnings, his love life, his island and now his resort and energy project. He felt awful. He hadn't tried to do that and he had never even realized it along the way. He thought through all the times that he had been with them, especially after they left Madison. Finally, he heard a voice coming from above him and opened his eyes to see Ellen standing over him. He opened his eyes but didn't lift up his head yet. She looked down at him and grinned, "Hey, Mr. Renewable Energy, not very energetic this morning, are you?"

He responded, "Ahhhhhhhh...shuuuuush...softly now".

She chuckled. "Open your eyes," she said. "I brought you a tall glass of water which I want you to drink first and then I brought you a cup of coffee. You still drink coffee, don't you, Island boy?"

He slowly sat up on the couch while keeping his eyes half shut and looked at Ellen. Without saying a word, he smiled up at her and took the glass of water. As he started drinking, he realized that the altitude had gotten to him again and he ended up gulping down the water. Damn altitude. She went to get him another glass of water and he took a small sip of the coffee. He realized that the coffee he had been getting on the island was nothing close to good coffee. He hazely wondered if they could grow their own beans on the island – or if perhaps he could get Starbucks to sponsor his resort coffeeshop someday. He yelled (which was a mistake) out to Ellen in the kitchen, "This coffee is great! Oh, my head! What brand is it?"

He heard her chuckling and she said, "Well, it is the incredibly good but inexpensive Peaberry's coffee, Mr. Castaway! I get it at the grocery store." She wandered back into the living room to see him looking down into his coffee cup as if unable to believe that something good could be in there as if his eyes would give validation to his tastebuds.

He said, "What time is it?"

"Just about ten."

"Hey. You should be at work by now, shouldn't you? I mean, isn't it Wednesday today?"

Ellen replied, "Well, I decided to be a nurse at home today and take care of you a little bit. It would be bad if Mr. Renewables died on our couch before he was able to complete his mission to save the world - one tropical paradise at a time."

Jim started to shake his head and chuckle as he hazily recalled a rather loud declaration at the bar during which he declared renewable energy to be his mission. "Hey, you shouldn't kick a man when he's down you know."

Then, he stopped talking and reminded himself of what was really making him sick this morning and he started, "Ellen, I realized this morning that I haven't been very good, actually bad, at listening to what you and Dean are up to when I'm not around. Everything is about me and what is going on with me and I'm so sorry about that. I want to hear about you and Dean now. For example, did you guys have a good time last night?"

Ellen sat there for a minute and looked kind of surprised and looked out the window before turning back to face Jim. "Thanks for saying that, Jim. That's very sweet. The truth of the matter is that we are always happy when you come and we're excited about your life because it gives us something else to think about besides our lives. Frankly, our lives are not all that great at the moment. I mean, nothing specific is wrong...but Dean is always, always at the hospital. He's always, always tired. He really tries to not be

210

cranky and short but it happens. We haven't had a chance to make a group of friends here in Denver yet, which is another reason why we love it when you come to visit."

She handed him the new glass of water in a large blue tumbler. She continued, "I think that we can make it, but some days, I am just not sure. It is only another two years like this and then he should have more time and better hours. I guess that being a resident is supposed to suck. We both knew that, but it just takes so damn long and it seems endless when you're in the middle of it. My work is going pretty well but the people I work with all have worked together for a long time. It's going to take awhile to get in their inner circle.

We make all the rent payments and pay the bills but we don't have enough extra to buy a 4x4 truck, for example, which would be really great for getting up in the mountains on the days when Dean is free to get away. Anyway, It's just hard but it's all supposedly normal."

And she paused for a second looking into her coffee cup, obviously wondering what else to tell Jim. Then, she stood up rather forcefully and continued, "But, that's what makes it so great when you come. You make us feel special again and get us out of our rut. Dean will stop at nothing to leave work early and come home to be with you. Bottom line: We like being part of your fairy tale. It reminds us of those times in Madison and reminds us of what our life might be like someday."

Jim just sat there for a few seconds. The richest man in Denver was sitting there enjoying his grocery store coffee and contemplating Ellen's words. Finally, he said, "Well, I'm sorry that things are hard for you both at the moment. I've never seen two people more in love than you guys so I'm very confident you can make it. And, I am very, very happy that you guys are part of my fairy tale. Actually, at times it feels more like a nightmare and I'm so glad to have you guys to lean on when that happens."

Ellen said, "You can lean on us at anytime. Speaking of leaning on me, do you want to lean on me into the kitchen for some breakfast?"

Jim said, "Sure, that sounds like a good idea. Wait, what are you making?"

Ellen said, "How about my famous cinnamon, apple, oatmeal pancakes?"

He said, "I think I can keep those down. Actually, my stomach is fine. Just my head hurts from this altitude and the severe lack of water in this country!"

As they settled down at the little two person table in the kitchen, Jim realized that it was a good thing Dean wasn't here or they wouldn't all fit at the table. Ellen started making the pancakes and soon the kitchen was filled with the smell of cinnamon and apples. It was small but tidy and it looked like they had spent some time painting some neutral yellow paint over whatever imaginably horrid color was on the kitchen walls and cabinets previously. It was actually very cozy.

Ellen said, "Hey, so now that I told you all the intimate details of our lives, what's going on with you..." and she looked over her shoulder to actually look at him when she said, " on the inside. What's going on inside of you right now?"

Jim said, "Hey, we are supposed to NOT be talking about me but rather you and Dean!"

Ellen turned away from where she was making pancake batter to look at Jim sitting at the table, gave him a quick shake of the head and said "No, I mean it. Where are you at?"

Jim paused for a long while staring into his coffee and playing with the placemat in front of him. Finally, he said, "You know what? Everything is totally weird – but in a good way. For the first time in as long as I can remember, I have a purpose and I have real responsibilities. And, more importantly, I like it. I really care about those people on the island, and the water and the land. You know, I went there just to get away from everything...again. But, I really think that I found something special for me there. I'm really enjoying it. But, on the other hand, it gets a little lonely being the only white American on the island. I am getting to know a bunch of the islanders more than just superficially and now that they think I'm really doing things for the island, they're less wary of me."

Ellen broke in," OK, I don't want to interrupt but if you could grab plates out of the cupboard, I think we'll be having the first pancakes pretty soon."

As Jim started setting two spots at the table, he continued, "These plates? Anyway, what I was saying was that sometimes it would be good just to talk to someone about baseball or basketball or watch Seinfeld reruns with someone. I do have internet and satellite TV now but Maria, the maid, isn't much in the way of company. On the flip side, I haven't gotten so much accomplished in such a short period of time before in my life! I'm learning tons of new stuff and really feel like I can make a difference, on the island at least. "

And with that, Ellen dropped the first two pancakes on their plates and started two more.

Between forkfuls and groans of appreciation, Jim said, "I don't know if Dean told you this, but in college, I used to be a pretty active environmentalist but I dropped it at the end of college, for several reasons I guess, but partly because it didn't seem like it was making any difference. People were still buying bigger and bigger cars, the rivers were still polluted and the government didn't seem at all able to do much of anything even when it tried. Now, I feel like there is something very immediate and tangible that I can do for these specific people. No offense, but in some ways, they're my whole world. I think that makes it a lot easier to get stuff done when you can see the immediate results in your own community. Of course, some days I think the whole thing is just silly and crazy and I should just buy a place in Malibu and live happily ever after with the other rich folk. Anyway, what do you think? You've been giving me crap about renewables since I woke up but I figured that was more about what I said last night."

Ellen walked across the room, dropped two more pancakes on the plates and then bent over and gave Jim a great big hug, "Thanks Jim. That was the most serious conversation we have ever had and I appreciate that. As for what I think, I think that you've really started to take ownership of your world, which is something that no one in Malibu gets to do. In fact, I misjudged you before because you didn't seem to care about much besides yourself since I met you."

Jim said, "Well, gee, I didn't mean to make you all mushy, but you asked! Funny, you only met me on the day I won the lottery so it would have been interesting to have known you before that. Of course, my life was pretty boring before that happened though. Now, are there going to be more pancakes coming? These are delicious. More syrup too, when you get a chance."

And more pancakes came off the griddle and more coffee was brewed and more orange juice was poured and the two of them spent the morning at the kitchen table talking about the island and med school and Ellen's job – what she liked and what she didn't like about it. Sometimes in life, everything comes together and the setting is just right for the perfect conversation. It can happen in a kitchen or on the street or in bed or at the top of a mountain peak. It can happen at any time of day. If you try to plan it, it seems forced and it doesn't work. You can try not to plan it and it doesn't happen. But, when it does, you need to talk until the talking is done and the moment is over. Jim and Ellen did that, sitting on the hard benches in the kitchen – at first eating pancakes and eventually just nursing lukewarm coffee until it worked its way to the end.

Finally, breakfast had to end. Ellen couldn't skip the whole day at work and Jim needed to check in on his email and phone messages. Ellen let him use their computer in the second bedroom and she left for work assuring him that she would be home by six and hoped he would be available for dinner again. He said, "Sure; that sounds great" and she left. Two seconds later and she would have heard a huge curse word boom through the house as Jim reacted to the email that he got:

214

Dear Jim,

Problems on the island. We paid the islanders their first paycheck yesterday (three days after you left) and none of the island workers have done any work since that moment. They are either spending all their money in the bar or are making some kind of huge feast. Nixon cannot get them to do anything either, no matter how much he coaxes and cajoles.

I don't want to give up on having them work on the project but I am just a few days away from calling in my own people and cutting the islanders out of the project. Some of them were more trouble than they were worth to begin with, but this is ridiculous.

The project has stopped until this is resolved or I bring in more guys. I am still billing you to pay my guys for sitting out on the island, that are already there. You can reach me at the Auckland office, as normal. Please respond one way or the other as soon as you can.

Mark

Mark Smithson
Smithson Energy LLC

With that, Jim made a couple of quick phone calls to Auckland (which isn't all that different in the number of hours difference – just in the day), sent a few emails, wrote Ellen and Dean a quick note and headed for the airport. He made one stop along the way though.

Later that night, Dean hussled to get home at six and Ellen arrived home just after him. They were somewhat puzzled that Jim wasn't there. Then, they saw the note on the kitchen table:

Dean and Ellen,

Thanks as always for the hospitality. You're my port in a storm and my link to normality. I got an email that the islanders are all drunk and not working for the contractor. As time is of the essence with the contractor on the clock, I am headed back out there tonight. I will email when I get there. I quickly made a reservation at the Chop House in Denver for you and under this note is money for you guys to have a dinner, unfortunately, without me

Sorry I had to leave so quickly.

Will be back as soon as I can!!

Jim

The stop that Jim made on the way out of town was to get Dean and Ellen a present. A few days later, Ellen came home to find a man sitting outside their house in a brand new Toyota Hybrid Highlander – the most fuel-efficient SUV on the market. The man explained that Jim had stopped by the store and had written a check for the car, which was to be delivered to them, at this address, as a surprise. He gave her the keys, the title and gave her a tour of the car and made sure she understood about it's hybrid features. After an hour or so, when they were done he gave her a note from Jim that said:

Surprise!!! You guys will definitely make it through this damn residency thing if I can do anything about it!! Jim

Chapter 17: Coming Home

In many ways, the Old Testament of the Bible is a testament to impatience. From Adam to the Israelites, everyone was impatient with God and his timeframe. They wanted what they wanted when they wanted it and if it seemed like God or his emissaries weren't getting around to it fast enough, they tried to take it a little faster. When Adam wanted to be more than what he was, he and Eve ate the apple. When the Israelite kings wanted to become small Gods in their own right, God had to send prophets and judges to get them all back on track. Even while Moses was up on Mount Ararat getting the ten commandments from God, the Israelites were making little golden Gods to worship because they couldn't wait for Moses to get back without panicking.

Jim was no Bible scholar but he thought about this as he quickly but still slowly traveled back to the island. When he had left, he had felt like everything was going smoothly. Everyone had been excited about the project. It seemed as if everyone was behind him on the new venture. But now, it seemed that everyone had gone round the bend. On the phone, the contractor said that even the individuals who had not started to shirk their duty were pressured into leaving their jobs as well, by the other islanders. Not to mention that the impression that the contractor had given him was that there was a real orgy of drunkenness occurring on the island.

Jim had replied to the contractor's message asking if it would be possible to pay the islanders at the end of each day. Jim also thought that everyone might be better off if he explained to them about saving for the future and to buy things or even about owning property. Anything but ruining their livers and delaying the project that will only improve their lives. Maybe, thought Jim, they don't want their lives improved or they think this project is just for me. I will have to change that. And so Jim spent the four different flights back not watching the movie but rather drafting a new plan.

As the little plane circled the island, Jim was shocked by the changes. Several towers were sticking out of the former sugar field in the center of the island and he could see a crane slowly raising another section of tower. He could also see a large section of ground that had been cleared for the photovoltaic array which would also be mounted. Jim knew that at the edge of town a small building was being built to house all the controls and electronics for the entire island's electrical grid but he couldn't see much of that. As the plane continued to circle, he saw a large group of people on the beach with a large fire burning. When they saw the plane, they started to jump up and down. The pilot turned to Jim and said, "So, seems like someone heard you were coming home, Jimbo. Shall I set down right in front of them?"

Jim was suddenly angry that, while nothing was seemingly happening on the project, the islanders had created a huge beach party for him. "Setting down right on top of them would be even better." Then, he realized that the islanders were going down this road to development for the first time – because of him and he settled down some. He said, "Of course, right in front of them would be great. Actually, can you buzz them first for fun? Not too low, just a little exciting?"

The island pilots in this part of the world didn't feel very constrained usually by the words "prudent" and "regulations" (neither of which would allow him to buzz the villagers) so down they went and the pilot ran up the beach about 50 feet in the air, right above the villagers. There was a combination of cheers and fears resulting in a patchwork of

219

individuals jumping up and down or trying to crawl under the beach. Jim smiled broadly as the pilot settled into the relatively calm waters here on the leeward side of the island and beached the seaplane on the shore.

He said, "Jim, you gotta get them to build a plane dock if you ever want Paris Hilton to come here!"

Jim replied as he started to jump into the shallow water and get some help to unload the various supplies and luggage, "Yeap, you're right, but there are a few things to get done first – like getting the lights on!"

And with the next step, Jim was ashore and back on the island. Again now, it was like the rest of the world was millions of miles away once he stepped off the plane. However, when he'd arrived here the last time, he'd come to harvest what the island had to offer in relaxation, privacy and tranquility. Now, he came back to a burden of responsibility and leadership which he unfortunately had to bear on his own, or so it seemed.

The islanders were very jubilant that he was back. Several of the older boys ran to grab everything for him off the plane and carry it to shore. Most of it would go directly to his house but he had them set one very special cardboard box, very carefully, on the beach and stand guard over it so that no one could step on it. Meanwhile, Jim greeted all of the village elders as he walked up the beach.

He got to Nixon about the same time as the seaplane was pushed back into the surf and was revving his engines to take off forcing Jim to lean close to Nixon's ear to be heard. At first, Nixon failed to look up at him at all but kept his eyes on Jim's feet.

Jim leaned into his ear and said, "Nixon, what do you say happened?" wanting to corroborate the contractors story.

Nixon spoke into Jim's shirt so no one could hear and in very quick sentences said, "The people got their checks and then went crazy with all the money. They all got drunk. I couldn't get them back to work. Only when they heard that you were arriving today did they stop drinking and put together this party. They know you like a good party. I'm sorry to have failed you, sir."

Jim leaned in again and said, "Don't blame yourself Nixon. This is my fault and the contractors fault for not handling the money in a proper way. You couldn't stop this and I didn't expect you to. You are my best help and I need you now more than ever. Put your chin up and help me lead these people back into line. Will you do that?"

Nixon looked Jim in the eye and smiled slightly, "Yes, I can do that."

Jim nodded, "Great. By the way, I picked up something in Australia that I think will help keep them motivated."

And, with that, Nixon did pick his head up off his chest and squared his jaw. He looked Jim in the face and said, "You can count on me, boss."

Jim found a rock upon the beach and stood up tall on it and raised his hand. In the island elder meetings that he had been too, Jack the bartender raised his hand when he wanted to start the meeting and get everyone to stop talking. So, Jim raised his fist into the air and looked out across the villagers until they all stopped talking and faced him. Nixon came forward to translate for anyone who couldn't speak English very well.

Jim began nicely, "Thank you for the wonderful reception. That means a great deal to me. As always, I feel very welcome and at home here on the island. The fact that you honor me so makes me want to work hard to make the life on this island better for all of us. Please, give yourselves a hand for creating such a nice welcome home party." And Jim clapped and several of the villagers clapped as well.

Jim started to get serious now and they were not perhaps expecting the next set of sentences. "This great party cannot change the fact that you all have dishonored me and, more importantly, yourselves and the community by not doing your work anymore after you received your checks." Jim paused for a few seconds to let those words sink in and for the many who didn't understand English to have it translated for them. He finally continued, "The

221

contractor wrote to me in America and said that you were not working. He says that you've been drinking ever since you got the money for working. "

"This is not good for the island! If the project falls behind, it will take longer for us to get electricity
…and longer to get the resort started
... and longer to get real jobs for everyone
Every day we delay means it will be longer to get a good schoolteacher
…and longer to get everyone a real house
…and longer to save money for the future
…and longer before more people come to live on the island for work.

I was disappointed and embarrassed that I had to come home to try and get you all to go back to work! So, from now on, I'm going to change a few things to keep this from happening again:

Number 1: Jack will stop selling alcohol to people who are obviously drunk."

Jim paused as a few groans rose from the crowd but he continued, " I know this seems like it should only be a rule for drunken fishermen but it will be better for everyone. And also, no one can buy any alcohol at all for the next two weeks at least. From what I hear, that shouldn't be a problem as you have all drunk everything already.

Number 2: Jack will not sell anyone more than one bottle of hard alcohol or 6 beers per day. We don't want anyone to be drunk all the time.

Number 3: Everyone who works will get paid, in cash, at the end of every day. If you want, Nixon and I are going to start a bank so that you can keep your money somewhere safe. I heard that some money was stolen and that wouldn't happen if most of your money was in the bank. Also, if you keep your money in the bank and don't spend it right away, you'll have more money when you do decide to use it later. You can ask myself or Nixon questions about the bank.

Number 4: Anyone who does not work on a day doesn't get paid. If you are sick or need to do something else, tell the contractor the day before. If you continue not to work, you may not be able to get a job in the resort once it opens. We only want hard workers that we can depend on to work at the resort.

OK? Does everyone see that these rules are for the best? For everyone's own good? Sometime in the future, I and the elders will probably change the rules but for now, these are the new rules."

Jim looked around the crowd and everyone was looking down at the ground and exchanging glances with the people around them. Jim realized they were quite embarrassed about being so drunk and making Jim upset. Anyway, no one protested so Jim continued:

"OK, now some fun changes!

New rule number 5! Every week, the contractor's men will vote on who the best island worker is. That person, and a guest that they choose, will get to have dinner with me that night. We'll eat and then we can watch a movie on my television."

With that statement, there was a quiet that fell across the crowd. Only a very few of them had ever been in the Owner's mansion and only Nixon and Maria had ever watched TV with Jim. This was something quite strange for them and Jim knew it. However, he felt that this would give them an opportunity to get to know him as a person and build a little bit of a world-view for them via the movies and television.

Frankly, Jim had not let them watch TV because he didn't want them all to see the outside world and leave. But, with a resort and the other people who were coming to the island, the outside world was coming to them.

He continued, "Rule Number 6: Every week, one of the worker teams – including both islanders and contractor's men – will be selected to go out on the sailboat with me. This will happen on either Saturday or Sunday after church depending on the weather.

Finally, Number 7, which is not a rule but a promise. When the energy project is finished and we have all the electricity we can use, I'll put the contents of this box up in the bar for everyone to watch." The boys lifted up the box, Jim opened it and pulled out a brand new 42" LCD flat screen TV and raised it over his head. "This, my friends, is a new television. Everyone will be able to come and watch football or movies or other things about the world on this television. However, not before the project is complete. And, there'll be several more surprises when the resort is finished. Enough surprises for everyone."

These rules were even more of a surprise. Suddenly, the islanders were crazy with the desire to work. They were not even sure what the TV would do for them but they knew they wanted to watch it. They seemed desperate to know what lay beyond the shoreline of this island; most had never been anywhere else.

Jim concluded, "I want you to know that I am not building this energy system for myself. I could leave the island whenever I want and never come back and eventually sell the island to another owner. You could all stay here just getting by and buying diesel and Nixon and the elders could probably keep things running.

I think that we can do better! I think we can have an island where people have jobs that they love. I think we can have an island where the lagoon and the fish are the same for many more generations. I think we can have an island where we bring other people, tourists, the happiness that they cannot find in their normal lives. I want an island where you are so well-paid that you can move away, if you want, but so happy that you stay here. I want an island where your children are educated and able to read and write in English and where you know enough about the rest of the world to know how great things are here. I may go away when I have to but I am always coming back. You need to know that as well. So, will you join me?"

And he paused and they said nothing.

He repeated, "Will you join me in making this an island we are all proud to live on?"

Finally, someone caught on and yelled "Yes!" from the back. A split second later, they all yelled "Yes!"

Jim continued, "Will you join me in making an island that doesn't need the help of anyone?"

"Yes!"

"Will you join me in getting a job for everyone on the island?"

"Yes!"

"Will you join me?" "Yes!"

"Will you really join me?" "Yes!"

"Thank you. Now, let's have a party to the future of the island!" And so the feast began and the eating and drinking commenced. And they all sat in a circle and a few of the women volunteered to bring food and drink to everyone else. And so it continued. And, as the eating continued, the drinking was more minimal. Jim led the way by only drinking one beer and then a bottled water.

Jim sat back and looked around the circle. He thought, "This will be hard but at least we aren't going backwards anymore."

After the party, Jim went to visit the contractor's men who were all staying in the visitors' bunkhouse up by the owner's mansion. They were happy to see him and hoped he could get this project moving again. Their leader was named Jamison and he walked up to Jim away from the circle of men talking and playing cards. "Jim, glad to see you back here again so quickly. Certainly hope that you can get this project going again."

Jim smiled, "well, I certainly hope so. I brought back some carrots and some sticks. I just was on the beach with everyone and we made some new rules about limiting alcohol sales. I also made some incentives. For example, the best performers get to go out on the sailboat once a week. Plus, everyone gets paid every day so there isn't a big paycheck that they can dump into a bottle. Oh, and I'm setting up a bank."

Jamison was a no-nonsense construction manager with a military background. He didn't believe in carrots and sticks but only in everyone doing what they are told. He gave Jim a half-smile and cocked his sunbaked, buzzcut head to the side. "Well, I hope it helps. I have doubts about some simple treats getting those folks to shape up but we'll give it a try. Frankly, I'm worried about trying to pay all these guys every day. Sounds like it could take an hour every day."

Jim nodded, "OK, I'll take care of paying them based on what you say. I'm hoping we can just do that for a week or two and get everyone signed up for the bank quickly. If it doesn't work, we'll do something else."

Jim turned to the whole group of men who were now listening, "I want to apologize for the islanders. I'm hoping that we can get back on track first thing in the morning. I'd like to apologize additionally by inviting you all up to the house for dinner and perhaps some Playstation or pool or something? Would you be interested."

They all jumpedup at the chance to do something besides sit around and play cards. As they all moved off towards Jim's house, Jamison whispered in his ear, "Well, it's your dime. Frankly, I'd just bring in more of my own boys to get this job knocked out. Let me know if you change your mind."

Jim grinned, "Oh, I appreciate that but I've got faith that it will work out now."

And so the weeks and months continued as both the renewable power system and the first phase of the resort, including six luxury bungalows and the spa center, were built. By day, Jim was out watching the construction or talking to Jamison and his contractors. Jim was walking up and talking to all the islander workers and off-island workers - cajoling them and encouraging them no matter what they were doing. Often, the contractor complained that the islanders were so unskilled, they were more trouble than they were worth. However, Jim kept reminding him that the more the islanders learn about the various systems, especially the wind systems, the fewer times the contractor might have to come to fix something. Jamison remained unimpressed. By night, Jim was entertaining the contractor's men at his house or the islanders who won the employee of the week award or both.

Chapter 18: Look Who's Coming to Dinner

Pheromones are chemicals secreted by all animals. Strange chemical compounds that are then detected in the nostrils of another animal. Studies show that when certain females emit the proper pheromones, the male of the species is overcome by feeling of attraction for the female. Evolutionarily, the pheromones are seem to help create couples with a high likelihood of raising offspring that then reproduce again. Of course, for humans, these chemicals are just one of many factors in an incredibly complex and seemingly capricious process that brings men and women together. In the end, most people feel that it's more about luck than any chemicals or science.

     Jim was watching the construction of the wind turbine towers just up from the beach on the windy side of the island. They were putting up five wind turbines, all in a line. The wind was very consistent on the island much of the year so they were able to put the turbines closer together by assuming that typically the wind would come from across the ocean. Sure, there were storms and times of the year when the wind actually did blow from a different direction but this allowed the wind turbines to be put closer together and not impinge on the rest of the island as much. Plus, there was room for expansion this way – if the island needed more power in the future. Jim would actually have liked to put them up out in the ocean itself but those turbines cost a lot more and would be harder to service.

However, even as Jim was watching the tower construction, his eyes kept scanning the sky. Kelli Nelson was supposed to arrive today from NREL for her first of many visits hopefully to install monitoring equipment and start collecting information and data on the project. Jim found himself involuntarily getting excited about her visit to the point of tapping his finger on the chair he was sitting on – and glancing into the sky. Finally, he realized what he was doing and shook his head to clear the thought. "She's just coming for work," he reminded himself. He chuckled to himself again. "It's like that old Brad Pitt movie – Legends of the Fall – where all the brothers fall in love with the same woman. The only woman seemingly in Montana." He chuckled again.

Just as they were getting close to finished up the second tower structure, he heard the plane on the horizon. He tried to make it look like he was just bored with watching the tower construction as he slowly left his chair, grabbed his mountain bike and started riding like a bat out of hell towards the landing area by the lagoon. He burst onto the beach just as the plane was coasting in to beach itself lightly on the shore. Down the beach a few hundred yards, they could see where the construction team had started to put in pilings for the real dock that would be there soon. But, at the moment, Kelli still had to jump into the shallow water from the plane while several of the village boys had raced down to help with luggage when they saw the plane coming in.

Jim walked up to Kelli as she jumped ashore and said, "Welcome to the island, Kelli. I'm so glad you made it."

Kelli stood there looking down at her now-soaking tennis shoes and the jeans that were now half wet and said. "Well, it serves me right for wearing something other than a swimsuit at a resort, doesn't it."

Jim smiled as reveled in the sight of the first attractive woman that was his peer, since he had flown back

230

from Denver, "Yeah, but you never know when the temperature is going to drop below 80."

As they followed the boys up the beach with all of Kelli's luggage and equipment, Kelli said, "I'm glad to be here. Thanks for the invitation and the funding, Mr. Wells."

Jim coughed in astonishment. "What? Mr. Wells? Call me Jim. Sure, I'm paying the bills but you and NREL are the one's doing me a favor. I certainly appreciate all the help and hints that you guys have given me."

Kelli said, "It was our pleasure. Plus, everyone wants to see if they can get a trip down here. You have a project filled with perks as far as we are concerned. Most government projects are devoid of perks."

Jim invited Kelli to stay at his house. Although one might think otherwise, his motives were purely logistical. The bunkhouse and servants quarters were all filled by contractors, whom he didn't want to leave Kelli alone with. He also didn't want her staying down in the village where there wasn't consistent running water, electricity, etc. She needed the internet and the satellite phone, which were still only available at his house. He would have liked to put her in one of the new resort bungalows but they weren't completed - let alone furnished.

Jim had Monica cook an extra-special dinner that night for himself and Kelli. He didn't invite any of the contractors or village people to dinner except for Nixon and his wife. He wanted Kelli to get to know Nixon as she would be working with him closely, in addition to Jim.

Nixon was very gracious and started by saying, "Kelli, it is very wonderful that you are here. We need as much help and advice as we can get. Where are you from originally?"

Kelli smiled, "Well, Nixon, I'm very glad to be here. I just hope that I can be of assistance. It looks like you guys have everything well in hand. And to answer your question, I'm originally from Iowa. Do you know where that is?"

Nixon looked at Jim and said, "Jim, isn't Iowa in the middle like Wisconsin."

231

Jim smiled, "Exactly. In fact, Iowa touches Wisconsin."

Nixon was pleased with himself and his wife smiled as well. Unfortunately, Nixon's wife, Margerite, had poor English and so she missed much of the conversation unless Nixon quickly translated for her.

Kelli took that as a challenge and turned to Margerite and said, "And Margerite, do you and Nixon have any children?"

Margerite continued to smile at Kelli while Nixon translated into her ear. She spoke to Kelli in small chunks so that Nixon could translate, "Thank you for asking. We have four children. Two boys, Nixon Jr. and Billie, and two girls, Suzanne and Christine. Nixon is 11, Suzanne is 8, Christine is 7 and Billie is 4."

Kelli looked at Nixon and Jim but continued, "That must keep you very busy."

Margerite smiled again, "Yes, it keeps me and Nixon very busy. Luckily, they are all out of diapers now." She now turned to Jim and said, "Mr. Jim, what about getting a new teacher for the school. Will that happen soon?"

Nixon seemed a little displeased by having to translate something that could be a criticism of Jim, but he did it. Nixon was a father first and an employee second.

Jim shrugged his shoulders, "I have spoken with the company that sent the previous teacher and they said that they had no one who could come for a whole school year. I also have tried to contact the United States Peace Corps about sending a teacher but they only send teachers to locations where they can have a contingent of volunteers within a country and generally more than one volunteer within a day's travel of other volunteers. However, I promise that within the next few months, we will have at least a beginning to a solution."

Nixon took the conversation back to Kelli again and asked her about her previous experience. Kelli related her previous international experiences. Nixon and Jim and even Margerite were mesmerized by her captivating storytelling.

After a delicious dinner of local fish, local vegetables and pie for dessert, Jim suggested a nightcap on the deck. Nixon and Margerite declined saying that they needed to get back to the children before it got too late. That left Kelli and Jim to sit on the big wrap around deck looking out at the ocean and splitting a bottle of a nice dessert wine.

Kelli said, " Nixon and Margerite seem really great. I'm glad to see that you have such talented local staff."

Jim shook his head affirmatively as he sat down in a big white wicker chair as Kelli sat down on the white wicker couch next to his chair. They sat such that they both could look out at the moon reflecting on the ocean. "Yes, you're right. Nixon is a godsend. I'm not sure I would have gotten anywhere without him."

Kelli looked over at Jim in the moonlight. "Jim, I've been dying to ask you a question. If you don't want to answer, that's fine. We can just talk about something else or nothing at all. Is that ok?"

Jim's gaze spun around to look her in the eye. Suddenly, he found himself wondering if this was a romantic opening already. He wasn't sure he was ready, for a second. All he could say was, "Shoot. I doubt there's anything you can ask that hasn't already been asked."

Kelli squirmed on the wicker couch a little. "What did it feel like when you found out that you had won the lottery? I mean, was it a rush or did you pass out or did it not hit you right away?"

Jim smiled as he realized that the question was easy and that, in fact, it was too early for a romantic opening. "That's a softball question. I had gone to bed and my old roommate Dean was the one watching the Powerball drawing for me on TV at the end of the first date with a woman named Ellen. After they realized the ticket was a winner, they came bounding up the stairs, woke me up and told me. So, to answer the question, I was groggy and sleepy when I found out. I did throw up after a few minutes though so I guess it was quite a rush. It slowly sank in over the next few weeks and months. I kept running into points that took me by surprise. When I bought a house. When I bought a car. When I realized that I no longer ever had to cook for myself or clean the house. Those were big moments. Of course, there was also the moment when I realized that a mansion can be lonelier the bigger it is."

Kelli smiled, "Is that why you asked me to stay up here instead of in the village, so that you wouldn't be lonely?"

"No, no. I just know you're not supposed to drink alone and I really wanted to have a few drinks in the evenings."

Kelli raised her glass chuckling, "In that case, a toast to imported drinking buddies."

Jim raised his glass as well, "I'll definitely drink to that."

After the toast, Jim turned to her and said, " I really am happy that you are here though. It will be nice to have someone to discuss ordinary things with. For example, how is your dog doing?"

And so they talked and talked. After an hour or so, Kelli's eyes started to droop from her endless day of traveling and so they called it a night. Jim went to bed thinking about something other than the island and its many projects for the first time in weeks.

As the days went by, Kelli proved herself to be an invaluable resource both for Jim and Nixon but also for the contractors....

After about two weeks, Jim and Kelli had drunk enough wine and eaten enough dinner together to know each other pretty well. Jim was enjoying being able to discuss his observations of the islanders with someone else who might understand. The incredible popularity of travelogues on the TV compared to the complete lack of interest in any comedies. For her part, Kelli was enjoying this lifestyle quite a bit. She was able to accomplish helping people and with Jim, Nixon and all the others, she felt like the was really an integral part of a community for the first time in years.

It was a Sunday. Sundays on the island started with a service at the church. There wasn't an official minister on the island so the village leaders took turns leading the service. There were several prayers and songs followed by a Bible reading and a short message. Depending on who was leading the service, it could be anywhere from a half hour to an hour and a half. The value of the message was a little hit or miss as well. At the very end of the service, there were some announcements made as well. The announcements had gotten longer and longer with all the recent activity on the island and Jim often had to stand up and give announcements about what was happening with the construction and the resort as well as announcing who was winning what employee award or dinner.

However, at the end of a short service by Jack the bartender (who ironically was dealt a passage about Jesus turning water into wine and related that to Jim turning a rum island into a resort somehow), Kelli jumped up to announce that she would like to play soccer or football that afternoon for whoever might be interested. All of the boys almost jumped out of their pews with something finally interesting to them happening at the church. Kelli had even bought a soccer ball with her to the island. Jim looked over at her quite impressed with her initiative.

At about 2 o'clock that afternoon, after everyone went home for the family Sunday dinner, about two dozen boys and young men met on the grassy field next to the big photovoltaic array. The contractors leveled a much larger area than was necessary for future expansion and now a nice field of wild grasses and ground cover were growing up making almost a perfect soccer field. Kelli and Jim pulled up on a motorcycle along with the freshly inflated ball.

Kelli was the only woman but that didn't hold her back at all. She had been on the varsity team in high school and played on club teams ever since so she had good skills and was quite fast. She also was good at organizing and soon had the local boys picking two teams.

235

Soon they were playing and, even though half the boys had never even seen the game, they moved out quickly and passionately - although sometimes in the wrong direction. They didn't really keep score and most of the game both teams were just following the ball around the field. Kelli was trying to encourage them towards a more organized strategy along with Jim and a few of the older boys who had played before or watched on TV, but generally it was a free for all.

At one point in the game, Kelli and Jim were covering each other. Jim had the ball and Kelli moved in really close to try and steal it away from him (the young boys shrieked with delight whenever someone stole the ball away). In the process, their legs became entangled and Kelli fell down on top of Jim and the ball went sailing away into the possession of one of Jim's teammates. Kelli looked down and Jim and her gaze lingered in his for what he felt was just a second too long to not be personal. Then, she said, "Are you ok?"

He responded, "Yeap, fine as ever. Just getting old."

She started to run off and said, "You're not old!"

Jim smiled after her thinking, "Was that what I thought it was?"

That night, several of the locals joined Jim and Kelli for dinner at the house for being the outstanding workers of the previous week. They had been working on erecting the new tracks that the car would ride on up from the beach to the ridge where the resort would be. They had spent the whole week with machetes hacking out a path and then pouring footings for these rails. You could still see the remains of all the bug stings on their faces.

After dinner, they all went out to the balcony. It was a full moon which made it seem like daylight on the surrounding jungle and the ocean below. Theo, one of the workers, asked Jim "Mr. Jim, do you feel like a swim tonight? We often swim in the lagoon during a full moon before going to bed."

236

Jim looked a little surprised, "Really? You go out at night?"

Theo said, "Yes, you can see everything at night and then you sleep very well afterwards."

Jim looked at Kelli who said, "Well, when in Rome. Cooling off sounds good to me." Jim's house had fans and caught all the breezes but there was always a little extra heat when you were lying in bed.

So, off they went down the trail to the beach. Kelli ran and grabbed her swimsuit as did Jim but the other guys just stripped down at the beach and dove into the water. Kelli looked discretely away until they were all safely submerged.

They all swam out into the lagoon and played in the water. The men were all splashing each other like little boys and Jim and Kelli joined in as well.

Suddenly, Jim asked, "Hey, is that something glowing out there in the water? What is that?"

One of the men turned at said something that Jim didn't understand. Theo swam over and looked out and said, "Oh, that is, I think, all-G or something. Little tiny green things that drift with the current and it glows at night. Should we fetch some of it for you?"

Jim said, "No, no need to do that. It just looks really strange."

Shortly, the village men decided to have a race into the lagoon and back. Jim and Kelli joined in for awhile but soon tired and turned back. As they got back to where they could touch, Jim suddenly was splashed from behind. He looked back to see Kelli laughing at him. "It wasn't me," she said smiling.

Jim took the opportunity in hand and splashed her until she had to finally turn away. He stopped and she moved closer to him until she finally splashed him again. At this point, Jim grabbed her around the waist and dropped her in the water dunking her completely. She stayed under for several seconds until she rose up right in front of him.

She put her hands on the side of his face and gave him a big kiss right on the lips.

Jim just stood there. The waves were lapping in around them and the village men were slowly swimming back towards them. He said nothing because he had been so focused on getting to this point he had no idea what would come afterwards.

Finally, Kelli looked at him and said, "Gee Jim, I hope that wasn't too forward. I didn't mean to misread the signals."

Jim stuttered, "No, no, definitely not too forward. I just wasn't sure you were at all interested."

Kelli laughed, "Do you think I'd be out here swimming with you if I wasn't interested. Heck, you've got playstation and the internet up at the house – just us and glowing pond scum out here!"

With that, Jim's shock was over and he leaned over and kissed her back. It was neither long nor lingering as the village men returned from their swim just at that point. They were quite vigorous at the end trying to best each other. Theo and another man, Bart, made a break for it with Bart diving onto the beach to inch out Theo. Jim declared Bart the winner but everyone was very happy – although no one had seen Jim quite that happy for some time.

As Jim and Kelli made their way back to the house, both of them suddenly realized that they were living in the same house which makes things a little tricky for a new relationship. As they got to the house, the village men turned off on another trail and headed down to the village beyond the big house. Kell and Jim walked in quietly. Jim turned to her and they kissed again in the hallway in their wet swimsuits enveloped in the warm island air again. Jim said, "Normally, I'd be waiting for you to ask me in to your place at this point but we already are staying in the same house."

Kelli said, "Jim, I really like you. I have really enjoyed our time together and I really want to see where this goes. I don't think I'm quite ready to sleep with you yet though."

Jim took a step back but kept smiling. "That sounds like a smart idea. I don't want to screw this up either. Especially since this is the first date I've had in a long time."

Kelli kissed him again and it lasted longer than a few heartbeats but not quite long enough. She pulled away from him and said, "Jim, I think that everything you're trying to do here is so sexy."

Jim replied, "and you likewise. I thought it was great what you did with the soccer game today. That was really great for them and I never would have thought of it."

Kelli smiled, "Humm, good teamwork I guess. So, I'm a little wound up to sleep. Wanna take me on with some video games?"

Jim wrapped his arm around her and escorted her into the living room where he said, "You do realize that I was living here alone, playing these games, for months before you arrived, right?"

Kelli replied, "Well, now you have someone to play against so perhaps it won't be as easy."

They waited two whole weeks before they finally shared the same bedroom. That's an eternity on an island, sharing the same house. But waiting enhanced the trust and helped them realize this wasn't a big mistake. Making a mistake with someone that you were living with means you can't walk away easily.

As Jim lay there holding Kelli and watching the ceiling fan spin, he realized that he hadn't felt this intensely about someone since Sable. And the intensity that he felt with Kelli was free of the confusion and inappropriateness that he had felt with Sable. Plus, he wasn't drunk as he'd been with Sable on that fateful night.

Chapter 19: The First Customers

When you see dolphins skipping in the wake of a ship or just flipping up in the air, one can only conclude that they are playing. Anyone who's watched otters playing on the shoreline and splashing each other in the water can only assume they are playing. Dogs love to play and run and chase. In fact, they look bored and melancholy at all other times. Animals love to play. They enjoy interacting with each other. In many ways, it is the playing that makes all the rest of life worthwhile.

Dean slept most of the way, which was good as his last few weeks at the hospital were some of the worst. It seems that once people know you are finishing your residency and leaving town for several months, they think you should get several months of work done before you leave. That, plus the final medical boards examination and the other paperwork and requirements to complete his residency, had more than filled his time the last few weeks. Ellen, on the other hand, had been completely bored and lonely for the last few weeks as Dean disappeared for days at a time with the only evidence he had been home at all being a change of clothes on the floor and a hastily written note on the table. Ellen was practically vibrating with the excitement of Dean being done with his residency and the prospect of a new life for them both and a nice long vacation, courtesy of Jim. And so, as they hurtled through the air, Dean reclined almost completely on the first class leather seats while Ellen sat up with headphones on watching the third movie of the flight and wondering how soon she could ask for more champagne without seeming like a lush. At 600 MPH, not a drop of the champagne spilled. Amazing, the technology of airplanes, Ellen thought. Still, they were on the second of four flights to get out to Jim's island and she wasn't really sure if even the super-rich would travel this far to visit Jim's resort. Just as she was thinking this, the steward came around again and asked her if she needed more champagne and she realized that she didn't have to worry about being a lush if he kept pushing the champagne on her. So, she went back to watching the movie and thinking about Brad Pitt, and if he had ever flown in this plane, first class.

Twelve hours later, they were circling into the island onboard the same small plane that Jim had flown in on months before. Unlike when Jim flew in, they were not alone. A rather rotund older gentleman and his wife were also flying out with them. They explained to Dean and Ellen that they were very excited to be coming out to Jim's island. They were from New Zealand and were friends with Jim's energy system developer, Mark Smithson. They had been to many of the different island resorts and had even created some website reviews of various resorts. Jim had invited them to come as some of the very first guests for free in exchange for giving both an entrance and exit interview to discuss their expectations and how the expectations had been met. Jim had extended the same invitation to Dean and Ellen but told them they could not come if they didn't stay at least a month! They leaped at the chance both to spend some real time with their friend Jim and also decompress after the intensity of the last three years.

From the air, Dean and Ellen did not see the partly constructed mess that Jim had seen on his flight in after the workers had gotten drunk and stopped working. Jim had been on the island constantly since he had last visited them because he really was too afraid of leaving for more than a few days. He did go on several short sailing trips but often brought the best island workers along with him. He was slowly trying to get the islanders out on the water and broaden their horizons. At least, he was trying to get the islanders out that were willing – a lot of them were deathly afraid of being on the water which struck Jim as supremely ironic. Another reason, which Jim kept to himself, was that he realized that sailing trips and lessons could be a major draw to this island. Most resort islands didn't have much more than fins, masks and boogie boards for people who wanted to be more active.

So, Jim had not seen from the air what they were now seeing. What they saw were five major wind turbines located on the western side of the island where the winds were normally strongest. These turbines had a combined capacity of 7.5 megawatts at their highest output, they found out later. In addition, they saw a large black field in the center of the island which they realized must be the solar field that worked together with the wind turbines to provide the power. There was what looked like a small harbor with a cluster of buildings around it. Then, off to the south side of the island in the most wooded area, running along the ridge that overlooked the lagoon, they could make out several large buildings mostly hidden within the trees. These buildings must have an incredible view of the ocean and beach by being raised several hundred feet up from the beach on a ridge. These must be the bungalows for the resort, they thought. They could more clearly see a few larger buildings in a clearing that also contained a pool and tennis courts. They continued to circle around and down until the pilot skillfully nestled the plane into the waves and taxied to the new dock which had been built purposefully for the arrival of guests.

This dock was located directly below the new bungalows so that the guests wouldn't have to do anything but go immediately to their bungalows. If they were allowed to get on the plane, back on the mainland, that meant they had a reservation and had enough money to pay for their trip to the resort. No one was allowed on the plane without the resort's permission.

Several of the young island men ran up to them as they were slowly extricating themselves from the airplane onto the dock. One of them presented himself to Dean and Ellen and said, "My name is Jeremiah and I am your personal assistant while you are here on the island. I take you to your bungalow now and tell you of the many spectacular possibilities available to you." And with that, two other young men came forward and picked up their luggage (which wasn't all that much considering their long stay but Jim had said they would not need much and that the staff could do laundry for them if they needed it). Jeremiah turned on a dime and started to lead them off the dock. The New Zealand couple also was being led forward by another young island man named Jeffery. Dean wondered if these were their real names or just names they took on for the visitors. He didn't wonder long, though, as Jeremiah started to inundate them with the hundreds of options they had to keep themselves occupied including:
- full spa services like pedicures, facials, manicures, waxing
     - mineral mud baths
              - massages – hot stone massage, full body massage, scalp massage
- tennis
  - swimming in the pool
    - golf driving range
      - snorkeling
        - scubadiving
          - hiking around the island
            - windsurfing
              - etc., etc.

While Jeremiah prattled on and on, they walked up the dock which ran back to shore and up the beach and into the trees in one long straight line. As they disappeared into the trees at the edge of the beach, Jeremiah didn't even drop a step. Dean and Ellen slowed down to let their eyes adjust. The beach sand slipped up under the edge of the trees and the wooden path continued. It was cooler within the cover of the trees and Ellen realized why the bungalows were covered by the trees above them on the ridge. The direct blazing sun could eventually get quite brutal here if they were outside and in the sun all day long.

After about fifty yards, Jeremiah came to a stop and it seemed that the boardwalk through the trees also came to an end. Jeremiah turned and said, "We must wait here for just a second for the carriage to arrive." Dean looked closer and saw that there were three little tracks leading up the hill. Within seconds, a small open-air funicular came zipping down from above and stopped in front of them. It was exactly like the type in Zermatt because Jim had ordered from the same exact company. The small car was large enough for Dean, Ellen, Jeremiah and their porters and luggage. They all climbed aboard and sat down. Jeremiah said, "Please let me know if we're moving up the hill too quickly, as I can control the speed."

And they moved off up the hill with a small start. The pace seemed actually quite slow and the ride was not all that long. Jeremiah continued rattling off the many options that they had but by now, he had started listing all the different foods they could eat and the special diets they were equipped to deal with here. So, Dean and Ellen were looking around at the tropical trees. They could also start to get a glimpse of the ocean through the canopy but not for more than a few seconds at a time. Finally, in looking around, their eyes came to rest on each other and they had a quick kiss before they realized that the three young men were staring at them. They pulled apart a little self-consciously and Ellen said, "Isn't it just amazingly green here!? God, every time we leave Colorado, I realize how dry it is. Everything here is sooooo lush!" And, it was lush. The tropical forest went on as far as they could see in every direction. The undergrowth was mossy and thick all around as if the carriage rode up a green slide to the ridge above.

After about ten minutes or so, with Jeremiah talking the entire time, the carriage came to a stop with trees still encroaching above them. They filed out and the carriage was sent back to the bottom, traveling much faster downwards, to get the New Zealand couple and their entourage. Jeremiah led them down another walkway. Still, the pathway had been straight from the dock to their current location. They walked about three hundred yards through these trees and along the pathway until they followed a path marked "1-4" and walked down towards the left. They went along past a path marked "1" and a path marked "2" and finally turned onto the path marked "3". They walked along this for just a short way and the path wove back and forth a little until it ended at the doorway to a large brown structure that seemed like a cross between a Thai Wot temple and a Colorado ski lodge. Browns and golds and extensive windows were what greeted them as they approached from the jungle towards the door of the bungalow. In fact, they couldn't see around the sides of the bungalow as this side was buried in the jungle as if it had been there for hundreds of years and not months.

Jeremiah motioned them into the bungalow ahead of him for the first time. He opened the door and Dean and Ellen started walking inside and both of them just came to a quick stop and their jaws just dropped open. In their minds, the entire bungalow wasn't there. Across from the entrance, the view of the ocean shot through the wall of windows across from them and directly into their eyes. They were totally blown away by the view before them. Dean went forward and slid the windows apart and felt the breeze from the ocean wash over him and the sun shine down on him. Dean thought he could just stand there, at that spot, forever. He looked over at Ellen, who was just staring out the window with her hand over her mouth and suddenly, they looked at each other and started laughing. They hugged. They kept laughing.

Jeremiah stepped into the bungalow behind them. The resort had just opened but Jeremiah was already getting used to the look of surprise and glee when the visitors saw the view from the bungalow for the first time. He knew that Jim had made sure that the entire pathway up from the dock would be covered in trees (to the point of moving about twenty trees to new positions) so they would not get a good view of the ocean until they entered their own bungalow. However, he didn't understand one thing and so he asked, "Excuse me. You like the view, yes? What is so funny?"

Dean stopped chuckling and turned to Jeremiah and said, "My good man, most of your guests probably feel like they belong here, with a view like this, because they have spent a lot of money to get here. So, when they enter the bungalow, they are expecting a lot. Ellen and I were just laughing because we, frankly, have no idea how we got here and it is just the luck of knowing Jim Wells. Do you understand? We have no idea how we got here, but we love it!" Ellen nodded her agreement without taking her eyes off the windows.

Jeremiah smiled broadly, still without understanding but then broke the spell by starting to talk about the bungalow, which he brought back into their reality forcefully. Off to their left, there was a large living space with an incredible view of the ocean of course, a small fireplace between a slew of comfortable chairs and couches ideally placed for spending the day reading a book or napping with the person of your dreams in this dream location. The fireplace was connected to a fan and a series of vents which could warm the entire bungalow if need be on the occasional cool evening. Jeremiah explained that there also was a bunch of fans and a whole house fan that could be used for the minimal air conditioning that was ever needed here on the island.

Also in the living room was a large painting over the fireplace. What Jeremiah showed them though was that the painting slid aside and revealed a flat panel television. Jeremiah told them that the island had satellite TV that was routed to each of the bungalows if they really wanted to be in touch with the outside world. The island also currently had email, phone and fax access at the main spa building, in the business center, but eventually the internet would be available at each of the bungalows as well, if people were demanding it in the future. Jeremiah said, "I think they come here to get away from their email, but I suppose they may not be able to completely get away all the time."

Dean replied, "We had no idea, so we told everyone that there was no way of getting a hold of us down here. In fact, most people don't even know where we are. They think we went to New Zealand. What happens if something incredible were to happen in the outside world? How would we know?"

Jeremiah replied, "Well, it wouldn't be a problem. We have someone who keeps an eye on the major news sources to let the guests know if any major disasters happen in the home areas of our guests. So far, that hasn't happened."

While Dean and Ellen envisioned Jeremiah solemnly coming to tell them about the outcome of a terrorist attack in Colorado, he continued on his tour of the bungalow. He pointed out that across from the living room, facing the hill, were two bedrooms each with its own full bathroom and king size bed. Jeremiah said that they probably would never need to go into these rooms but it would work well for when they come back with their children. (He said the last part with a smile.)

He brought them to the other end of the bungalow where there also was a section that faced out onto the ocean. Here sat a large rough-hewn wooden table and chairs. Jeremiah said that normally, a cook would track them down wherever they were on the island and ask them what and when they would like to eat based on a variety of options for the day. The kitchen, which sat across the dining room from the ocean, was fully stocked as well. The cook used mostly the items here in the bungalow but the kitchen was also stocked in case the guests wanted to make their own breakfast or midnight snacks.

Continuing through the bungalow and past the dining room and kitchen was a door into what Dean and Ellen agreed was the best room in the house. It was the master bedroom. The bed seemingly hung over the edge of the cliff into the ocean. The full-length glass windows were doors in here as well. Jeremiah opened them. The entire wall of windows seemed to move out of the way so that the ocean breeze flew right across the bed on a warm evening. On closer inspection, the bed actually was nowhere close to the edge of the cliff. Rather, there was a deck that ran along the front of the bedroom. It was sunken down from the edge of the bedroom so you couldn't see it but even if you launched yourself out of bed, you still wouldn't fall past the edge of the deck. In fact, following the deck around from the master bedroom towards the dining room, Ellen noticed a hot tub sitting out on the deck. Jeremiah said that it was solar-heated but that they would need to tell someone to start a wood fire an hour or so before if it wasn't hot enough or during a cloudy week. Dean smiled because he and Ellen had spent half a night in the hot tub on their short little honeymoon that they had squeezed in before residency.

Behind the bedroom was the master bath which contained both a shower and a Jacuzzi tub and steam room in a large room with rough granite tile everywhere and skylights making the room seem almost open to the sky. The toilets and shower were low flow to conserve the freshwater. The shower water and hot tub water were all used to water the plants around the bungalow.

Finally, Jeremiah left and Dean and Ellen sat and stared out the window at the ocean for a half an hour. They were just about to either head down to the ocean or make love on the bed (they really were torn about it) when there was a knock at the door. Dean thought it was poor timing for Jeremiah to come to the door again or maybe it was the cook. So, Ellen stayed in the bedroom. However, Dean was incredibly and pleasantly surprised by the sight at the door. Ellen heard him scream from the other room, "Dammit! It's great to see you!" and she heard Jim's voice back at him, "Even better to see you! I'm so glad you guys made it. Is Ellen here?"

Ellen yelled back as she finished putting her swimsuit on and one of Dean's t-shirts over the top, "Jim, I love this place! I'll be out in a minute!"

Suddenly, in mid-wriggle, Ellen stopped cold because she heard another voice. Somewhat quieter than the two male voices, a woman said, "Ahh, yes, Dean the doctor. It's excellent to see you again! We met in Denver at the National Renewable Energy Lab, if you remember. I'm Kelli. I've been out here monitoring the renewable energy system and taking data about the experiences of getting the islanders to use and maintain the systems."

By this point, Ellen was just standing behind the door. When she heard Jim say, "Actually, Ellen's being modest. She has had a big hand in getting the systems up and running not just taking the data. It's been really great having her help out with the power systems…and, it's just been great having her here…".

And with this, Ellen emerged from the bedroom and said, "Jim, thank you soooo much!!! This is really great! I love it! " And she stopped talking for two reasons. One, she saw that Jim had an uncharacteristically huge smile and a loud Hawaiian shirt to match. Second, she realized that the woman standing in front of her was the same one that Jim had hit on that night in Denver but that she looked almost shockingly different. She was more tan and had a bikini instead of ready-to-wear business clothes. Plus, she now had her hand interlocked with Jim's instead of her nose upturned at him. She also seemed to be gushingly happy. Ellen wondered momentarily if it's the location making these people happy and therefore allowing them to fall in love or if they would have fallen in love even in Detroit in March. She would ask Dean about that later.

Jim said, "Ellen, I'd like to reintroduce Kelli Nelson from the National Renewable Energy Lab. "

Ellen and Kelli shook hands in an oddly formal way for two women standing in swimsuits. Ellen said, "Of course I remember you. I'm surprised you came out here after how drunk Jim was that night at the bar!" She cast a sideways glance at Jim but with a playful smile. Jim smiled back.

Kelli skipped over that comment with a smile and said, "Ellen, it's good to see you again and I have to say, it is nice to have another young American woman on the island. The visitors so far to the resort are all old biddies from New

Zealand. They're fun but they aren't really into snorkeling or sailing or anything active."

Ellen said, "Then I'm your woman! Although, I'm probably not in the shape that you guys are at this point."

Jim said, "Great. I was thinking that we could go get some drinks at the bar "downtown" (making air quotes to say that downtown was a bit of a misnomer), tour around the island a little and then come back and go for a swim?? But, you guys are probably pretty exhausted from your trip so it is really up to you. Whatever you want to do is fine and we will just see you whenever."

Dean said, "Don't be ridiculous. We'd love to get the tour and a drink would be great after all that traveling."

So, off they went. Jim said that before they got to Dean and Ellen's bungalow they had given the entrance interview to the other couple from the plane and found them to be fun but very particular about their resorts, which was good. Anyway, they had been handed off to the staff and so Jim and Ellen were completely free to hang out.

The four of them headed down to the village. As they drove into the village, Jim explained, "We've had to upgrade a lot of the facilities and infrastructure both for the resort and the harbor but also to make the most out of the power systems. For example, we found that a lot of the electricity we were generating was just lost in the distribution system before it ever got to the homes. We redid the city grid plus we made it a lot safer. So, you'll see lots of new power poles everywhere. We dredged the harbor to get the sailboat in and then rebuilt all the docks and facilities so that we can easily accommodate six to ten visiting sailboats."

As they parked and walked towards the bar, Jim continued, "We also upgraded the bar to meet the typical health standards of these luxury resorts and we had to build some bunkhouses for the temporary workers for the resort and the power system. I guess that some of the staff people are starting to improve their own houses with the money that we are giving them. Even though I now own the land, we're starting to figure out how to get some long-term (like 100 years) leases for the residents so that no matter who owns the island after me, the residents can still be assured that they will get to stay in their homes. "

Dean asked, "Why don't you just sell plots of land to them directly?"

Jim replied, "Well, we thought about that. Frankly, they can't afford it yet. Also, if I sold or gave them the land, then they could legally turn around and sell it to Starbucks or something. Frankly, I want to keep control of the resort and everything else, at least for the moment."

They walked into the bar and Jim himself was again impressed with the upgrades. The booths had been all reupholstered to get rid of the duck tape. The main room had been expanded. The fluorescent tube lights had been replaced with individual compact fluorescent light fixtures over the booths and elsewhere. They had also installed a variety of skylights and enlarged the windows. This was done so that they wouldn't have to have the lights on during the day. Jim had mandated as much daylight as possible in all the new buildings and the rebuilt buildings. He explained it (quickly, as the beers had started to arrive) as a cost saving measure. He said that the cost of putting in the windows and the skylights was quite low. But, the cost of putting in more electrical generation – photovoltaics or wind turbines – was really high. Plus, the new resort and everything related was creating a lot of new power usage – more than expected. So, skylights. Jim said, "We have a few leaky skylights but it is worth it. Plus, we have the ideal rain patterns because it typically rains starting just after the sunset and finishes before the morning. We rarely need heating and we can do most of the cooling with fans."

By this point, they were sitting in one of the booths and Jack the bartender was waiting on them. Jim looked around and realized that the improvements were lost on Ellen and Dean. Jim was happy that Kelli had been here for eight months now because she had seen a lot of the changes and finishing touches develop. Jim had realized from even the few guests that had already come to visit that they didn't care at all about how far he had come or how big his future plans were. They were only interested in the state of the resort when they were there. They were not invested and neither are Ellen and Dean. But, Jim was excited about the improvements and the villagers, especially Jack, were ecstatic.

Jim looked around while Ellen and Dean quizzed Kelli on her background – which Jim, of course, knew. He looked at the natural light falling into the bar, the flat screen TV which hung on the wall in the back of the room and the half dozen people watching a travelogue DVD on New Zealand. Of all the DVD's that Jim had ordered and made available at the bar, the travelogues and educational programs were the most fascinating to the villagers. They couldn't really identify with the dramas or the comedies but they had an unquenchable thirst for knowledge about places off the island. And, the rich detail of this new TV sucked them into the picture itself, as if they were actually transported to New Zealand.

Jim turned back to the conversation to hear them say, "Wow, you've really been to a lot of places for your work. That's so great. I'm totally jealous." And to hear Kelli respond in the same way she had to him when he said that several months ago, "Yeah, but being on the road gets a little old. That's one reason I'm glad to have been here for such a long, continuous period. Plus, I get to hang out with Jim." And she grabbed his hand. And Jim grabbed it back and he was surprised again about how it felt. Most people look for some kind of electric feeling when they hold hands with their lover. To Jim, it just felt "correct". It felt natural and normal and he didn't feel strange or unusual but just "correct".

They finished their beers and Jim showed them around the harbor with the boat. Dean and Ellen hadn't seen the boat since everything with Sable had happened. They were careful not to talk about Sable but rather focused on what a great addition to the resort the sailing must be. Dean did notice that Jim had changed the name of the boat, from "Lucky Ticket" to "Little Mago" - implying it is an extension of the island experience.

They toured the rest of the island and Jim drove them by the large photovoltaic array and the wind turbines and showed them the huge battery shed. He let Kelli explain most of the system as he drove around. Ellen and Dean were appreciative but were starting to fade from the touring and the traveling before that. So, they all drove back to the resort. Jim and Kelli took them down to the beach and found them a two-person hammock in the shade overlooking the water and left them alone. Jim had to make some phone calls and Kelli wanted to watch the plant operators simulate a wind turbine failure's impact on the electric grid.

And so a long period of sleeping and relaxing began for Dean and Ellen. They slept through the afternoon and went up to meet their chef who was preparing the dinner they had requested earlier. Then, the evening somehow disappeared into the rug in front of the fireplace. And the next day disappeared into the hammock. Finally, they met up with Jim and Kelli again for dinner. The alcohol flowed and Jim and Dean told stories of the time before the money and medical residencies. They thought back fondly of their old apartment in Madison with the beat up furniture.

Jim said, "Seems like basically we did a bunch of drinking!"

Dean looked at him and said – almost soberly- "Yeap, you were something of a drinking couch potato. Remember? You used to have a favorite TV show for each night of the week. Not to mention all the baseball games and other sports you used to watch."

Jim stared into his drink, "Gosh, that's right. I used to play fantasy baseball and football and follow all the sports and all the teams. I haven't been doing that at all down here, I've been so busy. You know, I wouldn't have needed any money at all to NOT do all of that stuff."

Dean looked at Ellen and Kelli and raised his glass – which wobbled only slightly – into the warm night air with the light of the tiki torches reflecting off of it. "I'd like to raise a toast to my friend Jim who, through the grace of millions of dollars, got up off his ass and made something of himself."

Ellen and Kelli cheered and Jim tilted his head back and let out a roar of a laugh. Everyone thrust their glasses into the air in a toast and downed them. The staff was standing around and clapping as well and then rushed forward to refill everyone's glass.

Chapter 20: Finally Coming Home

It is the rare creature in nature that prefers to be alone. From anteaters to zebras, most creatures prefer to be living as part of a community. Many mate for life. One example is the American Loon, the state bird of Minnesota, known for its call echoing across the 10,000 lakes of Minnesota all summer long. Black and white with a very proper white collar, the loon mates for life.

The boat still handled the same way but sailing on the ocean, even if it was just around the island, was still radically different than sailing around Lake Michigan. The waves were larger, the winds were much more even and stronger and, of course, the spray was salty and the water was a little harder on the boat. Jim was still "lovin' the sailin'" as the islanders called it. Many of them had been out on the boat and several were becoming good sailors. Jim still missed a good sailing companion like Dean, though, because even though the islanders were very happy to be on the boat with him, they hated it when he got it going so fast that it started to heel over so much that they couldn't stand up on the decking.

Jim took Dean out and they sailed all the way around the island, which took about an hour even with a decent wind. Then, they sailed a long way upwind away from the island for almost another hour. Finally, Jim looked off the front of the boat and said, "See there Dean? That...right there...yeah, about 11:30 off the front. That, my friend, is Wanakana – the closest other piece of land to us. It's about 25 miles away from our island. I talk to them on the two-way radio a little. There are a bunch of Germans on that island trying to create a German retreat. Unfortunately, they don't have the capital to really make a place where the uber-rich would want to go. No one really wants a hostel after they've come this far into the islands and off the beaten path. They're good guys though and are having a great time doing it."

Dean looked over at him as they started to turn the boat around and said, "Damn, I bet you never believed you would end up here five years ago, did you? Jim, this is pretty awesome and you seem to be so happy. So, now that we're alone and I promise not to tell Ellen anything but, what is the deal with Kelli?"

Jim took his eye off the horizon just enough to shoot him a look and a grin. "She's pretty great, isn't she? I think she's wonderful. She's passionate about her work. She's so damn smart it makes me nervous that I'm too dumb for her. She's really gotten into the groove here and is very good with the islanders. They respect her and she really respects them for what they're trying to do here by becoming self-sufficient. And....well...OK... I know it hasn't been all that long but I love her, OK?"

Dean said, "OK? That is more than ok. That's great! In the short time that we've known her, Ellen and I both think she's just wonderful. You seem so ... alive now. I couldn't decide if it was her or the island or the projects but I guess it is probably all of the above, right? "

Jim thought for a second as he winched in the sail a little tighter on the tack and finally said, "Yeah, I think it is partly the island. It is partly Kelli. It is partly the perfect weather too, but you know what? It is really about being a part of something that I really care about – that I really think is important. It is all a part of doing the right thing for a change. I felt really adrift after I won the money, then there was Sable but everything I am doing now is so much more pure and it means so much to the islanders. I think that, at least for me, I'm a part of something good and not just on my own."

Dean asked again, "But, what about Kelli? Are you thinking this thing with her is going to last?"

Jim shrugged his shoulders and said, "If there is anything I can do about it, then definitely it's going to continue. And frankly, there's a fair amount that I can do about it. Buy a house in Denver, commute back and forth, something. It's a little unfortunate because I can't really leave this project alone very long without having problems but I really love her and I'm going to figure out a way to make it work. One day at a time if I have to."

They sailed back down to the island and around to the side where the wind turbines were spinning in the strong breeze that was now blowing. As they sailed within just yards of the shore and the base of several of the turbines, Jim said, "These are five 750 kilowatt turbines sitting right there on the very edge of the island. They cost me a bundle, almost a million bucks per turbine, but we (hopefully) will never have to buy barrels of diesel oil again. You know what else? Those fishermen have never come back and we, on the island, now have more fish in the lagoon and more rare turtles coming ashore than ever. This resurgence in the marine populations will really be a boon for our snorkeling and scuba-diving. Have you guys gone snorkeling yet? We will take you tomorrow, if you want. And, let me know if there is anything else that you want to try and we can arrange it, of course."

As they stared at the wind turbines turning slowly in the breeze and continued to tack along the side of the island, Dean suddenly snorted and started to chuckle.

Jim asked "What?"

"Well, I just remembered that I was so worried that you bought this place to come down here and be a hermit!"

Jim laughed too and said, "Yeah, the really funny thing is that was exactly my plan." Jim looked at his watch and suddenly became a little urgent, adding, "Hey, we need to get back. I have something to do with Kelli and it has to happen at sunset and I have to get ready for it first."

Dean said, "What is it?"

Jim looked at the equipment and said, "Oh, we're just going for a sunset sail. Something that we started doing to get some privacy but we really enjoy just stepping off the island for a little while. You guys can come with us on another day if you would like."

Dean said, "Nice. Very romantic. We'll see you both when you get back from your sail for dinner then?"

Jim said, "Sure, I usually start heading back as soon as the sun dips under the horizon so we should be ready for dinner around eight, I guess."

Meanwhile, Ellen and Kelli had gone "shopping" together to help get Ellen some little gifts to bring back to her co-workers and their family and friends in Wisconsin and Colorado. The women of the island made crafts from a combination of materials they could find on the island and a few things that they were ordering from off-island. Jim had gone to several other resort islands as a guest and brought back samples of what had been selling at those places for the ladies to look at and see what they could copy. Jim had also built a series of huts along the path where they could lay out their wares as guests moved between the bungalow area and the spa area. They were slowly creating a variety of necklaces, earrings and bracelets featuring weathered stones, shells and glass beads ordered from off-island. They also were starting to weave hammocks for people to buy and take home a "piece of the island" with them. They were also weaving palm baskets and big purses for people to take home for decoration. Of course, there were the required postcards, t-shirts, baseball hats and swimsuits. Jim was very pleased about the offerings and the women were almost overeager to sell to the guests. So far, there hadn't been very many guests but they should start selling more as the number of guests became more consistent over time.

Ellen and Kelli were trying to decide between two different necklaces for Ellen's mom. Kelli said, "Does your Mom have your coloring? This blue glass necklace with the small shells looks really good on you so it might be good on your mom."

259

Ellen said, "I think so. Although, I'm getting a little tan and her hair is mostly grey."

"Nevertheless, I think it'd work really well for her. What about a ring?"

Ellen picked up some of the rings, "I don't know, she has several rings already that she wears constantly so that might not work. By the way, speaking of getting a ring...do you think things with you and Jim are maybe headed in that direction?" As soon as she said it, Ellen realized she didn't really know Kelli all that well so she quickly added "Of course, you don't have to say if you don't want to".

Kelli blushed and focused on the jewelry. "Well....it has been a little quick I guess but Jim's just so wonderful. He's so much fun and kind and caring. He's been through a lot in the last few years but I think that what I'm seeing every day is the real Jim. So, I guess we'll see but, just between us, I really, really love him. We actually have talked several times about having a future together but I don't think we've really decided anything. "

Ellen smiled and said, "That's great. I haven't seen him this fundamentally happy with a woman for as long as I've known him. I think you guys are really well matched. Anyway, even if it doesn't work out, it seems like you guys are having a great time together."

And so they continued and bought Dean some t-shirts and Ellen bought him a hammock to put up at the hospital as a joke. She also bought some stuff for the other nurses that she had been working with and a few postcards although she wasn't sure if postcards and mail actually would beat them back to Colorado or not.

A few hours later, Jim was sailing the "Little Mago" directly at the setting sun with Kelli wrapped around him from behind with her arms around his chest. One could almost envision them on a motorcycle heading down the road into the sunset. Within a few minutes, Jim turned up into the wind so that the boat slowly came to a rest with the sun setting on the port side of the boat. Jim luffed the sail and the waves were small so they barely moved once they came to a stop. Jim was uncharacteristically quiet this evening and Kelli finally stopped talking and held his hand and watched the sun going down. Just as the bottom curve of the sun hit the waves, Jim, who had been standing behind Kelli in the cockpit said, "Kell? Can you look at me?" and as she turned around, she realized that Jim was down on one knee and he had a huge diamond in a box in his hand.

She gasped.

Jim, his voice starting to quaver, said, "Kel, I love you. I have never enjoyed anything more than the time that we have spent together these last six months. Even though it might seem a little early, I feel like I know you better than anyone I ever have. I know we are a great team already and I know we can be a great team into the future. Will you do me the honor of being my wife?" By this time, Jim's voice was starting to crack. Kelli still had her hand over her mouth but she was exhibiting the greatest contradiction of all – tears were welling up in her eyes while a smile was tugging at the corners of her mouth. Jim looked up at her and felt that no matter what, he was so glad he had asked her.

Finally, she said, "Oh, Jim! I love you so much. I love you so much. I would love to be your wife. Yes, Yes, YES." And Jim slipped the ring on her finger and they gave each other a big hug and a long, lingering kiss. And they were both all teary-eyed and she laughed, "I can't believe I was just looking at rings with Ellen this afternoon and we talked about this!"

Jim smiled, "Yeah, Dean asked me about us as well. They must have been trying to see if the stories matched."

"Should we tell them or just wait to see if they notice?"

"Well, with the size of that diamond, I hope they notice! I'm also hoping you can use it to cut some glass for the new greenhouse too! Just kidding."

And, after the very top of the sun dipped below the horizon, Jim jumped up to get underway. For obvious reasons, he didn't like to be out at sea too late at night unless he was planning to stay out overnight and had extra help.

He stood up and pulled in the line for the main sail. The sailboat immediately tipped back into the waves headed away from the glow where the sun had been for that crossroads moment. It headed back towards the island, whose lights were barely visible on the horizon.

Kelli helped with the lines for the bow sail to get it set to go home. They both wanted to share their news with their extended family – Dean and Ellen and the whole island. As they headed back, Kelli wrapped herself again around Jim as he held the wheel. She felt the ring with her right hand and smiled from ear to ear. Jim was smiling too and thinking about how wonderful it would be to have this great memory associated with this sailboat – the reincarnated "Lucky Ticket". He willed the wind to blow a little stronger because he was so excited to get back and start a new chapter in his life with this woman.

Made in the USA
Las Vegas, NV
13 January 2022

41352477R00144